Praise for the  by

THE DEVIL IN DENIM

"[A] strong debut . . . Scott does a fine job of balancing sports and passion, giving readers plenty to look forward to in the next installment in the series."

—*Publishers Weekly*

"Sexy, well-written, layered, and engaging . . . Emotional intensity and dynamic conflict combined with a lively setting make this baseball-themed romance a hit."

—*Kirkus Reviews*

"Sports and romance. What more could you want? *The Devil in Denim* is a page-turner . . . an awesome summer sports read. I'm looking forward to more in the series."

—*Night Owl Reviews*

"Deliciously sexy . . . a quick and entertaining read."

—*Ereadica*

"An amazing read!"

—Deirdre Martin, *New York Times*
bestselling author of the New York Blades series

Also by
Melanie Scott

The Devil in Denim
Angel in Armani

Lawless in Leather

Melanie Scott

St. Martin's Paperbacks

LAWLESS IN LEATHER

Copyright © 2015 by Melanie Scott.
Excerpt from *Playing Hard* copyright © 2015 by Melanie Scott.

For information address St. Martin's Press, 175 Fifth Avenue, New York, NY 10010.

ISBN: 978-1-250-04041-1

Printed in the United States of America

St. Martin's Paperbacks edition / May 2015

St. Martin's Paperbacks are published by St. Martin's Press, 175 Fifth Avenue, New York, NY 10010.

10 9 8 7 6 5 4 3 2 1

For everyone who ever believed that, to misquote *Field of Dreams*, "If you build it, they will come." Keep making those dreams come true, dreamers.

Acknowledgments

If it takes a village to raise a child, it takes at least half that many people to bring a book to life. As always, many thanks to my lovely editor Jennifer Enderlin, who is brilliant and makes these books better. And to Miriam Kriss, super agent, who is the publishing equivalent of a star pitcher and I am very thankful she is on my team. Thank you also to the wonderful team at St. Martin's Press who give me divine covers and get my books out into the world for readers to find. You all deserve cookies.

Thank you also to my writing pals who keep me sane and cheer me on. There are many of you, but extra special smooches to Keri, Carolyn, Robyn, Freya, Chris, Anne, Sarah, Kelly, and Barbara.

And to my ever-patient non-writing friends and family who have put up with my crazy writing schedule for the last twenty-two months or so, who also are always there for me, and come by to haul me out of the writing cave every so often to have fun.

Last, but never least, thank you to all the readers out there who read my stuff and let me (and others) know you like it. Readers rock!

Chapter One

Damn. It smelled like a ballpark. Malachi Coulter breathed deeper, closed his eyes, and let the grin spread across his face as he took in the mix of sweat and grass and old beer and well-worn wood and leather that spelled baseball.

It made his palms itch for a bat.

It made his gut twist as, once again, he contemplated the possible monumental insanity that had led him to buy a baseball team with his two best friends. He still suspected Alex had put something in that very good bourbon they'd been drinking when he'd gotten Mal to say yes to his crazy proposal. Or maybe Lucas. Lucas was the doctor. He had plenty of access to drugs.

Still, here he was. New York. Though, right at this moment, Staten Island. Part owner of the worst team in the major leagues. The New York Saints. And currently in charge of bringing the security in their stadium up to scratch.

That wiped the grin from his face. Deacon Field was a rabbit warren. A beat-up crazy rabbit warren. Figuring out how to keep it, the players, and the people who would fill the seats safe—because if one thing was for damned sure, it was that no one was getting hurt in his ballpark—had been keeping him awake at night for months now.

Rabbit warren or not, Deacon would be safe.

There would be no repeat of the attack that had changed his life, and the life of his two best friends, now his partners in the rabbit warren and the team that played in it. No explosions and fire and death caused by deluded evil.

Not on his watch.

He'd had practically half a squadron of contractors in here doing what they could but there were limits to what could be achieved without some major remodeling.

Which wasn't feasible with their budget or the time they'd had before the season started. In fact, he was starting to think the only way it would be feasible to do the work that really needed to be done was if the Saints relocated to a different field for a season. A choice that wasn't going to be popular with their fans. If it could be done at all.

Yet another thing to worry about.

And now there was only one week left until the first game and he had a to-do list that was so long, he didn't want to think about it.

Lack of sleep wouldn't kill him, though, and he found himself arriving for work at the crack of dawn each day, heading for Deacon Field first instead of his own offices and climbing to a different part of the stadium to sit and smell the air. Today, finally, he'd let himself into the owners' box, sliding back the windows to let the early-morning air seep in and carry the smell up to him.

It was the closest to peaceful things got these days, these first few minutes. The rest was sheer chaos.

Good thing he liked chaos.

OOH, BABY, SHAKE IT!

Music smashed through the morning silence. His eyes flew open. What the fuck?

SHAKE, BABY, SHAKE IT!

Mal stalked to the front of the box, stared down at the field. Took in the twenty or so women wearing skimpy little gym bras and leggings and shorts and groaned. He'd forgotten the damned cheerleaders.

SHAKE IT LIKE YOU MEAN IT!

He gritted his teeth. Cheerleaders. Hell. Baseball teams didn't have cheerleaders. Alex could call 'em a dance troupe and spout off about getting butts on seats all he wanted but they were cheerleaders and they didn't belong in baseball. No matter how good they might look prancing around down there, all long legs and long hair and big boobs.

He allowed himself a moment to appreciate the view and found his eyes drawn to the woman at the front of the squad. The one in charge, judging by the way the others were following her moves as she bent and stretched in ways that were arresting despite the goddamned annoying music.

Half a foot shorter than the shortest of the others, her hair a vivid slick of cropped scarlet—unlike the long falls of blond and brunette surrounding her—she was also built sleeker. She lacked the curves that were testing the limits of the Lycra worn by the rest, but as the music changed to some sort of sinuous beat and she started to demonstrate a kind of twisting hip-shimmy thing, he felt his mouth go bone-dry.

Da-a-amn.

It was surprising the turf beneath her feet wasn't scorching with each coiling move she made.

Sex on legs.

He blinked, tried to bring his mind back to the job at hand.

Hot or not, he didn't remember clearing a cheerleading practice for this morning. That meant he had to go down there and find out what the hell she was doing on his field.

"And five, six, seven, eight." Raina Easton bounced to her left, expecting the squad of dancers in front of her to mirror the move. Instead, to a woman they stayed right where they were standing, looking past her shoulder, varying expressions of surprise, approval, and assessment on their faces. *Uh-oh.* She spun on her heel and took in the very tall man striding across the ballpark toward them, wearing jeans, a dark-gray T-shirt, a perfectly beaten-up black leather jacket, and a thunderous expression.

She knew who he was. The other one. She'd met Alex Winters—he of the shirt/blazer/jeans/*GQ* good looks— when he'd interviewed her for this position. She'd met Lucas Angelo—six feet plus of immaculate suit, gorgeous Italian model face, and divine blue eyes—when she'd been talking to the team doctor about the training plans for her dance squad. But she hadn't yet met the last of the three men who'd bought the Saints.

Malachi Coulter. She'd wondered about him. A girl would have to be made of stone not to wonder what the last third of the trio might be like when the first two were so delectable. And she'd never claimed to be made of stone. Not in the slightest.

Though the man walking toward her might be. His expression was pretty stony. It didn't make his face, which was angles and jaw and deep dark eyes, any less appealing. He looked, as her grandma might have said, like a big ol' parcel of man trouble. Her favorite kind. Or rather, her *former* favorite kind.

Bad boy written all over him.

Pity he was sort of her boss. No. Not a pity. A very good thing. It would help her remember that bad boy was her former preference. Still, regardless of her stance on bosses or bad boys, there was nothing to say she couldn't enjoy the view. Or the irony of his approach being backed by a song about men who drove you crazy.

She summoned her best knock-'em-dead-in-the-back-stalls smile as he reached her and extended her hand. "Hi. I'm Raina Easton, your dance director."

He didn't take her hand. She raised an eyebrow. He didn't change his expression. She sighed and dropped her hand back to her side. "What can I do for you, Mr. Coulter?"

"I didn't clear anyone for the field this morning."

Damn. His voice fit the rest of him. It rumbled pleasingly. It made her girl parts want to shake pom-poms and she wasn't a cheerleader. Imagine what it might do if he didn't sound so pissed.

She squelched the thought. She wasn't going to imagine any such thing.

"The dance practice schedule was agreed a week ago," she said, wishing she wasn't in practice clothes and very flat dance sneakers. With a few-inch boost from her favorite heels, he wouldn't loom over her quite so much.

"You're supposed to get a security clearance from me before entering the stadium."

Oh dear. He was going to be one of those. Tall, dark, and grim. Pity. She didn't do humorless. Life was too short for men who couldn't make you laugh. And right now she didn't do men at all.

"I'm sorry, nobody told me." She tried a smile. "I swear we're not some other team's troupe sneaking in for illicit practice." She was tempted to add a line about it being pretty hard to conceal a weapon in a crop top but figured that would be pushing her luck. Besides, if he announced he was going to search everyone, she'd likely be trampled by the dancers behind her stampeding to be first in line.

Mal's gaze lifted, scanned the women behind her, then returned to her, looking no more pleased than previously. "Other baseball teams don't have cheerleaders."

He sounded like he thought that was a very good thing. She wasn't going to let on that she agreed with him. Alex Winters was paying her a boatload of money to whip his dancers into a lean mean cheering machine, and she was keeping her opinions about cheerleaders and baseball being sacrilege firmly to herself. She had plans for that boatload of money. Which meant she also had to make nice to Malachi Coulter. "Dance troupe, not cheerleaders," she said, tilting her head back to meet his eyes. "Now, we've only got another hour of practice. Can we stay or do you need us to leave?" She hit him with another smile.

"You can stay," he said after a pause in which the only noise was the pounding of drums and squealing guitars as the song on the sound system built to a crescendo. "But come and see me when you're done."

"Sure," she said after a little pause of her own. "I look forward to it." Then she turned back to the dancers so she wouldn't watch him walk away.

Two hours later, Raina finished slicking on lip gloss and decided that she'd needed to stop procrastinating. She'd spent longer than she should showering and changing after the practice session and talking to the women in the squad. She'd only met most of them a week ago at the auditions and she was still trying to get a feel for their personalities and strengths. They could all dance. She'd put her foot down about that and nixed a couple of the more blond and busty candidates who had looked freaking spectacular but had been less than blessed in the coordination and moving to music with some understanding of the basics of a beat and rhythm department. But just being able to dance wouldn't necessarily turn them into a team fast enough for her liking.

It took time for personalities to gel and right now it wasn't helping her cause that the best dancer of them all—the truly stunning green-eyed, dark-haired Ana—was shaping up to a be a diva of the pit viper temperament variety.

Still, this was a rush job and she didn't have time to hire any more dancers, let alone give up one as good as

Ana, so she was just going to have to do her best. Think of the very nice chunk of change she would be earning and give up on the idea of spare time for a couple of months.

But none of that changed the fact that she still had to beard the boss man in his den, so to speak. The tall, dark, grumpy, and disturbingly handsome boss man.

No chickening out just because he'd sent her hormones ratcheting into high alert.

Damn it.

He had that bad-boy vibe practically radiating for miles around him. There was the slightly too long hair. The jeans and T-shirt *I don't care* outfit. Alex Winters had worn jeans and a dark-gray blazer when she'd met him, but his jeans had been 100 percent designer. Whereas she was pretty certain that Malachi Coulter's were well-worn Levi's that had come by their faded patches and mysterious stains honestly.

There was also the tattoo snaking down his arm. She hadn't let herself focus on the design, only noticing the bold color and geometric black edges before she'd looked away.

And if she'd had to put money on it, she would have bet a fair portion of her next Saints paycheck that the big black motorcycle she'd spotted in the parking lot earlier belonged to him, too. He was, after all, wearing a well-worn pair of biker boots.

So the bad boy. Even if he was bad boy made good—he was part owner of a baseball team—he was still a bad boy.

And she'd sworn off bad boys.

Pity.

But necessary for her sanity.

She grabbed her things, stuffed them into her bag, and headed out of the locker room—which she suspected, based on the aroma of fresh paint, hadn't been a female locker room until shortly before Alex had hired her and held his auditions.

The next week in particular was going to be hell. By taking this job at the last minute, she'd managed to give herself the mother of all scheduling headaches. Her next big themed review at the club was starting the same weekend as baseball season. Which meant days here on Staten Island making the Fallen Angels—she hadn't been able to change Alex Winter's mind about the ridiculousness of that name—baseball's next big thing in dance troupes, and then nights and any other spare seconds rehearsing at Madame R before they opened for the night.

Which left her, as far as she could figure it, maybe six hours a day for sleeping, eating, and basic hygiene.

She was going to need a lot of caffeine. And possibly a clone army.

She reached the reception desk after riding the creaky lift up to the office tower where the Saints' management and administration operated and smiled to discover the blonde she'd met earlier in the week wasn't there. Instead a woman with shoulder-length light-brown hair and blue eyes was sitting behind the desk. "Hi. Where might I find Malachi Coulter's office?"

The woman looked up from her computer screen. "Does Mal know what this is about?"

"He asked me to come by," Raina said. "The name's Raina Easton."

Blue eyes lit. "You're the dance coach? Is that the right word?"

"It's as good as any," Raina said. "And yes, guilty as charged."

"I've been hearing all about you," the woman said. "I'm Sara. Sara Charles. I fly the team's helicopter."

"And man reception?"

Sara shrugged. "Just helping out while Tora has her break. Anyway, I'll let Mal know you're here." She picked up the headset on the desk—which gave Raina a lovely view of the sizable diamond gracing the ring finger of her left hand, a diamond that was an amazing shimmering blue that matched Sara's eyes—put it on, and touched something on the computer screen in front of her.

"Mal," Sara said after a moment. "Raina Easton is here to see you. Okay, I'll send her around."

She touched the screen again and pulled the headset off with ease. Once again the ring sparked in the light.

"He said to come 'round. You take this corridor then the second turn right, and his office is the end of the row."

"Thanks," Raina said. "Nice ring, by the way."

Sara went pink. "It's kind of big. Lucas insisted."

"You're engaged to Lucas Angelo?" Raina gave herself a mental smack. She should have known that. It paid to know the people hiring you.

"Yeah. It's still sinking in."

"Well, congratulations. He obviously has excellent taste in jewelry and women, if not baseball teams."

"You're not a Saints fan?" Sara grinned at her.

"Born and bred by die-hard Yankees supporters. I think I'd have been disowned if I didn't follow the family tradition."

Sara laughed. "Well, at least you understand baseball," she said. "I didn't know a catcher from a curveball a few months ago."

"You don't like baseball?"

"Spent my formative years at airfields, not ballparks."

"That much, I understand," Raina said. "I spent most of mine in dance studios and auditoriums. But with three baseball-mad brothers, it's hard to avoid it completely. Listen, I should get going, but you'll have to tell me about helicopters sometime."

"You like to fly?"

"Never been in a chopper. Did a bit of ultragliding back in my misspent youth."

Sara's smile widened. "I prefer something with a nice solid motor keeping me up in the air."

"These days, so do I," Raina said. Not that she'd had time to fly anywhere in anything lately. Madame R kept her pretty busy. "But I'd better go or the boss man will be cranky."

"His bark is worse than his bite," Sara said.

"Oh, I figured that part out," Raina said. "But he's still signing the paycheck."

She smiled a good-bye and headed off in the direction Sara had given. In the minute or two it took her to find her way, the nerves returned, a fleet of butterflies apparently trying out their step-ball-change skills in her stomach.

Malachi Coulter's bark might be worse than his bite but she had the feeling she didn't want to really see him growling.

She wasn't sure that she wanted to see him in a good mood, either. Add a smile to the chiseled lines of that face and a girl might be in serious trouble, anti-bad-boy resolutions or not.

The door to the office at the end of the hall was open. She took a breath and stepped into the doorway.

Malachi was sitting at a desk, but his chair was turned to face a bank of monitors showing what she assumed was security footage of the ballpark.

"I thought security offices were always down in the basement," she said. "They are in the movies."

The chair swung back around to her. She tried to ignore the tiny curl in her stomach as she took in that face again.

"Ms. Easton. Done with your practice?" Mal said.

"For now." She walked into the office, not waiting for his invitation, and put her bag down near the desk. She jerked her chin at the bank of screens, feeling a little bit of tech envy. She had security as good as she could afford at her club but that was still limited to cameras on the main floor, with a few others covering strategic points in the building and the entrances and exits. The twelve monitors behind Malachi's desk each showed views from four cameras, and she suspected they rotated through even more than that. "Nice setup."

His eyebrows rose. "Just the key feeds," he said. "Our main monitoring room is on one of the lower levels. Close enough to a basement, I guess."

"I can't imagine having to run crowd control for a place this size," Raina said. "Must take a hell of a lot of people."

"Yes, it does." Malachi said. He tilted his head at her. "Security isn't a subject I'd expect a dancer to know a lot about."

She shrugged. "Maybe I ran away with a rock band when I was a teenager and spent my formative years hanging out with roadies and security teams."

He shook his head. "According to your background check, you spent your teenage years in a number of different schools around the country until you landed in New York for Juilliard. Where you lasted a year before you started working on Broadway."

They'd done a background check on her? Well, she shouldn't be surprised. Alex Winters wasn't the kind of guy not to obtain all the information he needed. And Malachi didn't strike her as any more easygoing. "Busted. No rock bands for me. Well, not the kind with arena tours. But dancers spend their lives in theaters and other venues. And these days, those come with security. I pay attention."

"I guess burlesque clubs come with security, too," he said.

"Yes, they do," she said. So he knew about the club. And what she did these days. She waited to see what he said next. A lot of people assumed burlesque meant stripper. Mal said nothing. "But not like this," she added, nodding at the monitors as she tried to figure out what silence meant.

"That might be a good thing," Mal said. Then he waved a hand at the chair. "Please, sit."

She waited for him to say something else, but he didn't. Man of little words, this one. "So, you asked to see me?" she said as she sank into the chair. The dark brown leather was old and soft and she ran her hand over the arm, appreciating the feel of it. "Is there a problem?"

"Just thought we should get things straight about the security protocol around here."

"O-kay." She leaned back in the chair. "I'm sorry, no one told me that I had to do anything about security. I sent my practice schedule to Alex days ago."

"It's probably still sitting in his in-box," Mal said. "He's been flying back and forth to Florida every other day with the end of spring training."

"So I should send it to you as well?"

He nodded. "Then you'll be in the system and we can leave passes for you all at the gate for next time."

She rummaged in her bag for her phone and then opened her contacts. Held it out to him. "Fine. Give me your email and we'll be all set."

He took the phone. As his head bent as he typed, his hair fell forward over his face and she had another flash of *Oh Lord, he's attractive.* In a perfect world he'd be giving her his details for a whole 'nother reason . . . but this wasn't a perfect world, and she'd learned over the years that men like Mal were among the least perfect things in it.

Damn it.

"There." He passed the phone back to her and his fingers brushed hers. Brushed and lingered. Just for a second or two. Then she pulled her hand back, resisting the urge to shake it to get rid of the tingle in her skin.

"Thanks," she said. "I'll send you that schedule."

"Good. And I'll send you where you'll be practicing."

"What do you mean where?"

"You can't use the main field every time."

She sat up a little straighter. "Why not? It's best for

the girls to be familiar with where they're going to be performing."

"Sometimes it's not available. The ground staff will be doing things to the field or the team might need to use it. They'll be back from Florida this week. Which reminds me, I'd appreciate it if you'd tell your dancers that the players are off limits."

"Excuse me?"

"You heard me."

"How about you tell your baseball players that the dancers are off limits?" she said. "In my experience it's more likely to be the guys hitting on the girls, rather than the other way around."

Mal shrugged. "Well, in my experience when the guy comes with a nice fat bank account, that's less likely to be true."

"You did not just say that," she said. "You think that my dancers will be panting after your baseballers?" She had to admit it wasn't entirely out of the realm of possibility; a couple of the girls on the squad were single. Still, in her experience, professional dancers were just that. Professional. They wanted to dance. And they wanted the paycheck.

"This is Major League Baseball. Girls are always after the players."

"Poor things. Obviously they're incapable of resisting the wiles of evil women?"

Mal shook his head. "I didn't mean that. I just meant it's not unheard of for women to go after rich athletes for their money."

Raina narrowed her eyes. "This is New York. There

are two other baseball teams in town where the guys are a lot better paid than the Saints players." The Saints were just about the worst team in the league. She knew that much. Her mom's dad had been a Saints fan.

"True. But our guys are still earning more money than a lot of people. Things will be simpler for everyone if everyone just keeps their distance."

"Which brings me back to how about you give this speech to your guys. They can keep it zipped." She was starting to think that she'd been right in her initial assessment. He was tall, dark, and grumpy. Which was a good thing, she told herself. It would make his exterior much easier to ignore if he was going to be cranky all the time.

"Trust me, I will be," Mal said.

"Good," Raina said. "I'll tell the squad, too." Her phone buzzed in her hand and she glanced down at the screen. Message from Luis. Damn. That meant something was going on at the club.

"Something wrong?" Mal asked.

She shook her head. "No. Just business." She stood. "Was there anything else? I'm sure you have a lot on your plate."

He studied her a moment, dark eyes inscrutable. She wondered, because she was clearly an idiot, if she'd see any other colors in that very dark brown if she got up close. Which she wasn't going to do. Ever. Though even as she thought it she felt the first tiny move of her muscles swaying toward him.

Not going to happen. Dancer's instinct saved her and she froze before she could make the movement for real. Feeling heat rise in her face, she took a step back, then bent to grab her bag again to disguise both the retreat and the blush.

"Nothing else. For now."

There was a world of interpretation that could be made of those last two words and the deep rumble of the voice saying them. Her cheeks went hotter, and she forced herself to hang on to the most sensible version. That he really did have nothing more to say.

She made herself smile as she straightened. Tried to look like she wasn't thinking illicit thoughts. Professional—that was what it was all about. He'd made his views on dancers mixing with his team pretty clear, and no doubt those views extended to himself. No mixing business with pleasure.

Apparently he didn't take after his partner. Alex Winters was dating Maggie Jameson, the daughter of the former owner of the Saints. She still worked for the team. And, having met Alex a few times, Raina was damned certain it wasn't his money that Maggie found irresistible. The man had charm by the bucketload. After all, he'd talked her into taking on this crazy job after he'd seen her at Madame R at a friend's stag night. Convincing her that she was just what he needed to train a squad of baseball cheerleaders had taken a lot of charm.

Maybe he should lend some of it to his partner. Then again, maybe not. The man had way too much dangerous charm of his own even when he was being cranky. Which meant the only sensible thing to do was to stay out of his way.

Chapter Two

Mal emerged from his office about an hour after Raina had left, in search of coffee and the latest update from the crew replacing the last few sets of security gates in the stadium.

He passed by the reception desk and saw Sara typing something on a laptop.

"Where's Tora?" he asked.

Sara looked up but she kept typing. "She had a half day. I said I'd cover for a while."

"You know you don't have to do that."

She shrugged. "I like helping out. I'm flying Maggie back into Manhattan later. Did you need me to take you anywhere?"

Mal shook his head. "No, I have my bike."

"You will go home tonight?" Sara nailed him with a disapproving look.

Mal hid a wince. He thought he'd hidden the fact that he'd spent a couple of nights in his office lately from Alex or Lucas but apparently not. If Sara knew, then Lucas must know.

"Yes, Mom," he said.

"Not your mom. Just an interested onlooker. The three of you are going to be burned out before the start of the season."

"Only a few more days. I think we'll survive."

"I hope so." Her expression softened a little. "What did you want with the dance coach?"

"What?"

Sara's gaze sharpened. "The dance coach? Raina. You know, short, red hair, smokin' bod. Was in your office about an hour ago? That one."

"Just a scheduling mixup," Mal muttered. "I fixed it." He tried not to think about the "smokin' bod," as Sara had so neatly put it. He'd been trying not to think about it since Raina had left his office.

"She's pretty," Sara said.

Pretty was not the word Mal would use to describe Raina Easton. Her face was too sharp for pretty. She was all cheekbones and dark angled brows above slightly tilted eyes that were somewhere between bronze and green and razor-sharp red hair sleeking around her face. Then there was the mouth. Curved and bowed in contrast with the straight lines everywhere else. Painted a shiny version of her hair color. He'd found it hard to look away from that mouth. Until she moved. Because when she moved—particularly when she walked—every last one of his male instincts went on alert.

He'd watched the practice a little while longer from the safety of the stands after he'd spoken to her. In the sea of dancers, she'd been the only one he'd seen.

Bad news.

Alex and Lucas had both gotten themselves tangled up with women who worked for the Saints since they'd bought the team. He had no intention of continuing that trend.

A woman was the last thing on earth he had time for.

And a woman like Raina Easton? A redheaded, sex-on-legs, owner of a goddamned burlesque club of all things, firecracker? No. Just no.

She wasn't the sort of woman you'd get out of your mind easily if you let her in.

So he wasn't going to.

"Hello? Earth to Malachi?"

He realized he was still standing by the desk. Sara was looking amused.

"Sorry, what?"

"I said Raina's pretty," Sara repeated.

He forced a shrug, and Sara's smile widened. "I suppose. If you like that type."

"The hot-as-hell redhead type?" Sara said. "Don't most men?"

"Why are we talking about this? She's not going to be here for long."

Sara frowned. "I thought Alex had hired the Fallen Angels for the season?"

Mal fought the urge to roll his eyes when she said the name. He still couldn't believe Alex wanted to use cheerleaders at their home games. Cheerleaders weren't a baseball thing. But Alex thought they'd be good publicity, and he'd managed to convince Maggie to take his side; then the two of them had managed to convince Lucas as well. So Mal had been outvoted.

"I doubt we'll use them that long," Mal said.

"That doesn't seem fair."

"Oh, we'll pay them anyway," Mal said. He wasn't going to rip them off when Alex came to his senses and changed his mind.

"Alex seems pretty set on the idea," Sara said.

"I'm sure he is," Mal said. "But if it doesn't go down well with the fans, then he'll see sense."

"If they all look like Raina, then I think they'll be popular with the fans," Sara said.

"We'll see."

"Lucas said she owns a burlesque club. That's pretty cool. Maggie and I thought we might check it out. Have you ever seen it? You live in Brooklyn, right?"

"Yes. Not much time for burlesque clubs, though." Not much time for any nightlife recently, in fact. He wasn't entirely sure what burlesque was exactly. He had mental images of girls in corsets and fishnets and hairdos like old movie stars, but Alex had stressed that it had nothing to do with stripping.

Not that it was any business of his what Raina Easton did with her life. Any more than it was his business imagining what she might look like in a corset.

"You should come with us, when we go," Sara said.

He shook his head. "That sounds like a girls' night out. Take Hana. Or Shelly." Hell, anyone who was female and not him.

"Chicken. I bet Alex would come with us."

"Then ask him." If Alex had any sense he'd leave girls' night alone too. Then again Alex was the one who thought the cheerleaders were a good idea in the first place, so apparently he had given up on sense for a while.

* * *

It was after ten when Mal finally left Deacon. At least working late meant there was no traffic to get in his way as he aimed the bike toward home. He liked riding at night, out on the road with fewer idiot drivers to get in his way. The only problem was keeping the Harley at the speed limit instead of opening it right up and indulging his taste for fast bikes. But he wasn't out to kill himself or anybody else, and the last thing the Saints needed was the press having a field day because he'd been stupid enough to get a ticket. So he held it down and let the roar of the bike and the rumble of the road beneath him clear his head.

By the time he reached the streets of Brooklyn he was more relaxed but also more awake than he'd been when he'd left Staten Island. The thought of going back to his apartment and crawling into bed had lost its appeal. He steered the bike through the streets, not sure what exactly he wanted to do. Once upon a time, this itchy feeling would have been easily solved with a bar and a drink and a willing woman to take his mind off things. But his taste for wild lost nights died three years ago.

And lost nights weren't a habit he wanted to reacquire. He'd worked through the grief now. Come to terms with the fact that Ally was never going to walk through his door again. He was never going to see bright-blue eyes and wild blond hair sauntering in on long, long legs, laughing at him as she outlined her latest plot for adventure. It hadn't been easy but he'd done it. So no, no more need for lost nights with too much bourbon and the nearest woman to ease the pain.

And no more wild girls. Ally had been wild, at her deepest core. Wild and it had killed her. That was the infuriating senseless part. She'd survived the army, survived three tours, and then she'd come home and whether she'd always been that way or whether she was chasing the adrenaline high she couldn't get in civilian life, she'd started doing crazy things. And it had been one of those—her impulsive decision to take up paragliding—that had killed her.

Stupid. All because she had an itch under her skin that couldn't be scratched. A need to fly or a need for escape. He'd never figured out what exactly had driven her into the sky with nothing but flimsy fabric to hold her up. Where a simple change of weather had stolen her from him. At least that's what the accident investigation had determined.

He'd never entirely believed it. Part of him wondered if she'd just let the wildness carry her all the way down into the dark to try to drive out whatever had been eating at her soul.

He'd never know now.

So no. No more wild girls.

No one who made his skin itch.

The next woman in his life had to be calm and easy and looking for a good solid life. Not that he'd ever told anyone those were his criteria. Definitely not Alex and Lucas. They'd either laugh at him or, more likely, decide that he needed some more therapy.

Which he didn't.

All he needed was a life that wasn't crazy.

Come to think of it, maybe he did need more therapy. Because buying a baseball team wasn't exactly designed to deliver a life of peace and quiet. But the craziness would die down, he hoped, once they got everything running to their satisfaction. Then it would just be the long slow process of building the Saints back up to the team they should be. The team they would be if he had anything to say about it.

That wouldn't be crazy. Just a process. A considered and logical process if you listened to Alex and Lucas and Dan Ellis, the Saints' manager.

So, a calm and steady life. That sounded good.

But he was pretty sure that *calm and steady* ruled out women like Raina Easton. She owned a nightclub, of all things. He didn't know what happened there but it wasn't exactly mainstream USA.

Not that he could claim to be mainstream USA, either. But he could get there.

So he needed to stop thinking about Raina Easton. Yes, she was sexy. Yes, he already liked her style. Yes, there might be a little itch there. But that didn't mean he had to indulge it.

The lights changed and he gunned the bike down the near-empty street—only to land in a detour due to construction work on the cross street. He turned right, in obedience to the signs and the guy directing traffic, and went down the next street at a more sedate pace. He pulled up at a set of lights and glanced down the next street as he waited for the green. And there, winking at him like an invitation, was a discreet sign lit in shades of blue and green that read MADAME R. The R stood out because it was outlined in pink, unlike the rest of the lights.

Madame R.

Raina Easton's club. He knew the name from the résumé he'd read when they hired her.

Keep moving, Coulter.

Just keep moving.

But despite the better urgings of his brain, he turned the bike as the lights turned green and rode toward that bright pink R like it was a magnet, cursing himself while he did it.

It was late but the club was still open. For another hour, or so the guy at the door—who was wearing skintight black apart from the braces holding up his trousers; those matched the shiny dark-pink door—informed him. Okay. One hour. That was time to have a drink and regain control of his senses and go home. He paid the cover charge and walked up a half flight of stairs toward the sound of music and laughter. It was a Tuesday night, but apparently that wasn't deterring anyone from going out and having a good time.

At the top of the stairs there was a heavy velvet curtain in a deep shade of greeny blue, half hooked back with a cord that ended in tassels with tiny deep-red fabric lips hanging from them.

He moved through the opening, ducking to avoid the curtain's fringe, and stepped into the club.

The inside of the club wasn't what he had expected. He'd expected red and gold. The bordello school of sexy . . . well, he really hadn't thought about it that much. But this space wasn't that. No, this was sleek and sensual. Black lacquered furniture and low lighting from both lamps and candles and soft fabrics in deep gray and jewel tones. There were mirrors here and there in aged silver frames, set in places that reflected both light and the people within, making it hard to tell exactly where the room ended. There were lights above, too, high in the air. Black chandeliers dripping with crystals that mirrored the other colors in the room. It all said, *Come in. Sit down. Let us entertain you. You'll like it. We promise.*

Intriguing. How had she managed to achieve that with just furniture and paint and fabric?

But the furniture wasn't really what he was interested in. Nope.

Not even slightly. Not when the second thing he'd spotted after walking into the club, after the chandelier, was Raina Easton standing on the stage in a very short, very tight sequined silver dress and fishnet stockings, sparkly microphone in one hand, mouth painted a siren red even brighter than her hair. A wicked grin that made his temperature rise a few degrees brightened her face.

She had her head slightly tilted to one side and whatever she'd done with her makeup made her eyes look far greener than they had earlier.

She was listening to something someone in the audience was saying, which Mal couldn't quite make out.

But apparently Raina could. She laughed, a throaty, deep-down laugh that had no business coming out of such a small woman, and then shrugged and did a little shimmy that made the shiny fringe of her dress, which he hadn't noticed before, spark light in all directions.

It wasn't all that was sparking. He felt his mouth go dry and his brain go foggy as she purred, "Sorry, sweetie, but that's all you're getting tonight."

The audience laughed along and Mal found himself

suddenly scanning the crowd, trying to figure out who it was who'd made the comment—it had obviously been some sort of invitation.

Shit. What the hell was he doing?

This wasn't good news.

He shouldn't be bristling over something some complete stranger said to a woman he barely knew. Not when he hadn't even heard the comment to know whether there was something actually worth bristling over.

He made himself look back at the stage, where Raina was bending down to give a round of applause to the tiny band—a drummer, a guitarist, a sax player, and a keyboardist—nestled next to one corner of the curving stage.

The audience applauded again and started to call for more.

Raina shrugged. "No can do, my lovelies. The neighbors get a little difficult about noise restrictions around here, and your favorite gals need their beauty sleep." She gestured down the length of her body and mock-pouted. "All this takes work, you know."

The audience protested some more and she wagged a finger. "You'll be happy to know that the bar is open for another hour. So you have time for a little more booze. But you'll have to entertain yourselves." She laughed that wicked laugh again. "I have faith that you'll all be up to the task. You never know what little secrets the person next to you might be harboring." She leaned over and whispered mock-conspiratorially, "If you ask very nicely, they just might tell you."

God, he really wanted to know what little secrets she might be harboring.

The interesting kind, he thought. Possibly the *very* interesting kind.

He turned away as she bowed, needing to gain some distance. A beer. He needed a beer.

Actually he wanted something stronger but he wasn't going to indulge when he was riding home.

He made his way over to the bar. The bartender, thank God, proved to be speedy. The beer was cold and crisp and the glass was chilled, the moisture cooling his hand at least. Hopefully the rest of him would cool down, too.

This had definitely been a bad idea.

So he would drink his beer and disappear before he could get himself into any more trouble.

He took another mouthful.

"Well, well, well," a voice said from beside him. Raina's voice.

Hell.

"I wasn't expecting to see you here tonight, Mr. Coulter," she continued.

He turned on the bar stool.

She stood there in that goddamned ridiculous dress, sparkling gently in the flickering light of the candles in the lamps over his head.

"It's Mal, not Mr. Coulter," he said.

Red lips pursed. "I think I'll stick to Mr. Coulter for now," she said. "What brings you to my humble establishment? Did you manage to convince Alex that cheerleaders are a bad idea after all?" There were nerves in the big eyes despite her bravado.

Damn. He hadn't thought about what she might make of him coming to see her.

"No," he said. "Your cheerleaders are safe." He left off

for now. Then he tipped his glass toward the room. "And if this is what you call humble, I'm not sure I want to see what you think fancy is."

One side of her mouth lifted. "Fancy involves me wearing far more comfortable shoes. Surrounded by servants fulfilling my every whim. And far less dealing with drunks."

"You seemed to have them under control." She did indeed. He'd worked a bar or two in his youth and when he'd first been kicking off his security firm. Raina obviously knew what she was doing handling an audience.

He scanned the room again. Actually, for midnight on a weekday—which meant those who were here were probably serious about enjoying the evening and consuming booze to match that aim—the room seemed well controlled. No one was obviously plastered that he could spot, and the vibe was cheerful, not dangerous.

She wrinkled her nose. "Lots of practice." She gazed up at him and muttered something that he thought might have been "Damn, he's big," then she hitched herself up onto the bar stool next to him, crossing her legs. Which gave him an eyeful of what was a very, very nice thigh encased in fishnets as she leaned over to the bartender and asked for mineral water.

Danger zone.

He looked back up at her face. That was somewhat safer. Only somewhat, but looking at her face, if he tried hard enough, he could pretend that she was wearing something that more closely resembled clothing from the neck down.

At least the dress—skimpy as it was—wasn't a corset.

He was pretty sure if he saw her in a corset he would be in a world of trouble.

Raina took her glass from the bartender and took a long sip. "So how long have you been here, Mr. Coulter?"

"Not long," he said. "I was riding home and passed the sign. I remembered the name of the club from your CV."

"That's an interesting route home," she said, tilting her head at him. "Don't you live in Park Slope?"

She knew where he lived? He frowned.

Raina waved a hand. "Don't worry, I'm not stalking you. It was in the papers when you bought the Saints. You live in Brooklyn and Alex and Lucas live in Manhattan. I thought you'd live on Staten Island."

He shrugged. "I grew up in Brooklyn," he said. "So I moved back here when I got the chance."

"If you grew up in Brooklyn, why aren't you a Yankees fan?"

"Ah. My dad grew up on Staten Island," Mal said. Baseball. That seemed a safe enough subject. "So he was a Saints fan. Got me young."

"Was?"

"He died about ten years ago," Mal said.

Her expression turned sad. "I'm sorry."

"Yeah. Life sucks sometimes. It was lung cancer. He never smoked but there you go. It was a long time ago, though."

She winced a little. "It's never a long time ago when you lose someone important," she murmured. "I guess he would've been pretty happy that you own the Saints now."

"Well, he'd be happy if I got them to win a World Series. So maybe in time, he will be."

"You're not trying to win the World Series this year? I thought you were meant to be the saviors of the Saints."

"We might have saved them, but we're not miracle workers. The team needs building up, and that takes time. Dan Ellis has done pretty well with not enough money for the last two seasons, so right now we'll take building on that."

"But you want to win the Series one day, right?"

"Of course." A World Series. It seemed like a crazy dream. Once upon a time he'd wanted to play in a World Series. He'd never gotten that far, but now he might get to own a winning team.

If they could get the team through this season.

"You like to win, then?"

"Ms. Easton, anyone who says they don't like to win is lying."

"There's a difference between liking to win and having to win."

"If I had to win, I think I would have spent my money on something other than the worst team in MLB, don't you?"

"Well, that would be the smart thing," she agreed, toying with the slice of lime on the edge of her glass.

God knew what she was thinking. He was being sized up, that much was clear. Which told him there was a brain heading up the pretty package. Which he'd kind of figured out earlier but it was good to have confirmation.

"I'm not sure that anyone has ever accused me of always doing the smart thing," he admitted. And if they had, right now he was proving them very wrong. The smart thing would be to run far, far away from Raina of the sleek curves and the plump lips and the goddamned endless legs. How did a woman so short manage to have such long legs? But instead he stayed put, halfway to mesmerized as she shifted on the stool and her sequins sparked little flecks of light everywhere. Including all over the acres of skin she had on display. She was pale to begin with. With the light flickering over her she was close to being moonlight personified.

And if the sight of her wasn't bad enough, he'd now noticed the smell of her as well. Her perfume was something deep and spicy with a hint of leather and something salty amid warmth. It smelled kind of like sex.

It made him want to lean in and press his nose into the curve of her neck and inhale her before he pulled her onto his lap and found out if she smelled good all over.

Really not smart.

Truly dumb, in fact.

"You don't seem to be doing too badly," she said with another one of those assessing looks. "So if you're prone to doing dumb things, you've survived your impulses so far."

"So far," he agreed. "Dumb luck maybe."

"Or skill," she said. "I'm not sure you survive in the special forces for as long as you did with just luck."

Right. She'd read about him. "Actually dumb luck has a lot more to do with that than you might imagine. I know plenty of guys far smarter than me who didn't make it back."

She winced again and he was forced to wonder exactly why he was telling her all this. Somehow she was getting past his guard. Or maybe that was just exhaustion and the beer finally getting to him.

Speaking of which, he really needed to leave before

he descended to a whole new level of dumb. He tipped his glass back and drained the last of his beer.

"I have to hit the road. And you must have things to do to close up here," he said.

"We have it down to a fine art," she said. "But yes, things need doing."

She slid off the stool at the same time as he did. Which left them standing very close together.

He took a deep breath, and more of her perfume snuck into his brain. He shook his head.

"What?" she asked softly.

"Nothing," he said.

"Ah," she replied.

Standing, she had to tilt her head back to look at him. Thank God her dress lay flat to her skin because if he'd gotten a peak of cleavage right at that moment he wasn't sure he wouldn't have just kissed her.

As it was he couldn't bring himself to move too far away from her. Or at all.

A minute passed as they just looked at each other. Far too long for the look to be open to any interpretation other than the obvious.

Eventually Raina shook her head and stepped back. "Well, this is inconvenient," she muttered.

He wasn't sure if he was supposed to have heard. "What's inconvenient?"

Another head shake. "I think you know. But I also think it's something that we shouldn't be discussing late at night." She looked disappointed but resolute. "Definitely not." She took a step back. "So I think we'll call this good night, Mr. Coulter."

"Mal," he corrected.

"Oh no," she said. "It's Mr. Coulter. Might help us both deal with the . . . inconvenience."

"If you go around calling me Mr. Coulter at Deacon, people are going to think it's weird."

"Well, there's really not that much reason we need to run into each other at Deacon, is there?" she asked. "Not now that I understand the rules of the schedule."

"I'm at Deacon about fourteen hours a day right now. I'm guessing we'll cross paths."

If he had anything to do with it, they would. Because he was pretty sure that somewhere back there in that unspoken conversation they'd been having, he'd decided the only way to get Raina Easton off his mind might be to convince her to climb into bed with him and not get out until they'd burned themselves out.

But apparently she had more sense than him. Or at least some sense of self-preservation.

"Well, we can deal with that when we have to," she said. "Good night, Mr. Coulter."

"Good night, Ms. Easton," he said. Then failed to leave until he'd finished watching her make her way back through the club and disappear though a door beside the stage.

Chapter Three

Raina let herself into her apartment at somewhere close to two a.m. As usual, she felt wide awake after a night at the club, riding the adrenaline of the audience and the performance. Being a night owl came in handy for a Broadway dancer and a nightclub owner. It was less convenient, though, when she had to be at Deacon field at nine in the morning for practice. Apparently she was going to have to get used to sleeping in shifts or something while she was training the Angels.

She padded over to her fridge and pulled out cheese, bread, and turkey. If she was going to be awake, she might as well eat something and catch up on her email. The opening of the fridge brought her cat, Wash, prowling over from his favorite spot on the sofa to see if perhaps there was turkey to spare for him.

She bent to pat him and tug at his smoky-gray plume of a tail but didn't give in. She'd fed him before she'd left for the club earlier. And even though he had a Maine

Coon–sized appetite, that didn't mean he could eat everything he wanted. He chirruped his displeasure a few times then stalked off again, probably to seek and destroy one of her stockings as vengeance for the lack of treats. She kept a stash of her ruined ones for him to find, so he couldn't wreak too much havoc.

Sandwich assembled, she wandered over to the nook where she kept her computer and flipped the laptop open.

For a moment, the pleasure of being alone washed over her. Of coming home to her own space. No one waiting for her other than Wash. No one wanting every detail of her life. No one to judge or control.

She shivered a little. Control. She hadn't thought about that word for a while. Hadn't thought of Jeremy. Jeremy who'd started off as the alluring bad boy and turned into a nightmare.

Jeremy who was long gone, she told herself firmly. And the reason she'd built this new life for herself at Madame R. In the aftermath of Jeremy, she'd wanted something more stable. More permanent. Not so full of the crazy as theater life. Though some might question the choice of a burlesque club as the saner option, it was hers.

She tried to let the memory of Jeremy dissolve back into past regrets where it belonged. Easy enough to figure what had conjured him tonight, though. The appearance of another man with that bad-boy edge. That touch of danger that drew her despite her better judgment. Despite the lessons she'd learned.

Which only went to show that she still needed to be alone. To keep learning that lesson. So Malachi Coulter and his big bad self were to be firmly kept at arm's length.

She took a bite of sandwich, chewed. She needed food and sleep. Not a man. But she wasn't sleepy yet.

There was a folder of paperwork she'd brought home from the club with her. She could spend an hour checking accounts and doing all that administrative crap that never seemed to end. That might be boring enough to reverse the effects of the night and send her to sleep.

Or maybe not. She was buzzed, her foot tapping restlessly against the leg of the chair.

Which, lessons learned or not, she knew wasn't entirely due to the usual performance rush. Nope. It was perfectly clear, when she let herself look squarely at the problem, that part of what had her body humming was the unexpected appearance of Malachi Coulter in her club.

Drinking her beer. Drinking her in with his eyes.

Making her want to eat him up.

Inconvenient was too mild a world for it. *Inappropriate* was closer.

Inadvisable closer still.

Or maybe just plain old insane. He was the wrong guy. She didn't need another wrong guy.

Been there, done that. Twice even.

So all this energy surging through her was going to have to be channeled elsewhere. She could take it out on the Angels in their rehearsals or else fit a daily run into her spare seconds. Brady had an elliptical trainer down in the club's basement. That would work. Or maybe even a dance class or two. She hadn't made it down to Evie's studio in far too long. She just had to work it off or wait it out. Eventually, it would wear off. Bad-boy buzz usually did.

But wearing off wouldn't help her tonight, so she needed a distraction. A new routine for one of the girls at the club? Or herself? Or a new costume. New costumes were always fun. She stretched an arm out to grab her tablet. Then looked around for the stylus. It wasn't in its usual place in the cup of pencils beside her monitor. Which meant that Wash had probably kidnapped it.

For reasons known only to his small feline brain, he had something of an obsession with her stylus. Maybe it was the shiny green color. Maybe it was the fact that he didn't like it when she sat on the couch and worked on her tablet instead of letting him sit on her lap, so he blamed it on the stylus. Either way, two days out of three the stylus went missing from her desk. It didn't matter if she hid it in a drawer—Wash could open drawers—and if she put it somewhere truly Maine Coon–proof, he would just steal something else. She'd resigned herself to playing hunt-the-stylus more regularly than she might have liked.

It looked like she would be playing tonight. She eased herself out of the seat, winced at the stiffness in her muscles setting in. Between the Angels and the club, she had been spending more time dancing than she had in a while. The return of the familiar aches and pains that had been her companions when she'd worked on Broadway, along with a few new friends they brought along for the ride, was reminding her exactly why she'd given up full time professional dancing.

She was thirty. Old for a dancer. And feeling it.

Perhaps she'd add a bath to the agenda. She'd showered at the club and rubbed herself down with her favorite stinky liniment but it hadn't quite done the job.

A bath. With the killer mineral salts and some laven-der oil or something to relax her. And a book, perhaps. But first the stylus.

When she was halfway to Wash's bed—his favored hiding spot for his prizes—her cell phone starting play-ing "Send Me An Angel." Which meant one of the girls or Brady had been messing with her settings again. They were all pretty amused by her Saints gig, and angel-themed ringtones, screensavers, and tchotchkes were appearing in strange places with alarming regularity.

Raina reversed direction and headed back to her kitchen counter, grabbing the phone just before it went to voice mail. Sure enough it was Brady.

"Shouldn't you be in bed with your new husband?" she said only half joking.

"Luis is doing something with the security cameras," Brady said. "So we're still at the club and I'm bored."

"Sew a sequin on something." Brady helped back-stage with makeup, costumes, and whatever else the girls needed to keep the Madame R show ticking over like clockwork. He also designed a lot of the costumes and turned the ideas Raina had into glorious shining reality.

"I'm off the clock," he retorted.

"You're never off the clock. Neither am I."

"Which is why I knew you'd be awake at this ungodly hour to talk me through my boredom."

"First, tell me about the security cameras," Raina said. The security system at the club was about as good as she could afford, but the setup she'd chosen had proven to have a number of quirks. Including cameras that seemed to decide at random to go on strike, the occasional spon-taneous wiping of the hard drives they used to record the images, and other niggles that kept Luis busy on a regular basis.

He'd threatened more than once to go down and knock the heads of the guys who'd sold her the system, but Raina had restrained him. She didn't want the trouble and suspected the reason she'd gotten a deal on the system in the first place was because it was perhaps not entirely from the original manufacturer. But it did the job for now. She'd replace it as soon as she could, but at the moment she was saving every possible penny.

"Luis says it's nothing to worry about," Brady said. "He'll fix it."

"Okay." She let go of the breath she'd been holding. She really couldn't afford the chunk of cash a new system would eat up. Well, technically she could because she had the Angels gig, but she needed that money for the down payment on the building where Madame R was housed. Phil, her weasel of a landlord, made muttering noises about selling every so often and Raina was determined to have a shot at buying it herself. The club was starting to do steady business, so she could just about squeak the loan if she had a good solid down payment.

"So tell me about the guy at the bar," Brady said in her ear.

"What guy?" Raina said.

"Mr. Tall Dark and Hot," Brady said.

For a moment she genuinely drew a blank—money woes apparently having chased thoughts of Malachi Coulter from her head—but then she remembered. "I hope Luis can't hear you."

"He can. He thought your bar guy was hot, too."

"He's not my bar guy."

"You were very chatty with him. You had that flirty look."

"I did not have a flirty look," Raina denied.

"Sweetheart, I know your flirty look. You had it. So, give. Who is he?"

"Can't I take the Fifth?"

"There's no taking the Fifth with your best friend," Brady said. "I'll just nag you into confessing."

He would, too. Dogged pursuit of a goal was an attribute that Brady shared with Wash. "His name is Malachi Coulter," Raina said.

"That's the baseball guy?" Brady said, sounding startled.

"Yes. I'm surprised you didn't know that already."

"I'm a Yankees fan. I don't pay attention to what those upstart Saints do."

"The Saints have been around just as long as the Yankees."

"Yeah, out on that island. That's not really New York."

"Says the boy who roots for the Yankees even though he was born and raised in New Jersey."

"Having said that, if all the Saints' management look like him, I could be persuaded to change my allegiance," Brady said with a laugh.

"Alex Winters is the really pretty one."

"Blond is not my thing."

"You're only saying that because Luis can hear you," Raina said. Though Luis had, in the time she'd known him, had hair pretty much every color of the rainbow, he had currently reverted to his natural deep brown.

"Nope, I don't think I've even ever dated a blond,"

Brady said. "But stop changing the subject. We were discussing you, Malachi Coulter, and the flirty look."

"Correction. You were attempting to discuss that. I was telling you there was nothing to discuss."

"Methinks the lady doth protest too much."

"Methinks you should remember that the lady has decided guys like that are not her thing anymore."

"Hmmm, rich, handsome, rides a hot motorcycle, owns a baseball team, it doesn't sound too terrible."

"Rich and handsome are fine," Raina said. "Rich and handsome would be good without the motorcycle. The motorcycle says bad boy." She paused a moment. "How do you know he rides a motorcycle?" She hated herself for asking. She'd sworn off motorcycles, too. Because of the guys that usually came attached to them.

"We checked out the security tape of him leaving. Gorgeous big black thing it was."

"I wasn't aware that *thing* was a brand," Raina said.

"Why do you care what brand of motorcycle it is, if you've sworn off guys like him?" Brady asked.

"Well, if it was some urban Honda number, maybe he isn't a bad boy. Maybe he's just having an early midlife crisis."

"Maybe he's just a nice hot guy who likes motorcycles. And you, judging by the fact he came calling. He didn't seem to be paying much attention to the other girls."

"He's in security, he's nosy," Raina said. "Probably trying to build a case against me so he can convince Alex to drop the Fallen Angels."

"He's not a fan of cheerleaders?" Brady said.

"No."

"So that's one thing you agree on him with."

"Maybe. But I'm not telling him that. Because then we don't get the nice fat check that comes along with the crazy cheerleader idea. And we want the nice fat check. Which is another reason to have no interest in Malachi Coulter. Bad boy or no bad boy, I definitely don't sleep with men who are hiring me."

Brady sighed. "And here I was hoping for some vicarious excitement."

"Dude, you've only been married a few months. You don't need vicarious excitement, you have Luis."

"This is true. But that doesn't mean I don't want you to have no fun."

"I hardly have time for fun at the moment."

"All work and no play make Raina a dull girl."

"All work and no play makes sure that we all have a roof over our heads and gainful employment at the moment. I can handle a little dull for a while."

"You've never handled dull very well."

"That was the old Raina. The new Raina is all about responsibility and sensible routine."

"Most people wouldn't call running a burlesque club all that routine, you know."

"Well, I'm modifying the old Raina, not throwing her under a bus." She changed positions and felt her back twinge a little. "Speaking of things that are old, my back is in need of some heat and TLC. Is Luis done yet?"

Brady sighed again. "Yeah, I think so."

"Then why don't you take your handsome husband home and get him to distract you?"

"All right. But don't think you've heard the end of this."

"I would never," Raina said. "Love you, see you to-morrow."

"Tomorrow," Brady said and hung up, leaving Raina all alone in her apartment with renewed thoughts of Malachi Coulter to subdue.

She had to stop looking up at the damned office tower. It was getting ridiculous. For one thing, the windows were covered with that reflective stuff that meant she couldn't see in. So even if she did know exactly which office was Mal's, there was no way she was going to spot him.

For another thing, if she didn't pay attention to what her feet were doing, she was likely to land flat on her ass. And that wasn't a good look for anyone.

Raina dragged her attention back down to the girls in front of her. Who were shimmying and shaking and ball changing pretty damned well.

She smiled approval and led the way into the next combination of the routine.

It was only five days since they'd first practiced to-gether and she was pretty happy with where they'd gotten to. She thought she had the measure of them all now.

Of course, the next step was to get them dancing in costumes. And given that Alex had insisted on wings being part of their outfits—at least for the first game they danced at—that was going to prove interesting.

She'd been working with Brady to come up with wings that would actually let the girls dance rather than just pa-rade around like Victoria's Secret models—or alterna-tively wouldn't look like dinky little Cupid's wings. If Alex wanted wings then goddamned wings she would give him. But it wasn't easy.

Nor was it that easy to figure out what they should wear. The Saints' colors were white, blue, yellow, and silver, which didn't exactly lend themselves to a Fallen Angels theme. But given this was baseball and had to be somewhat family-friendly, maybe that was a good thing.

She moved through the last sequence of steps by rote and then held up a hand as they all came to a stop.

"Okay, that was pretty good. Just remember to keep it sharp when you're doing those place transitions. You're going to be working in a big space, so if you're out of place, things are going to get wonky fast. But let's take five and then we'll come back for the next routine." She bent to grab her water bottle and swallowed gratefully. Then picked up her jacket and shrugged it on. It was almost April but the weather was still pretty bad.

The last two days, they'd ended up practicing inside due to rain, but today she'd made everyone get out on one of the training fields. The squad needed to be able to perform on grass and they didn't have all that much time up their sleeves to get the hang of it.

It was warm enough when they were moving but no point anyone catching pneumonia during the breaks. "Make sure you keep warm," she yelled as the dancers moved off toward the sidelines where they'd left their gear. She caught the eye-roll Ana sent her way but decided to let it go. She was going to have to pull her up sooner or later but an eye-roll wasn't enough to confront her over. Not yet.

Raina watched the girls go, trying to see if anyone was limping or doing anything unusual that would indicate that they'd hurt themselves.

She didn't need any walking wounded at this stage.

Everyone needed to be on top of their game to make the splash Alex wanted. But she couldn't spot anything so she made her way back over to the speakers and iPod dock she'd brought along to cue up the next song.

A woman with long dark hair stood waiting beside the equipment. She had a Saints scarf wrapped around her neck and wore a thigh-length dark-blue wool coat that Raina envied as a sudden gust of wind hit her and cut through her dance gear like it wasn't there.

The woman stuck out a hand. "Hi, we met once before. I'm Maggie Jameson."

Raina nodded, summoning a smile of her own, and shook Maggie's hand. Great, one of the boss types down to check out what she was doing. "I remember."

Maggie nodded toward the dancers, who were standing huddled together while they drank from water bottles and checked their phones.

"They look really good," she said.

"Thanks, I think it's coming together."

"You've done well. It's not like we gave you a long deadline."

"Comes with the territory," Raina said. "Outside of Broadway, I'm not sure I've ever had a job that came with quite enough rehearsal time. And even those get down to the wire if the show's not quite coming together."

"I can imagine," Maggie said. "Not that I know much about dance. The audience is about as close as I get. I did ballet for a couple of years when I was little but I think it was a relief for all concerned when I decided it wasn't for me."

"Well, you're definitely too tall for ballet," Raina said. Maggie had boots with a relatively sensible two-inch heel but she had to be close to six feet in them. Which made Raina feel like a midget, but around the Saints, she was starting to get used to that. She wasn't that short in the dance world but apparently everyone in baseball had been handed out the tall genes.

There'd been players wandering around the complex for the last few days and she'd yet to spot a short one.

"Yes," Maggie said. "Which is why it's good that I'm better at baseball. Anyway, I just wanted to come down and see if you needed anything. Is the schedule okay?"

"Yes," Raina said. "I'm trying to sneak in a few more sessions on the main field, so I have to get clearance from Mr. Coulter for those but otherwise everything is fine. Shonda got me set up for invoicing for the costumes and everything else."

"Mr. Coulter?" Maggie said. "Please tell me you call him that to his face?"

Raina wasn't sure what the joke was. "Well, he kind of does that tall-dark-and-very-focused thing. Doesn't really invite a first-name basis."

Maggie's eyebrows rose. "Oh really?"

"I've only met him a couple of times," Raina said.

"Interesting," Maggie said, and Raina had the sudden urge to shake her down for more information. Or at least to find out what she was thinking. Because Raina had the distinct feeling that Maggie was finding something funny. And she didn't quite know what.

"Not really," she said, putting on her best nothing-to-see-here face. The last thing she needed was to let anyone else at the Saints know that there was anything . . . inadvisable in the air between her and Mal. She was here to do a job, not sleep with one of the guys paying her.

Time to end the conversation. She waved toward the dancers. "Was there anything else you needed from me?" she asked. "Because we need to get going again before anyone stiffens up in this weather."

Maggie shook her head. "No. Of course, keep doing what you're doing. But give me a call if you do need anything."

"I will." Raina turned away.

"Maybe I'll see you at your club sometime soon," Maggie said.

Raina froze, then turned back. "You want to come to Madame R?"

"Sure. Well, Sara and I do. Not sure we'll drag the guys down. I've been to a couple of burlesque shows in Manhattan. They're great."

At least she wasn't a complete newbie. That was a relief. The last thing she needed was Maggie Jameson scandalized. Of course, if the Saints were going to be scandalized about burlesque, they wouldn't have hired her in the first place.

"I'll leave your name at the door," Raina said. "Come anytime."

Chapter Four

Mal actually left Deacon Field before the sun went down on Thursday night. Actually he left at three, because he had to go into Manhattan to meet with one of his MC Shield clients. Half the time it was hard to remember that life outside the Saints existed—but he did have another company to run. Before he could do that, however, he had to go home and change because he'd insisted on climbing into one of the service tunnels above the locker rooms and checking out why the security feed in that spot kept dying on him. In the process he'd covered himself in dust and grime and, although he wasn't an inveterate suit wearer like Lucas, even he had to draw the line somewhere.

The construction detour was still in place and he found himself slowing as he approached Madame R. He was almost past the club when his brain sent up a ping that something wasn't the same and he did a U-turn and rode back. He parked across the street and sat on the bike, staring at the club, trying to figure out what had snagged his attention. At this time of day, the club sign wasn't lit but that wasn't unexpected.

He took in the whole street. This part of Brooklyn wasn't the best area but it was one getting more and more gentrified. There were Realtor signs on a couple of the buildings and one construction site where the sign proclaimed that new and exclusive condos would soon be available to delight buyers.

Fairly standard stuff. He let his eyes drift back down the street to Raina's club, still trying to figure out what was different.

He narrowed his eyes, squinting against the sun, as he studied the building. Three rows of windows, the bottom two floors painted out, the top one with curtains that were drawn. And above the door, a silly little pink-and-black-striped awning. It shaded the very glossy black door. Bingo.

That was it. When he'd been to the club the first time, the door had been dark pink. The same pink as the stripes in the awning.

She'd repainted her door.

Why had she repainted her door?

None of your business, Coulter.

But even as the thought floated through his mind, his hand was killing the ignition on the Harley and he was swinging his leg free of the bike.

In his experience, the main reason a door got repainted in a business—other than a refurb of that business—was if it had been graffitied or damaged.

His gut tightened.

Was someone messing with Raina?

He didn't really have time to process why that pissed him off before he was across the street and pressing the intercom by the door after he'd tried the handle and found it locked.

The door smelled like fresh paint. But he couldn't see any signs of damage beneath the glossy surface.

If it was a whole new door, there'd be no paint smell. Graffiti then.

Which could be just teenagers being teenagers but he was going to find out what was going on.

The intercom crackled into life. "We're closed." A man's voice.

"I'm looking for Raina Easton," Mal said.

"Is she expecting you?" The tone was crackly and surly. Mal hoped, for Raina's sake, that this guy wasn't on her customer service team.

"No."

"Then we're closed. Come back at seven."

"Tell her it's Malachi Coulter."

"The Malachi Coulter who owns the Saints?" The voice was still crackly but no longer surly.

"That's the one."

"Hold on."

The crackling stopped. Mal stared at the door wondering if he was just going to be left standing there like an idiot. But then the door opened, revealing Raina in yoga pants, a vivid purple tank top that hugged her curves and momentarily distracted him, and sparkly pink shoes he thought might be tap shoes.

"What are you doing here?" she asked, dark brows

drawing together. Her cheeks were flushed, the pink glow making her eyes extra green. Apparently he'd caught her mid-rehearsal or something.

"I saw your door," Mal said.

She didn't look any more happy to see him. "My door?"

"You've repainted it. It was pink the other night."

"And you prefer pink to black?"

"I was wondering why the change."

"Maybe I prefer black to pink?"

He looked down at her shoes then back up at Raina, one brow lifting. "Somehow, I don't see it. Did someone tag your door?"

"Tag? You mean graffiti?"

"Yes."

"You came here to ask me if someone graffitied my door?"

"I did."

"Why?"

"Because in my experience, a repainted door means it got damaged. Damaged front doors usually aren't a good sign. I wanted to make sure you're okay."

This time her brows, which were a very dark brown that he guessed might be her actual hair color, lifted. "Well, that's very nice of you. And very nineteen-fifties of you, but as you can see, I'm fine."

She didn't look at him as she said it. Instead she seemed to find her sparkly shoes very interesting.

Scrap fine then. "Is someone making trouble here?" he asked.

"No." Her head lifted but she looked past him, not at him.

"Raina, I'm a security expert. And ex-special-forces.

I'm pretty good at spotting both trouble and when someone is lying to me."

She sighed. "It's nothing, just kids."

"What did they write?"

Her lips pressed together.

"I can stand here all day," Mal said.

"I bet you can't," Raina said. "Bet you have to be
somewhere else."

He folded his arms. "Just tell me, Raina."

This time her sigh sounded like it came all the way
from her toes. "Whores."

"Excuse me?"

"That's what they wrote. Whores."

"Someone is calling you a whore?"

"Well, maybe not me specifically. Some people
don't get burlesque. They think we're a strip club." She
tilted her head back, jaw set. "It's just a word."

"Well, to some people, naked women are naked
women," he said.

That earned him a flat look. "Are you one of those
people?"

"Do I think you're a stripper? No, I don't."

"Good. No lap dances here. Not all the girls take their
clothes off, and we do comedy and songs and other things
anyway, and—"

"You don't need to explain to me. I don't have a problem with what you do." Madame R wasn't a strip club and
he knew that Raina herself didn't tend to take her clothes
off there. Or not that the background check they'd done
on her could discover. Her face cleared a little and he
nodded at the door. "Is this the first time that's happened?"

"This is a big city, Mr. Coulter. Buildings get vandalized all the time."

"So people tell me," Mal said. "But not on my watch."

"I wasn't aware that I was on your watch," Raina said.

"You work for me."

"When I'm at the Saints, yes. Here, not so much."

He shrugged. "Doesn't make any difference."

She looked amused for a moment. "Well, you certainly chose the right career path, didn't you?"

"Excuse me?"

"Picking something to channel all those protective instincts into."

"It's a job," he said. "Did you see anybody on your security footage?" He scanned for the cameras that should, if she had any sense at all, be covering the front door. He spotted the mount, but the camera was gone. The back of his neck prickled. "Did they take your camera?"

"No," she said.

"Then where is it?"

"Being replaced."

"They cut the feed?"

She looked at him for a long moment. "They spray-painted the lens."

"So that's a no to there being any footage. And a no to it just being kids."

"What makes you say that?"

"Your average teenage vandal doesn't think about killing the security feeds," Mal said. "Have there been any other incidents?"

"Someone tried to jimmy the back door two weeks ago. They didn't succeed."

"I think I need to talk to your security guy," Mal said.

She blinked then pursed her lips. "You're not going to take no for an answer about this, are you?"

"Not likely, no."

That earned him an eye-roll. "I'm a big girl, Mr. Coulter. I can take care of my business. I've been taking care of my business for years now, in fact."

He looked down at her. "You're not that big. And now you have me to help." He added a smile, trying to look helpful.

"I have you?" Raina said. "Did I miss something here?"

"Are you going to be difficult about this?"

"Probably," she said. "I often am. But I'm starting to freeze out here on the street. So I'll make you a deal, Mr. Coulter—"

"Mal," he interjected.

"Mr. Coulter," she repeated firmly. "I will introduce you to Luis, who looks after my security, and you're welcome to offer some suggestions to help him. After which he and I will decide whether or not to take said advice. But first, however, I think you and I need to have a discussion about this other thing. So why don't you come up to my office?" She stepped back from the doorway.

"What other thing?" Mal said.

"The inconvenient thing," she said, eyes not shifting from his.

"What inconvenient thing?" he said, as his heart started to thud.

"The one that brought you charging to my rescue," she said. "Come inside, Mal. We need to talk."

"I told you, you're part of the Saints."

"And that's very nice of you but I'm also pretty sure that you're not personally checking out the security arrangements of any of your other contractors' businesses. So. There's that." She gestured to the doorway. "Come into my parlor."

"Said the spider to the fly?"

"I think that part is yet to be decided," Raina said. "But either we talk about this first or you can climb back on your very nice Harley and go back to Deacon Field."

"You like motorbikes?" he asked.

"For my sins, yes," she said. "Now, in or out?"

"Oh hell," he muttered, but he stepped past her and walked into the club.

Raina's office was tiny and the lack of space was emphasized by the decor. Everything was shiny black wood or velvet in various shades of dark pink and gray. The lighting came from low lamps. The desk had curved legs and looked like it had been lifted from one of those old-fashioned movies about the French Revolution or something. The chairs on either side of it looked equally delicate. He eyed the one closest to him dubiously.

"It's stronger than it looks," Raina said.

Okay. Let's not think too closely about what that might mean. He shut off the part of his brain suddenly imagining two people on the chair and took a seat.

Raina settled herself on the other side of the desk, folding her hands primly on the desk in front of her. She didn't say anything, just watched him for a moment.

He didn't look away. And the moment started to stretch and sway, turning from a casual glance to a locked gaze that was definitely far too long. His pulse thumped again, as he felt himself go hard under the weight of her gaze.

With an effort, he cleared his throat. "What was it you wanted to talk about?"

It seemed to take her a moment to come back to herself, too. She shook her head slightly and licked her lips.

"That," she said.

"What?" Maybe if he pretended that he had no idea what she was talking about, the whole thing would go away. Except he didn't want it to go away. No, he wanted to put his hands on Raina as soon as humanly possible. But he was pretty good at ignoring crazy impulses.

"The fact that we can't even look at each other for a few seconds without both of us wanting things we shouldn't want."

To hell with pretending. Raina obviously was the type of woman who laid her cards on the table. "Who says we shouldn't want them?"

"Well, we've already established that I'm currently working for you," she said. "So there's that."

"You're not working for me full-time," he countered. "So what's the problem?"

"Maybe I've given up bad boys who ride Harleys for Lent."

"Then that's not a problem, either, I'm one of the good guys."

Raina shook her head. "Oh no. You're really not. My bad-boy radar is well honed and you, Mr. Coulter, tick all the boxes."

"Isn't Lent over in a few days anyway?" he asked. The start of the season was coinciding with Good Friday and his hazy understanding of Lent was that it ended at

Easter. He wasn't exactly a churchgoer. His dad had been a firm atheist and his mom, though she'd been brought up Lutheran, had never exactly dragged them all to church.

"Let me rephrase that," Raina said. "I've given up bad boys permanently."

"At the risk of sounding repetitive, I'm not a bad boy," Mal said. "Protective instincts, remember? Charging in to save people. That's hardly a bad boy."

"Protective instincts can go too far," Raina said. "Become possession."

Hell, she had him there. He definitely wanted to possess her. Just not in the way she meant. Nope, more in the strip her naked and bury himself inside her for a few days way. But saying that out loud right now wasn't going to help his cause any. "I've never held on to anyone who wanted to walk away from me," he said.

"Oh good," Raina said. "Then we aren't going to have a problem."

He shook his head. "Nice theory. But there's a snag."

"Which is?"

"You don't want to walk away from me."

One side of her mouth curved up briefly before she got it under control and sent him a stern look. "I guess you weren't standing last in line when they handed out the self-confidence."

"You're the one who brought up the subject. In my experience, when a woman raises the subject of sex with a man, she's most often wanting to have sex. If you could walk away from this, you wouldn't even have brought it up. You would have just ignored me. You're hoping I'll do the walking away for you."

Her expression turned annoyed.

"Are you going to tell me I'm wrong?" he asked.

"A gentleman would walk away," she said.

"Well, that might be your problem. I'm not a bad boy. But I've never claimed to be a gentleman. Particularly not when a beautiful woman is sitting in front of me talking about sleeping with me."

Her eyes widened slightly at that and the color of her cheeks, already flushed from whatever she'd been doing in her exercise gear before he had arrived, deepened. Guilty as charged, it seemed.

"But the fact remains that I'm working for you. And that this would be a very bad idea."

"You think it's a bad idea," he said. "I'm inclined to regard it favorably."

"That's because you're a man. You think great sex is enough."

He raised an eyebrow. "It isn't?"

She shrugged. "Once upon a time, I would've said it was all that was needed. But I'm not twenty-two anymore. I want more than just sex."

"You're looking to settle down?"

"I don't know," she said. "But I want more than just scratching an itch. Hence no bad boys. Bad boys are great for itches but they don't do much more than that."

"I see."

"And now you're worried," she said. "You think here's a crazy woman who wants to get married after dating for two weeks. Well, I don't. I'm just saying I'm not starting anything if I don't think there's potential for something more."

"You don't think I have potential?

She shrugged. "I don't know. But my life is this." She gestured at the office. "Sequins and late nights and women who like to wear very expensive lingerie and even take it off in public sometimes. Add in quite a bit of weird. It's a little off center. And you might be a long streak of Harley-riding bad judgment but you're also baseball and money and defending your country. Not so big on the weird. That's another thing that, in my experience, doesn't work so well."

"That's a lot of things you've made up your mind about when we haven't done anything even approaching holding hands," Mal objected. Some part of him thought that her arguments made sense. Like went with like or something. But a bigger part of him was thinking that opposites attract. That the more she talked about sequins and weirdness and called him a long streak of trouble, the more he wanted to sit here and listen to her talk. Listen to that little rasp in her voice and watch the way her eyes sparked when she got passionate about something.

It made him kind of wonder just how they might look if the thing she was getting passionate about was him.

"I'm just telling you why this isn't a good idea," Raina said.

"I get that," he said. "But it's a lot of talking. You're trying to convince yourself. Which tells me you don't quite believe what you're saying." She started to look indignant again. He held up a hand. "Look, I'm not going to push this if you truly don't want to. You say no and I'll turn around and go talk to your security guy and get things sorted out and that will be all I'll do. No harm, no foul, as they say. But I have to tell you, I'm kind of hoping that you won't. Because the more you keep talking, the more I want to put your theories to the test. Find out exactly what there is between us before we walk away from it. Maybe that's perverse of me—my mom always says I've got more contrary in me than is good for me—but there it is."

Raina stared at him. Her tongue darted out to lick her lips again. Whatever lipstick she used was obviously stubborn stuff because the shiny red didn't budge. He wondered what that mouth might taste like. She reached up and tugged at one of the longer pieces of hair that curled in front of her ears.

"What exactly would putting it to the test involve?"

"I'm a fan of keeping things simple," he said, trying to sound calm. He wasn't calm. Her words had somehow set him on fire. She was actually considering this. He might get to touch her. If he didn't fuck this next part up. "So we could start with kissing."

"Kissing?" she said, sounding slightly foggy.

Foggy was good. Foggy meant that her brain was working along the same lines as his.

"Yeah, kissing," he said softly. "You know. My mouth on yours." Blood roared in his ears suddenly as he thought about it. Hell. Maybe she was right. Maybe this was a terrible idea. He couldn't remember the last time he'd felt this horny just thinking about kissing someone.

Her hand drifted up to her mouth. "Kissing," she repeated.

"If you're not familiar with the concept then you can just come over here and I'd be happy to show you?" he offered.

That coaxed a laugh to those very red lips. "Believe me, I'm familiar."

"Well then, how about you come over here anyway and we can get this over with? Who knows, maybe you'll luck out and it will be a terrible kiss and all your troubles will be over."

Her smile turned wry. "If I were a bookie, I wouldn't be giving great odds on it being terrible."

"Bookies are wrong all the time." He leaned back a little in the chair, still wary of its delicate frame. "Or maybe you're just chicken?"

"I'm not chicken."

He crooked a finger at her. "Then come over here and prove it."

She blew out a breath. For a moment he thought she was going to send him packing, but then she stood and moved around the desk with her graceful dancer's walk. She stopped in front of his knees. "Just remember this was your idea," she said. "And you only have yourself to blame." Then she sort of flowed onto his lap, took his face in her hands, and pressed her mouth to his.

Chapter Five

She'd had some first kisses in her time. Good first kisses, average first kisses, terrible first kisses, and some first kisses she'd classified as pretty darned great. But as Mal tightened his hands on her waist and kissed her back, she realized she'd been wrong about those. Those weren't great kisses. This was a great kiss.

Hot and sweet and slow as they explored each other.

His hand moved a little and hit the skin at her waist bared by her tank top and leggings and she shivered and wriggled a little closer.

Which made his hands pull her even tighter and suddenly there was no room between them at all.

It stole her breath and set her skin alight and in two point nothing seconds flat, the kiss went from great to unforgettable. Mal's mouth opened and so did hers and the deep seductive taste of him burned indelibly into her brain.

As did the feel of him right where their bodies pressed

together. Leggings weren't much of a barrier, and it was abundantly clear that Mal was enjoying the kiss as much as she was.

Even as she thought it, he growled a little, a deep hum in the back of his throat, then settled her more firmly against him and took the kiss to a whole new level again.

Supernova.

Turning her into a spark of nothing but heat and the taste of Mal. Brain-meltingly good.

Wait. There was something wrong with her brain melting.

What was it?

She tried to think but he was hard against her and her thoughts collided, skittered, and dissolved when he moved and the hard length of him under his clothes hit her exactly right.

God.

No.

She had to think.

Think.

But he felt so good.

With some shred of self-preservation gathered from who knows where, she disentangled her hands from where they clutched his shirt, put them on his chest, ignoring the urge to grip him again, and pushed herself away from him. The effort left her breathless as she stared down at him.

He stared back, his eyes gone dark and dangerous, pupils wide, chest moving as rapidly as hers.

Crap.

So much for trying to scare him off with a kiss.

She should have remembered that kissing men like

Mal rarely did anything but encourage them. It was the nice ones who were scared away by her being flirtatious and forward.

Though, as she looked at Mal and he looked at her, clearly just as dazed by that damned kiss as she was, she was struggling to remember exactly why she wanted a nice boy when there was a man like Mal at her fingertips.

Sanity.

Safety.

That was why. She was going for grown-up and adult. Going for stable. She was too old for the roaming insecure life of a Broadway dancer; that was why she'd started Madame R. And that meant she was responsible for people. For everyone who worked for her, for the ones who hired the space, for the women who came here for classes and an escape, for the audiences that came every night, looking for a bit of sparkle and sizzle and mystery.

She couldn't let people down. Couldn't lose her bearings—or more—because of a man.

Or not a man like Malachi Coulter.

The weight of those deep, dark eyes rested on her, the banked heat in them warming her skin all over again.

He hadn't pulled her close again, hadn't made any demands. No, he was just waiting, his hands resting, so lightly she was only just able to feel them, at her hips.

Being a gentleman.

Being a good guy.

But he couldn't hide it. She'd kissed him now and she knew that spark when she felt it. There was the same wildness and need at the heart of this man as there was at hers.

Two sparks would make a fire.

An all-consuming, destroying fire. Leaving ashes and destruction and pain.

So. No Mal for her.

A deep breath. Then another.

"Well," she managed. "That was . . . nice. Useful. Thank you."

One of his eyebrows twitched upward and a dimple appeared in one cheek as his mouth curved. "Useful?"

"Informative," she said brightly, trying to ignore the urge to start kissing him again. Her cheeks were flaming, she was sure. And she hardly ever blushed. "Very."

"And what exactly did you learn?"

She slid off his lap. He didn't stop her.

"That my first instincts were right," she said. "That this is a bad idea."

"So you liked it, then."

She definitely wasn't going to dignify that statement with a response.

Two more retreating steps put some more much-needed distance between them. "I'll introduce you to Luis," she said firmly.

Mal looked at her another few seconds then nodded. "If you say so." He unfolded himself out of the chair, making her wish desperately for her stilettos once again. He was too tall. Too annoying. Too . . . tempting. Standing there, looking half amused by her, as though he hadn't just had his hands on her body and his tongue down her throat.

"Though," he said, running one hand through his hair before tugging the edges of his T-shirt down where she'd rumpled it up past his hip. "For the record, I'd like to state that I think that I disagree with your assessment of the situation."

"Noted. But when it comes to who kisses me, I get the deciding vote."

He smiled then, slow and sure, and she wasn't sure if it was lust or irritation heating her blood. Though it was probably lust. Irritation had never made her weak at the knees before.

"Well, then," he said with a drawl that made her think that at some point in his life he'd spent no little time either in the southern states or surrounded by southerners. "I guess I'll just have to work on changing your opinion."

Raina led Mal back down through the club to the back office where Luis was likely to be hiding, working hard not to turn back and look at him every few seconds. She was aware of him walking behind her, aware of the space he took up, of the boundaries and lines of his body.

Almost as though she could describe exactly where he was without looking. As though the tingle on her skin and the weight of his gaze on the back of her head drew a perfect image of him in her mind.

Unsettling.

Sometimes she'd gained that sort of awareness with a dance partner, the kind where you could reach out a hand and know where they were without looking. But that was a hard-won awareness, born out of hours of sweat and moving together. Of trusting and learning each other.

She couldn't remember it happening with a lover.

And Mal wasn't even her lover.

She intended it to stay that way. Luckily Madame R's

wasn't that big and she reached Luis's office and rapped on the door with relief. She didn't usually stand on ceremony around here but since Luis and Brady had gotten married, they were enjoying some sort of honeymoon frenzy. It wouldn't shock her to catch them wrapped around each other, but she couldn't be sure how Mal would react.

"Come on in." Luis's deep voice echoed from behind the door and she threw it open.

Luis was sitting at the desk in front of the bank of security screens, which were a lot older and less sophisticated than Mal's at Deacon. The pictures were gray and grainy, and Luis was frowning at one of the images, which had dissolved into static. A second screen was completely black. That one, Raina knew, was the feed the vandalized camera at the front door should have been producing. The one they'd need to replace if it couldn't be cleaned.

Raina joined Luis by his desk, trying not to make it too obvious that she was trying to put some distance between her and Mal. Luis shot her a quizzical look but didn't say anything.

"Luis, this is—"

"Malachi Coulter," Luis said. "He was at the door earlier." He levered himself out of his seat and held out a hand to Mal. "Mr. Coulter. Nice to meet you. How's that team of yours shaping up?"

Luis was a Saints fan. Damn, she'd forgotten that.

"Well, spring training went well. We've filled our roster, picked up a couple of good pitchers, so we'll see how it goes."

"I saw that Basara kid on one of the televised games," Luis said, nodding enthusiastically. "He's got an arm on him."

"He's got some potential," Mal agreed. "We'll see how he does."

Much as it was a relief to have some of Mal's attention focused on someone other than her for a little while, Raina knew she had to nip this particular topic of conversation in the bud. Otherwise Mal and Luis would be talking baseball for hours. Which wouldn't get him out of her club and out of her head anytime soon.

"Luis," she said. "Mal looks after security for the Saints. He noticed our door and the camera and offered to see if there was anything he could do."

Luis's dark eyes narrowed briefly and Raina wondered if she was going to be in the middle of some sort of male power game. But apparently baseball trumped any ego Luis might have about his systems, because he shrugged.

"Sure," he said. "Always good to have an expert opinion." He jerked his head toward one of the chairs near the desk where he did paperwork. "Pull up a seat."

"Did you get any footage of the guy who tagged your door?" Mal asked as he pulled up the chair.

"Nothin' but the first few seconds before he sprayed the camera," Luis said. "There's only the one out front. The queue isn't usually long enough to warrant more."

Mal nodded. "I see. Do you mind if I take a look?"

Raina felt herself bristle. "Luis has stuff to do. I told you, it was just a dumb kid."

"And I told you, I take the security of anyone associated with the Saints very seriously," Mal said. That earned

him an approving look from Luis. Damn, between baseball and acting all protective, Mal was winning brownie
points with Luis.

"I—"

Another knock on the door interrupted her. Brady
stuck his head into the office, smiled blindingly at Luis,
and then looked at Raina. "There you are. I ran the girls
through the rest of the routine but they're on break now.
Are you coming back to rehearsal? I want you to try on
the wings again. I've made some tweaks."

"Wings?" Mal said, looking startled. Maybe it
was Brady's hair, which was currently mostly brilliant
blue with a few black streaks. It set off his blue eyes very
nicely but still took some getting used to.

"Wings for your Angels," Brady said. "I'm helping
Raina with the costumes."

"Wings?" Mal repeated, turning toward Raina.

"It was Alex's idea," Raina said.

"I'm sure it was," Mal said, shaking his head.

"If you're going to have a baseball team called the
Saints and a dance squad called the Fallen Angels, then
you're just going to have to put up with all the bad heaven
and hell imagery," Raina said.

"I know that," Mal said. "I've been a Saints fan a long
time."

"Should've picked the Yankees," Brady said. "No
wings in the Yankees. Though, thank God you didn't.
Not sure what we would have done for costumes there."
He nailed Raina with a look of impatience. "So are you
coming back? Or do you have something more important to do?" He lifted an eyebrow then, his eyes flicking
to Mal.

Raina's face went hot again. Damn it. Brady had a supernatural sixth sense when it came to registering sexual tension. She should have hustled Mal out of the club as soon as possible. Because now she was going to get grilled six ways from Sunday about Mal and what she might or might not feel about him.

She bit her lip, torn. If she stayed, then Brady would be teasing her about being unable to keep her mind on the job with the big boss man in the house in about thirty seconds flat. Which was so not a conversation she wanted to have anywhere in the vicinity of Mal.

But if she went with Brady, then Mal would have free rein to wangle all of Madame R's security dilemmas out of Luis. Worse, he might then decide he needed to get involved in fixing them.

Damned if she did, damned if she didn't.

Where was the convenient wall to bang her head against while she decided which was the lesser of two evils.

"Raina?" Brady said again. "We need this routine down before tonight. Carla's sick, so she's out. Which means we need the extra group number. Unless you want to do ten minutes of flirting with the crowd to make up the time?"

No. No she didn't. She was tired and, while she was very used to working when she was tired and cold, and could, if needed, turn on the charm and the smile and the flirting and have an audience eating out of her hand even when she was nearly dead, she didn't want to. Between the Saints and the door and all the other balls she was trying to keep in the air, she'd save energy where she could.

"I'm coming," she said. "Just give me a couple more minutes."

"Five, max," Brady said. "The bloody wings take forever, so you need to sign off on the design tonight so I can get the seamstresses working on the white ones. The feathers are arriving tomorrow. Eighteen pairs of wings by Saturday week is cutting it pretty fine."

"What color is the pair you've made for Raina?" Mal said.

Brady smiled at him. A sneaky sort of smile that Raina didn't like the look of. "Why don't you come by the stage when you're done here and we'll show you?"

"I might just do that," Mal said.

Raina's heart sank. She wanted him to leave. But he was one of the people paying for the wings and the outfits and her time, so she could hardly tell him no.

Brady looked somewhat smug. "That would be awesome. Raina, five minutes." He spun on his heel and disappeared back out the door before she had time to object.

Luis was watching her with amusement in his eyes. He was obviously drawing the same sort of conclusions about her discomfort as Brady had.

Double damn. Or even worse words that she wasn't going to let herself think because she might just start saying them out loud.

Swearing at Mal wasn't exactly an option, either.

She turned back to Mal, who was waiting patiently. "Okay, you heard the man. I have five minutes."

"You could just go now," Luis said. "Mal and I can talk computer at each other and you won't be bored stupid."

"I speak geek," Raina said. She'd had to learn it. Running a business was easier if you understood computers.

"This will be über-geek," Luis said.

She frowned at him. He looked unrepentant. There was no graceful way to say *Okay, but don't tell this guy all my secrets*, so she made a frustrated noise and said, "Fine. Mal, don't keep him too long, we have a busy night ahead of us here, so Luis has plenty to do."

"Understood," Mal said. "I have to be on my way soon anyway."

Thank goodness for that. One small thing that was going her way, at least.

"I could just send you a picture of the wings. Send it to all three of you," she offered.

"Might as well look while I'm here." The dimple in his cheek flashed again. "Go on, or Blue Hair will be reading you the riot act."

"His name is Brady," Raina said. "And he works for me."

Luis snorted. "Don't you always say that a wise dancer doesn't piss off her choreographer?"

"Maybe. But who said I had to practice what I preach?"

Mal grinned at that. "Consistency builds morale."

"Morale is just fine," Raina said. "Everyone here gets to dress up in pretty things and have fun. It's not a baseball club."

"So I see," Mal said. "Well, go have your fun then. I'll come check out these wings after Luis and I have our conversation."

There was no point standing here arguing with the man. He clearly wasn't going to leave until he was good and ready, and she was going to be late for Brady. And that would just cause more drama.

She would give her right arm for a lack of drama right now.

And a lack of disturbingly attractive men damaging her calm.

Who would have thought that baseball would be so much trouble?

Raina had lost track of time when she noticed Mal standing at the back of the main room, behind the last row of tables, eyes fixed on her. She must have stiffened because Brady, who was doing something to the fit of the harness that held up the wings, made an annoyed sound.

"Stand still," he muttered through his mouthful of pins.

"I am," she said.

"No, you're not," he retorted. He pushed the wing forward and stuck his head out from behind it. "And now I see why. Mr. Tall Dark and Baseball is back." He came all the way out from behind Raina and beckoned at Mal. "Come on down here, Mr. Coulter."

"Call me Mal," Mal replied. He started weaving his way through the tables toward the stage.

Raina watched his approach and suddenly felt severely underdressed. Which was dumb because she was actually wearing more clothes than she had been earlier. She still had her leggings and crop top on, but Brady had insisted she slip on a sparkly black shift dress that approximated the length of the angel outfits he had made to go with the wings.

Somehow wearing the scrap of silk and sequins made

her feel naked. And then there were the wings themselves. The harness crossed between her breasts and
the tightness of it and the weight of the wings forced
her shoulders back so her boobs were front and center.
She might as well have been striking a *Playboy* pose.
She wasn't exactly huge in the breast department but the
combination was doing its best to highlight what she did
have.

The wings, which on the Angels would come down
just past their hips, almost reached her knees. Brady had
made them to scale for one of the universally tall dancers they'd hired, not her. The black and pink feathers surrounded her on either side and arced up over her head.

She felt like she was being served up to Mal's gaze on
a feathery platter.

What's worse, seeing him looking made her feel hot
and weak at the knees all over again.

Her body had no sense.

Mal reached the edge of the stage, stopped for a long
look that swept slowly up from her ankles to the top of
her head, then boosted himself up to stand beside her.

She was, at least, wearing dance shoes now, which
gave her a couple of extra inches of height.

"Impressive," Mal murmured. "That look has potential."

"The version for your dance squad will be white of
course," Raina said. "And the outfits are white, too. With
touches of silver and blue and yellow."

Mal reached out and touched one of the feathers near
her right ear softly.

There was something wrong with her because a shiver
ran over her skin as though he'd stroked her, not the wing.

"I have kind of a soft spot for black and pink," he said.

"Well, not sure your fans will go for those as team colors," she said briskly.

"They might if they saw you in this outfit," Mal said.

Behind her, Brady cleared his throat. "So you approve?" he asked.

Mal shrugged. "They look cool. But aren't wings hard to dance in?"

"They won't be wearing them for the whole routine," Raina said. "They come in doing this slow sort of walk and then there's a bit of a—" She demonstrated the slow-mo shimmy/twist/turn series of moves briefly, figuring that Mal wouldn't understand if she started spouting dance terminology at him. She hadn't thought about how he might react, though.

Which was to go still and deep while he watched her, his eyes once again full of wicked intentions. "Anyway," she said, trying to pretend she hadn't noticed, "imagine that with someone taller and blonder than me."

"I don't go for blondes," he said. Beside her Brady choked down a laugh.

"Anyway," she continued, soldiering on. "Then we do this." She hit the release on the wings, shrugged out of them, and let them flutter to the ground. "Fallen angels, get it? Which leaves the girls perfectly able to do the rest of the routines. It's like a big opening number. Get some attention, let the press get some good shots. Alex is using us for some publicity, so we're going for a bit of spectacle and razzle-dazzle."

Mal was still looking at her and she got the feeling he

was thinking about things very far removed from spectacle and razzle-dazzle. Things that were far more personal. Involving a much smaller cast and a much smaller set.

Damn it, now she was thinking about it, too. She bent down and picked up the wings. She didn't know quite how Brady had done it but they were light enough to be wearable without giving anyone a back injury but tough enough to survive being shed by the Angels during the routine.

She ran her hand down the wings, smoothing the feathers. The black with the odd brilliant pink one here and there was striking. Maybe she could come up with a way to use them in the show here.

One of her reasons for taking the job with the Saints was to try to get some publicity for the club as well, so it couldn't hurt to have a fallen-angel routine that was a little more burlesque and naughty than she could get away with on a baseball field.

"So, what do you think?" Brady said.

"I'm beginning to understand Alex's point of view on the cheerleader thing," Mal said.

"Fab," Brady said. He reached out and took the wings from Raina. "Well, I'll just put these bad boys away and leave you two to chat. Many wings to make before Saturday and all that." He disappeared behind the stage curtain before Raina could object. Leaving her alone with Mal again. Feeling even more naked without the wings.

Where exactly had she left her hoodie again?

She couldn't remember. And she wasn't going to give the Mal the satisfaction of hunting frantically for it to put it on so she felt less exposed. Instead she straightened her spine. "Thanks. That was helpful."

"I want to talk to you about the graffiti. Luis said it wasn't the first time."

"I thought we already discussed that. I'm not an idiot, Mr. Coulter—" She couldn't quite bring herself to use his name. Not with that kiss still tingling on her lips. "—if I thought there was an actual problem, I'd take steps. I take my safety and the safety of everyone who works here just as seriously as you take things as Deacon. Now, don't you have somewhere to be?"

"I do," he said. "But it can wait."

The implication being that he had all the time in the world to stand there and watch her while he grilled her about her security. But she didn't want him watching her any longer and she really didn't want to talk to him. When she talked to him, she apparently lost her mind the way she had earlier, in her office.

"That must be nice," she said. "But my schedule is pretty packed today." She made her way over to the stairs at the side of the stage and headed down. Normally she just hopped off the edge, but she didn't want to give Mal any chance to get his hands on her again in the guise of being gentlemanly and helping her.

When she was safely down on the floor, she turned back to him. And froze. He was standing under a spotlight, outlined in light against her black velvet stage curtain. Every long, lean inch of him perfectly outlined. Like a da Vinci drawing of the ideal male specimen.

Her brain adjusted the image by removing the clothes he was wearing and she blinked and turned away, heading for the door that led to the outside, spots dancing in front of her eyes from both the spotlights and the desire dancing through her veins.

She heard Mal follow her but this time she'd learned her lesson and didn't look back.

Chapter Six

Later that night Mal prowled through the tunnels below Deacon, trying to dislodge the image of Raina Easton as a very dark and sexy angel that was burned into his brain. He hadn't been able to shake it despite the hours that had passed since he'd seen her.

No more than he'd been able to forget that bloody kiss.

Maybe she'd been right.

Maybe it was a very bad idea.

But now that he'd had a taste of her it was an idea that he definitely wasn't going to be giving up on anytime soon. He came to the end of the tunnel and propelled up the set of stairs that led to the next level. He'd been pushing the pace of his inspection round, trying to wear off some of the energy pulsing through him.

Maybe he should just give up, go change into workout gear, and run a few dozen laps of the stadium itself. That might tire him out enough to actually sleep.

Not that Raina was the only thing likely to keep him

up at night right now. She was definitely the most pleasant, though.

But no, as the first game approached, he found himself getting more and more tense. He'd been upgrading the security here at the stadium for months now but the thought of something going wrong still gnawed at him.

He pulled the door from the lower levels shut and made sure it had locked behind him. He'd done everything possible given his time frame and the limitations on how much work he could do to the actual stadium infrastructure.

Until he could do more, he was just going to have to rely on the staff he'd hired and the systems he'd designed and make sure everyone who passed through the stadium gate stayed safe.

When he came out of the elevator to head back to his office, he met Alex and Lucas coming the other way.

"Well, this is just sad," he said. "Shouldn't you two be home at this hour?"

Alex shrugged. "Lots to do."

Lucas nodded agreement.

Mal shook his head. "It's amazing Maggie and Sara put up with the two of you."

"It's not like either of them works shorter hours than we do," Lucas said. "But you're here, too. Shouldn't you be out following our excellent examples and finding a woman to put up with you?"

"I don't recall you meeting Sara by crawling through bars on a weeknight," Mal said.

"I did kind of meet Maggie at a bar," Alex said, looking nostalgic.

"I thought you met her at the meeting where we signed the contracts with Tom to buy this place," Lucas said.

"Well, she was there," Alex said. "But she didn't do much more than look like she'd like to kill me at that meeting." He grinned. "Not that she was much friendlier in the bar, either. But that was the tequila."

"I don't aspire to drive women to drink," Mal said. Ally had liked a drink or two. They'd had quite a few wild nights in their time. But he'd been a lot younger then. And stupider. Now he preferred a clear head most of the time.

"She was drinking because of the deal, not because of me," Alex said. "But hey, it all worked out in the end."

"Still, you didn't meet her in a bar."

"Well, there are plenty of girls floating around at the moment with all those dancers," Lucas said. "Maybe one of them will take pity on you."

He didn't want Raina to take pity on him, he just wanted her to kiss him again. But he wasn't going to talk about that with Alex and Lucas. They'd found great women, yes, but that didn't mean he wanted them matchmaking for him.

Raina seemed skittish enough about things without him subjecting her to his friends. Who were also her employers.

"I'm a little too busy right now for that sort of thing," he said.

"If you're too busy for sex, then we really need to sort out your schedule," Alex said with another grin.

"We have our first game in a few days," Mal said. "I'm sure I can survive that long. So, given that we're all here rather than home in bed alone or otherwise, why don't we talk about where we're at with that?"

Lucas nodded. "Smooth subject change there. But

you're right. We're coming down to the end of the inning on this. Is the security system ready, Mal?"

He nodded. "Ready as it can be right now. I still want to upgrade the inner gates at some point, but the camera network is upgraded and the scanner systems at the entry points are operational. Tom already had the bag search and entry rules set up pretty well, so we're just building on those. And the patrol teams know what they're looking for."

"No one is going to try to blow us up," Alex said. "You've done what needed to be done. People will be safe."

Mal sucked in a breath. *Safe.*

That was his job. What he did. Kept people safe. But there were always lunatics and bastards out there who wanted to use fear as a weapon and didn't care who they hurt.

The three of them had learned that lesson young when the explosion had ripped through a stadium at the last college baseball game any of them had ever played. They'd been lucky, they'd survived. But it had changed all three of them. In a way, it was the reason that they'd all arrived back here now. Back then they'd all thought they knew what their lives were going to be. Major-league ballplayers. Stars. Bound for money and the high life. But instead that explosion had shattered that path and they'd all diverted. He'd joined the army a week after the explosion—once it had been clear that Alex and Lucas were going to be okay despite their injuries—determined to do his part in making the world a safer place. The army had led him to a whole different world. And to Ally.

And now full circle back to the world of baseball.

He wasn't going to let anyone else's world be shattered here.

Alex reached out and punched his arm gently. "We're all still standing. And no one's going to touch what's ours." He gestured at the space around them. "And this place, this team is ours."

Mal nodded and tried to make his shoulders relax. He'd been carrying around a load of tension ever since they'd bought the Saints. True, it was balanced by the joy he felt at the knowledge that he owned a freaking baseball team. But it was there, always, riding him.

Except for a few short minutes when Raina had climbed into his lap and kissed him. She'd made the world go away. Made him feel good.

The question was how to get her to do it again.

Raina stood in the tunnel that led onto the field and tried to quell the nerves in her stomach. From above them, the rumble of the crowd filling the stands sounding alarmingly loud. Deacon Field wasn't a huge stadium—it only held about thirty thousand people—but that was still far more than any theater she'd ever performed in. Not that she was performing today.

She gave herself a mental shake. She should be reassuring the Angels, who were about to make their debut, rather than standing here suffering nerves on their behalf. They'd worked really hard and she was pretty proud of what she'd gotten them to achieve—but at the end of the day, she knew, the reaction to them wouldn't be about the dancing, it would be about the fact that Alex was using cheerleaders in baseball to start a bit of good old-fashioned controversy.

He was relying on the publicity and a degree of scandal. There hadn't been any coverage of the Angels to date—somehow the Saints' media team had worked some voodoo to avoid the news leaking—just a promise of some entertainment between the innings.

And now they—Alex and Mal and Lucas and her and her dancers—were about to find out how good a judge Alex was of the mood of his team's fans.

"This is kind of ridiculous, huh?" Marly said, standing next to her.

Raina looked up at her—and it was a long way up. Marly was nearly the tallest dancer in the troupe, somewhere around five nine without the wings that added more to her height. Combined with the very blue eyes and very blond hair and the oomph Brady's costume had given her cleavage, she was an impressive sight. She was a great dancer, too. Really great. Nearly as good as Ana. And unlike Ana, Marly didn't have the personality of a narcissistic cobra.

Raina kept wondering if she should try to interest Marly in giving burlesque a go. Her height was almost enough to work against her on Broadway but it wouldn't be a hindrance at Madame R, where the burlesque artists came in all sorts of shapes and sizes.

"It's going to be great," Raina said. She looked back over her shoulder. The rest of the squad filled the tunnel that led back to the depths of the stadium, variously stretching or chatting. Ana, who would be at the head of the line when they finally walked out onto the field, was standing apart from all the others, looking supremely bored. Raina had practically had to wrestle her smartphone out of her hand when they'd left the locker room, and apparently life without her texts and social media accounts was too tedious to bear.

Behind Ana, Raina spotted Chen, the security guy Mal had assigned to the Angels. He, unlike Ana, looked alert and watchful and Raina tried to push away the nagging question in her mind about why Mal hadn't come down to wish her luck. Because the part of her brain coming up with that question was stupid. It was the same part that had kissed him. Best ignored.

She turned back to Marly. "It's going to be great," she repeated.

"It's going to be interesting at least," Marly said with a grin. "But still, it's been fun."

"It will keep being fun."

"I hope so. The money is nice. But they'll can us if the fans hate us."

That might be true but Raina had read the contracts before she'd signed up and she'd made sure the girls would still be paid a good chunk of their salary for the gig if the Angels did get canceled. Cheerleaders might get screwed over in some other sports, but she'd been determined that wasn't going to happen on her watch.

Dancers worked damned hard and they deserved to be paid for their efforts.

"Alex Winters isn't the type to give up easily," she said, trying to sound reassuring.

"Let's hope his partners agree," Marly said. She hitched a shoulder. "Can you check my harness at the back? It feels like it's twisted."

"Sure, turn around."

Marly did and Raina reached between the wings to

run her fingers along the straps. One section had folded over; she smoothed it into place.

"There. All done." She turned back from the wings and found herself face-to-chest with Malachi Coulter.

She'd avoided him since he'd come to the club. Since that kiss. It had been easy enough to do. Everything at the Saints had been frantically busy these last few crazy days, with no time for socializing. Just for wondering why he hadn't come to find her.

But absence, it seemed, hadn't made the body grow less fond. Her pulse went into double time. She stepped back and almost ran into Marly, who blocked her with a well-placed hand between her shoulder blades.

"Hello, Raina," Mal said.

She tilted her head back to look at him. He wore a sharply cut dark suit—in the glaring light of the tunnel, she couldn't tell if it was black or navy or a very dark gray—and a white shirt and a Saints tie. The suit outlined his shoulders and the long lines of his body with loving precision. His hair was, for once, tamed, combed back from his face, and he'd shaved the stubble he usually sported, leaving the strong clean angles of his face on display. And all those angles seemed to lead to his mouth. That delicious mouth that she'd been trying so hard not to think about.

The mouth smiled at her below brown eyes glinting with something that might have been him remembering their kiss, too.

Her mind went blank.

He'd looked pretty good in jeans and T-shirts. Dressed up, he was pushing *all* her buttons. Bad boy in good guy packaging.

"Um, hello," she said when she remembered how to speak. "What are you doing down here?"

"Came to see that everything was okay."

"We're good," she said. "Maggie came down to see us in the locker room."

"And the guys went through the security stuff with all of you?"

She nodded. "Yes. Chen explained everything."

Above them the crowd roared suddenly and she figured the inning had come to an end. Which meant any minute now she was going to get a cue and the Angels would be on.

"I think they're about to play our song," she said to Mal. "If you'll excuse me?"

"You're welcome to come up to the owners' box, after," he said.

"Thanks. Maggie already invited me." She didn't say that she'd tried to wriggle out of it as gracefully as possible—she'd figured that Mal might be there.

She looked at the dancers, who were starting to do the nervous little things that dancers did before they went on. Stretching and jogging in place and flexing hands and feet. Tugging at costumes and fussing at the tall white wings. Ana made her way up to the front of the tunnel and the rest of the squad lined up behind her.

"We're about to go on," Raina said, and Mal stepped back somewhat reluctantly. Raina made herself focus on the girls. "Okay, ladies. This is your big moment. So go out there and show them what an angel looks like, okay? Whatever happens, just smile and, for God's sake don't stop dancing." God, she wished she could go out with them, but she couldn't coach from the sidelines. No, she had to stay here in the mouth of the tunnel and let them do their thing.

"We're good," Marly said as she moved into her place behind Ana. "You go talk to the nice boss man some more." She winked at Raina and flicked her blond curls back into place.

"I don't need to talk to the boss man," Raina said. "I've got you all to wrangle."

"Everyone needs to talk to a tall drink of water like him," Marly said.

"Well, then, feel free."

"Sweetie, that man has barely looked at any of us the entire time we've been training. He does, however, do a lot of looking at you."

"He can look all he wants," Raina said. "Now, focus on the routine please."

"Sure," Marly said with another grin. "Easy for me to focus. Malachi Coulter isn't angling to get me into his bed."

"He isn't—" Raina started to protest but then she heard the cue from the guy talking in her headset, and a second later the opening bars of "Send Me an Angel" started to boom over the speaker system. She stepped out of Marly's way and watched as the entire line of dancers snapped into position, not a wing out of place.

"Break a leg," she muttered as they started their slow walk out onto the field. And then she sat back to watch the show.

It had gone pretty well. At least she thought it had.

The fans had been pretty enthusiastic and none of the

dancers had killed herself with her wings, so all in all, pretty good.

She'd balked on the invitation to go up to the owners' suite though. For one thing she hadn't really thought about bringing respectable clothes with her because she was driving straight to Madame R's after she was done with the performance. So she was in yoga pants and her favorite pair of foot-pampering trainers with a simple black tunic top and long red cardigan thrown on over them. Not ratty but hardly what you'd wear to hobnob with millionaires.

So she'd overseen the girls cleaning up and changing and helped stow all the sets of wings in the lockers that had been designed for them. They were all invited to a postgame event—an invitation also extended to her, but one she'd already declined—so they all primped madly and she had to sit there and listen to them talking about which of the players was cutest. Which had prompted her to remind them about Mal's warning about getting involved with a player.

At one point Marly came over, bringing with her a waft of freshly applied perfume and hair spray, and sat down next to her. "You're wasting your time hiding down here, you know. I heard him invite you up to the box."

"I am not interested in Malachi Coulter," Raina said.

"Yes, I could see that by how you went all tongue-tied and pink when he said hello to you in the tunnel."

Raina looked around, hoping desperately that no one else had overheard. "I don't date men I work for."

"You're not really working for him."

"He owns a third of this team. Of this bloody stadium. So yes, I'm working for him."

"Not forever, though," Marly said. "And not full-time. So it shouldn't be a problem. My grandma always said to make hay while the sun shines. And that man is worth making hay with."

"Not gonna happen," Raina said. "He's not a good long-term prospect. Not for someone like me."

"Maybe." Marly shrugged. "But think of how much fun you could have in the short term."

Raina narrowed her eyes at her. "Don't you need to flat-iron your hair or something? You gals need to look good at the party so the press has someone to take pretty pictures of. So why don't you worry about finding someone to make hay with yourself?"

"Not interested in a ballplayer," Marly said. "That's almost as bad as hooking up with an actor. Athletes are all about themselves. I like a man who's all about me."

"I didn't mean one of the players. I'm sure there'll be plenty of guys there who aren't on the team," Raina said. "They'll be inviting all the season ticket holders and sponsors—all kinds of men."

"Which raises the question of why, if you're really not interested in the boss man, you're not coming along."

"I have this minor detail called a business to run. You girls aren't the only dancers I've got to keep in order."

"You can't miss one night?"

"Not a Saturday. Saturday is our biggest night. I emcee the show."

"Well, your loss."

"I'll survive," Raina said. "It's not like I've never been to a party before." She had to admit to a certain amount of curiosity. She'd seen pictures from the fund-raiser the Saints had held at the Paragon earlier in the year. It had looked divine, with a steampunk-meets-angels theme that was right up her alley. Maggie had told her some of her plans for tonight and they sounded pretty good, too.

But hey, Saturday nights at the club were also a blast. And there, she wouldn't do anything stupid like drink too much champagne and throw herself at Malachi Coulter's feet. She glanced over at the screen in the corner of the room that was showing the game. "Hey, it looks like they're actually winning," she said. "I might sneak out and watch the end of the game. You want to come with me?"

Marly swept a hand down at the very short, very tight vivid-blue dress she'd squeezed herself into. "Not exactly designed for sitting in the bleachers."

Raina laughed. "I guess not. Well, I've got my phone, so text me if anyone needs anything. I'm staying for the press conference after the game, and then I'm out of here." Maggie had promised that Raina wouldn't have to say anything at the press conference but had insisted she come along in case anyone needed more info about the Angels. Maybe she should take Marly with her. The sight of her in that dress would distract the press from any negative things they might be planning to say about the performance or the squad.

But she'd worry about that later. Right now, she was going to see if she could find an empty seat and eat a hot dog and watch some ball.

Chapter Seven

Raina tried to slip away after the press conference, thankful that no one had actually come with a question about the Angels that Alex hadn't been able to answer. That meant she been able to dodge having to actually speak to the assembled reporters. She'd been sitting off to the side with Maggie rather than with Alex, Mal, and Lucas, which was also good because she'd managed to avoid talking to Mal again. Her plan was to get the hell out of Deacon and continue avoiding him. Sadly she didn't manage to get very far before Mal caught up to her.

"You're not coming to the party?" he asked as he appeared next to her in the corridor.

He was about the tenth person to ask her this since Marly had. She kept walking, trying to look like she had very important things to do. "It's Saturday night. I have to be at my club." She didn't look at him.

He and Alex and Lucas had been grinning like loons during the press conference. Only to be expected when the Saints had managed to just steal victory in the last inning. It wasn't the greatest performance in baseball ever but it was, at least, a promising start to the season.

Still, even though she felt happy for them, and happy that they seemed pleased with the Angels' reception, she was less happy to be confronted with a delighted Mal.

Because delighted Mal was even more appealing than ever, something of the tension he carried with him vanishing, and leaving a sort of loose vibe that made every inch of her quiver.

She knew loose and delightful and sexy. That was practically the hallmark of her particular brand of poison when it came to bad boys. She liked the charming ones. The witty ones. The ones who could disarm her with a wicked smile and a quick-fire punch line.

Pity that those particular characteristics seemed to come with wanderlust, no ability to commit, or what her grandmother would have called fecklessness. Or even less pleasant traits.

She'd sworn to herself that she wouldn't go there again. Not after Jeremy. But then she'd met Patrick. Also charming with that touch of an edge. Not the moody artistic version like Jeremy, more the never-quite-grown-up version. Seemingly a good guy who had a taste for very loud metal bands but no other obvious faults. Pity she hadn't seen the less obvious ones. She'd been so relieved to find someone not the kind of jealous over-controlling idiot Jeremy had been that she'd relaxed too quickly. Not kept her guard up. Trusted too soon.

Patrick had cleared out half her bank account on his way out of her life. Half a very hard-earned nest egg— thankfully not all of it as she'd had part of it safely squirreled away in a term deposit—but enough to put a dint in her financial security, her pride, and her faith in her instincts as far as men were concerned.

And then he'd managed to disappear into thin air as far as the cops were concerned. The money was gone as thoroughly as he was. A fact that still made her want to punch something whenever she thought about it.

She needed that money. Her plan to buy the building where Madame R was housed someday would give real security to her—as well as to her family, all the strays and dreamers who, like her, had devoted their lives to the mystery of theater or dance for mostly love.

The need to rebuild her nest egg as soon as possible was the reason she'd taken the crazy contract with the Saints.

Her landlord—Phil—had been particularly unpleasant lately and she wanted to be able to make him an offer he couldn't refuse if push came to shove and he tried to oust her. So that she wouldn't be thrown out on the street to start all over again. She was tired of that life. Of changing theaters and companies and shows and never knowing how long something might last. Jeremy and Patrick hadn't helped in that department.

She wanted some solid ground. Bedrock. Roots. Whatever you wanted to call it. Something that couldn't be snatched away from her. Which would've made most of her friends, who always held her up as a shining example of someone born to thrive in the firefly life of the theater, scream with laughter.

And here was Malachi Coulter. Seemingly solid. But she knew wild at heart when she smelled it.

Like called to like.

Or something.

Which was why it was so disturbing to see that so clearly and still want him like she wanted oxygen or music to dance to.

Malachi who was walking quietly beside her, apparently not going to argue with her.

Which made her even more nervous. She needed to ditch him asap. "I know my way back to the locker room."

He didn't change his pace, just glanced down at her with a half smile. "I know you do. But it's dark out now and I'm walking you to your car."

"It's not dark in the underground lot," she pointed out. "Gardner got me a space today."

Mal shrugged. "It will still be mostly deserted. My guys have done their last sweeps of the stadium to make sure everyone has cleared out but I'm not taking any chances."

She wondered if that was true. Was he being chivalrous or was he just finding an excuse to spend some time with her? And then she wondered which of those options was more disconcerting.

She didn't have an answer.

They reached the elevator. Raina pressed the button and held it for a few seconds too long, willing the aging lift to move faster than its usual glacial pace. The locker rooms were down in the lower levels, and the press conference had been held in one of the big meeting rooms on the executive floor.

The door slid open and Raina stepped in. Mal followed.

It wasn't a big elevator but it wasn't tiny. And yet Mal

seemed to take up a little too much space. Long legs and broad shoulders and altogether too much man still show-cased in that very nice suit. She moved back slightly, practically wedging herself into the corner.

The silence turned heavy and dense as they stood watching the numbers above the door go down slowly.

Say something.

Say something, idiot.

"You must be happy with the win," she managed. Safe subject. Hopefully. If he was like most sports-mad men she knew, he'd be able to talk for hours about the game. She liked baseball but she didn't feel any need to know every last detail about her team. In this case, though, she was willing to let Mal talk and to shut up and listen if it meant avoiding the heat practically light-ing the air between them.

Mal smiled then.

Damn. She'd forgotten about that delighted smile and its killer effect. She should've picked an unpleasant topic.

"It was a start," he said. "It would've been nice if they'd gotten some more runs on the board, locked it up earlier."

"That's a bit harsh. The Saints aren't exactly the great-est team in the league. You should be happy with the win." He laughed and she narrowed her eyes at him. "You're one of those never-satisfied types, aren't you?"

"No," he said. "But I'm a realist. It was a good start and the guys should be proud of themselves but they can do better. They will do better."

Heaven help them if they didn't.

Maggie had told her that Mal was the least intense of the terrible trio, as she called them. Either she was really wrong about that or Alex and Lucas were taking intense to a whole new level. Raina reminded herself not to bring up the team's performance in anything other than a glowing light around those two, just in case.

The elevator jolted to a stop and the door slid slowly open, the dinging sound that accompanied the action sounding distorted and weird.

Maybe Mal made it nervous, too.

Mal stepped out and put his palm on the edge of the door, waving her out. She scurried past him and headed off down the hallway to the locker room, not waiting to see if he was following her. Mostly because she knew he would be.

She swiped her pass at the door and went inside to grab her stuff. Which consisted of her coat and the huge old black case that housed her emergency kit. As usual, it looked a little worse for wear, stuffed to the gills with spare tights and cold packs and ibuprofen and eyedrops and every type of makeup anyone could possibly ever need backstage along with half a hundred other things that could come in handy in a performance emergency. But the zipper, though strained, was closed and she wasn't going to take the time to fuss with it with Mal looming at her side. She shrugged into the coat and flipped up the handle on the case.

Mal held out his hand. "I'll take your case."

"I can manage," she said.

"I know," he said. "But I'm offering."

"Are you going to get huffy if I say no?"

"I'm not sure I've ever been 'huffy' in my life. So no, probably not. If you're determined to drag that around by yourself, so be it."

She was tempted to put him to the test. But then she remembered just how awkward the case could be. And she had a show to do tonight. So conservation of energy was only sensible. She stepped out of his way. "Be my guest. Thank you," she added.

"My pleasure," he said. She waited for another grin. Or an eyebrow waggle. Or something. But no, he just lifted the case off the bench effortlessly and rolled it over to the door. Which he then held for her.

Her grandmother would be impressed. A polite big ol' parcel of man trouble. Which made a nice change. Though Raina was determined not to be impressed.

"The press was pretty good, about the Angels, I thought," she offered as they headed to the parking lot.

Mal nodded. "Yes. There'll probably be some really stupid puns in the headlines tomorrow but at least no one has thrown a fit." He looked down at her. "They looked good. I still think cheerleaders in baseball is a dumb idea, but you did a good job."

"Thanks." They'd reached the door to the parking lot and Mal swiped his pass to let them through. On the other side, he looked around the parking lot. "Which one is—no, wait. Let me guess. It's the hot-pink pickup?"

"Guilty," she said. Rose was hardly an extravagance; she'd bought her as a very hard-used dirt-cheap means of transporting herself once she'd moved out of Manhattan a few years ago. When she'd finally opened Madame R's, Brady and Luis had surprised her with the new paint job, an engine refit, and gleaming black leather upholstery as a business-warming present.

It still made her smile every time she saw her truck. It made her smile now as they crossed the lot.

"Do you want the case in back or inside?" Mal asked when they reached Rose.

"In this weather, inside," Raina said. She unlocked the passenger door. Mal lifted the case inside. As she shut the door, he said, "Nice truck. I like these old Fords."

"You'd just prefer it not to be pink?" she said.

"Not really my color," he said with another smile. Then, as Raina moved to skirt around him, his expression went grim.

She froze. "What?"

His chin jerked toward the hood. "You have a flat tire."

"What?" she repeated. "Really? Crap." She craned her neck to see, trying not to think of the time. Normally she was at Madame R midafternoon on Saturdays. And it was already close to six. They opened at eight and the show started around nine. But there was no denying the fact her tire was doing a pretty good pancake impersonation. So time to deal and get on with things. "It's okay," she said. "I have a spare. And Triple A."

Mal prowled around to the other side of the truck. His mouth went flat when he got there. "Do you have two spares?"

"Two?" She darted around to join him. The front tire on the driver's side was just as flat. "Fuck."

"Pretty much," Mal said. "One tire might be an accident. Two is deliberate."

"Or maybe just very bad luck," she said. "Maybe I drove over some glass or something."

Mal knelt by the tire and ran his hands over it. "Nope. Someone stabbed it." He stuck his finger into the side of the rubber, and the top joint disappeared inside the tire.

"Glass doesn't usually cut the sidewall." He scowled at the tire.

"Maybe someone didn't like the Angels so much after all," she said.

Mal pushed back up to his feet, shaking his head. "Pretty fast job of figuring out that you're the choreographer and this is your truck." He wiped his hand on his suit, leaving a smudge of grime across the leg.

Raina winced.

"What," he said.

"You just got mud and grease and God knows what else on what had to be a very expensive suit," Raina said.

"I'll get it cleaned," he said, voice holding a distinct rumble. "My suit is hardly our biggest problem right now."

"*My* biggest problem right now is how I'm going to get back to the club." Where she would now need to have a very good night to be able to squeeze two new tires into her very tight budget. She didn't want to dip into her Saints money if she could possibly avoid it.

"No, your biggest problem is whoever did this to your tires."

"It could've been anyone," she protested.

Another head shake. "This area is VIP only. I don't think anyone on the team or any of the sponsors or ticket holders slashed your tires. Which means whoever did this snuck in."

"Well, you have that whiz-bang security system," she said. "So you'll be able to see who did it, right? Which means we can deal with it. But that still leaves me with no ride and a club in Brooklyn about to open."

"I'll take you," Mal said.

"You," she said, doing some definite head shaking of her own, "have a party to go to. And a team to congratulate. And important baseball-team-owner stuff to do. You're can't go haring off to Brooklyn."

"Haring?" He looked amused. "You do like strange words. First I'm huffy, now I'm haring."

"I read," she said, sticking her chin out. "My folks believed in education, and you get a lot of spare time hanging around in theaters. So I read. And do crosswords. I'm betting I could beat your butt at Scrabble."

"Probably," he said. "Though I read, too."

"Security system manuals and computer programming books don't count," she said. "No one ever got a pithy phrase from one of those."

That made him laugh. "No, probably not," he said. "But we've strayed from the subject. Which was me taking you to Brooklyn."

"No, it was how you're not going to take me to Brooklyn. Because you are needed elsewhere. And besides, you ride a Harley. There's no room for my case on a Harley." God knows, she did not want to spend any time pressed up against Mal's body on the back of a motorcycle. "Just call me a cab. I'll be fine."

He looked distinctly displeased again. "Not a cab. I'll call my driver."

"You have a driver?"

"Yes. Sometimes I need to work, not drive."

She wasn't going to argue. But it was another reminder that he wasn't a good proposition. He was a bad boy, despite his manners, but he was a wealthy bad boy. Which meant that he probably wouldn't clear out her bank account, but he was likely to do some serious damage to her heart when he moved on to someone far more suitable to date the owner of the New York Saints than a thirty-year-old burlesque club owner.

"Okay," she said. "Call him."

"We're not done discussing who did this," Mal said.

"I didn't for a moment expect that we were," she said. "But Luis has fixed all the things you suggested at the club and Saturday's the night we have the most security staff, so I'm perfectly safe at Madame R's."

He looked as though he was going to argue but then he just pulled out his cell and made the call. When he'd hung up, he said, "Five minutes."

"You keep a driver on call here on Staten Island?"

"I'm going to a party," Mal said. "I'm not going to ride home after that, so yes, Ned's on call tonight. He came to the game. This will give him something to do while I'm schmoozing."

"He doesn't get to come to the party?"

"He was invited. He declined. He likes to watch movies on his laptop while he waits for me. Said he's got a new one he's been looking forward to. He's not much into socializing, Ned."

"Let me guess, he's ex-army, too?" Malachi seemed the type to employ one of his old army buddies.

"Yes," Mal said. He looked up as the doors slid open and a man wearing a neat dark-gray suit, his sandy-brown hair military-short, walked through carrying a briefcase in one hand and a set of keys in the other.

Mal extracted Raina's case from Rose, waited while she locked the truck, and then held out his hand. "Leave your keys with me."

"Why?"

"Because I know a guy with a garage near here. He'll come and fix your tires."

"Does everyone just jump when you snap your fingers?" she murmured. Still, she needed Rose, and if Mal's way meant getting her back faster, then so be it.

"Everyone but you," Mal said as she tugged her car key off her fob and handed it to him.

She wasn't sure if he was joking or not so she just kept quiet while she followed him across the lot to where the guy in the gray suit—Ned presumably—was standing beside a black Mercedes.

"Ned, this is Raina," Mal said. "She needs to go to Brooklyn." He reeled off the club's address. "See that she gets inside safely. I'm going to be at this party until about midnight, I'd say. So you don't need to be back until eleven at the earliest. Grab some dinner or something."

Raina had thought that the Saints had a game in Baltimore the next day, but maybe the team would go home early and the party would continue without them. Or maybe they were used to burning the candle at both ends. Not that she thought the terrible trio were likely to put up with any of their players doing the sorts of things that seemed to land pro athletes on the wrong side of the law and the media.

"Sure," Ned said. His voice was soft but deep. "Just call if you need me sooner."

"I will," Mal said. He turned his attention back to Raina. "I'm going to call the security team now, get them to look at the tapes. So we'll be talking about this."

"So you said." She still wasn't sure why he seemed to be taking this so personally. Was he upset because someone had gotten past his security system? Or because it was her who'd been targeted? The second possibility made no sense. They hardly knew each other. One kiss wasn't enough to make him bent out of shape about a flat tire or two, was it?

She didn't really want to know. There was a fine line between concern and control. She'd let a man drag her across that line once. Never again.

It was easier to think of Mal as pure chemistry. Heat that could flare up like rocket and fade just as quickly. Then he'd be easier to resist. And resisting him wasn't making her day any easier. So, time to hit the road. She held out her hand to Ned. "Hi, I'm Raina Easton. You must be Ned."

Ned nodded and took her case from Mal. "Yes, ma'am." He clicked something and the lights on the Merc came on as the lid of the trunk slowly eased upward.

"Raina," she said firmly. "Mr. Coulter, thank you for the help. I'm glad you liked the routine today." And then she fled into the safety of the backseat of the Mercedes and let Ned drive her away.

Chapter Eight

Mal arrived at Madame R just before midnight. He parked Raina's pickup—his excuse for coming to see her—in the street behind the club. If someone was harassing Raina, there was no point providing them with such a tempting target right out in the open.

He walked back around to the front entrance.

Luis was at the door. "Hey, man, congratulations on the game." He waved Mal through with a grin.

"Thanks." Mal nodded and slipped into the tiny foyer. He paid the cover charge and ascended the stairs. The sound of music and voices was much louder than it had been the other night. Figured. Saturday night was the busiest night for just about anywhere that served booze. Add in pretty women doing interesting things in the sort of dress Raina had been wearing the other night and the patrons would be rolling in. As he pushed through the curtain at the top of the stairs, he stopped, getting his bearings. The small stage was empty and it seemed the band was taking a break but there was music blasting from the sound system, Pink singing about blowing someone one last kiss.

He didn't want to think about last kisses.

He was much more focused on that first kiss. And the one after that. The next kiss.

But that meant convincing Raina that the next one had to happen.

Despite the noise, the crowd seemed tame enough. There wasn't the sort of vibe to the room that he associated with trouble. Between the army, security work, and traipsing around various dives after Ally, he had a pretty good radar for trouble when it was brewing.

But nothing was spiking his senses right now, so he relaxed a little and changed his surveillance of the room to something more targeted. Seeking out one bright-red head in the sea of heads.

It took longer than he'd thought. Raina wasn't exactly tall, not even if she strapped on four-inch heels. Hell, next to the girls from the Angels she was positively tiny, so she didn't stand out from the crowd. But eventually he caught a glimpse of red and started to work his way through the crowd toward it. As he got closer, he heard her laugh ring out.

The shock of it—of that moment of instant gut-tightening recognition—made his head feel light for a moment as his body tightened. God, that was a sexy laugh. No wonder he couldn't see her. She was ringed by a group of men, all of them likely—unless they were complete morons—trying to make her laugh again.

One of them must have succeeded because her laugh came again. He closed the last few feet then hesitated. He was trying to convince Raina to give him a shot. She was obviously nervous about him. Thought he was a bad boy. Charging in on her conversation like a caveman staking his claim wasn't going to improve that impression of him. The grouped men were standing near the bar. So maybe it was time for a bit of strategy while he scoped out the situation more thoroughly. He turned toward the bar and found a gap in the row of people trying to buy drinks. He slid into the space, just a foot or so from Raina and her admirers.

One of the bartenders leaned forward to hear Mal's order over the noise. He'd limited himself to a single glass of champagne at the Saints party for the toast that Alex had made but hadn't felt like anything more. Maybe in the back of his mind he'd been planning to come to Raina all along. Whatever the reason, he was in Brooklyn now, just a short cab ride home, so he could have another drink. "Scotch," he said. "Rocks."

He generally stuck to beer these days but standing here and listening to Raina laugh, he needed something stronger. Something that might have enough burn to dull the irresistible pull Raina seemed to exert on him.

Because, despite all the explanations and rationales he'd been giving himself for why exactly he was here again and why exactly he'd offered Tucker a hefty bonus to replace Raina's tires after hours on a Saturday, the driving force was the need to see her again. Of course, the fact that Tucker was an ex-cop who could check the tires and Raina's car for prints was also handy.

His desire to see her again was, to be fair, tempered

with a healthy dose of concern after her tires had been slashed. That had set all his instincts to high alert. Still, even if that hadn't happened, if Raina had just jumped in her hot-pink truck and driven off after the press conference, he was pretty sure he would have found himself back here anyway. Wanting to see that face. Wanting to see the green eyes light up when she thought she was putting him in his place. Wanting to hear that little rasp in her voice and taste that goddamn mouth.

And now here he was with no idea how to bring that about.

He turned, scotch in hand, but didn't give up his spot at the bar. Keeping half an ear on Raina and her group of admirers, he settled in to wait for the herd to thin a little. To occupy the time, he scanned the room and the crowd, seeing if anyone stood out. Someone was targeting Raina. Question was, Why? And were they ballsy enough to try to get close to her?

But he didn't spot anyone who made him pause. Everyone seemed to be enjoying themselves, in small groups and couples. Laughter and the clink of glasses filled the room. He didn't see anyone sitting by themselves. No men—or women—who seemed out of place.

Another mouthful of scotch, the peat-tinged burn of it warming his stomach. She served good liquor. He hadn't specified a brand yet what he was drinking was a decent single-malt. Not the blended cheap stuff that so many bars would try to fob off on the customers.

She'd want people to enjoy themselves. And that included drinks that were as good as the entertainment.

He heard Raina laugh again and turned toward the group. Just in time to see two of the men move away.

Which left a gap in the throng surrounding her. He could see the moment she spotted him. Her smile went a little stiff and then he saw her force herself to relax. To look like she didn't care.

It didn't work. He could also see the flush in her cheek and the sudden deepening of her eye color.

He waited.

She stayed where she was. Neither of them looked away.

One heartbeat. Two. Three. Four.

Then, to his relief, she gave the tiniest shake of her head, flashed a brilliant, apologetic smile at the men around her, and came toward him.

It didn't take many steps. Just barely long enough for Mal to register the looks of annoyance on the faces of the guys she was abandoning. And for him to enjoy the hit of satisfaction that hummed through his veins as they shot him looks that should have set his hair on fire.

He refrained from the smile he wanted to send back at them. The smug I-win smile. Because, while it would be undeniably satisfying, it might just send Raina turning on her heel and heading back to them.

So. Dismiss the other men from his mind. Focus on the woman. The one who had an equal chance of setting him on fire. Only in all the good ways.

"Ms. Easton," he said when she tilted her head to one side, put her hand on her hip, and looked up at him with challenge clear in her eyes.

"Mr. Coulter," she replied, letting the last word stretch out just a little. It put a slightly rougher note in her voice that was pure sex. "You developing a taste for burlesque?"

He let his smile go then. "Maybe." He returned the

look she was giving him. "Some of it anyway." Tonight she wore red. Red satin. A shade lighter than blood. The shade of femme fatale lipstick and expensive racing cars. Designed to stop a man in his tracks.

It was working.

The satin hugged her body more tightly than the fringed dress from the other night had. It shouldn't have made him feel like he'd been hit in the gut with a two-by-four. After all, he'd seen her in workout gear that revealed more of her than the dress did. He was familiar with the sleek lines of her and the curves.

But apparently red satin changed things. Especially paired with equally red lips and slicked-down hair and sparkling earrings that cascaded halfway down her neck, drawing attention to the curve where her neck met her shoulders with little squares of reflected light dancing over her pale skin. A perfect place to kiss.

His fingers curled into fists, resisting the urge to grab her and pull her up onto the bar so he could do just that.

He was having trouble remembering his name, let alone what his excuse for being here was, but he hadn't completely lost his reason.

"Nice dress," he managed.

"I'll tell Brady you like it," she said. "He designed it."

Mal made a note to tell Brady to keep up the good work. He obviously had a fine appreciation for the female form even if he didn't have any interest in getting up close and personal with it.

"Good job," he said.

Raina smiled and shifted her weight in a way that somehow made the satin pull even tighter across all sorts of interesting places.

"Was there something you wanted?" she asked.

And there was a leading question if ever he'd heard one. Which made him wonder if it was a test. He fished in his pocket for the keys to her truck, held them up. "I thought you might like these back."

"My keys?"

"Yup."

"My tires are fixed already?" She shook her head. "Let me guess, you said jump and the garage said how high?"

"Like I said, I know the guy." He wasn't going to explain to her about Tuck and his background. Not right now. "He was happy to do it. But if that's a problem, I can drive the truck right back out there and you can wait until morning to have it back."

She blinked at him. "No, I'd rather have it tonight."

"Then, as my mother would say, say thank you to the nice man." He grinned at her then.

She shook her head. "Oh no, you're not the nice man."

"What do you mean? I fixed your truck."

"You got someone to fix it, you mean."

"I delegated. Same difference."

"Not entirely."

"Still, it seems like a nice thing to do, to me."

"I rather think that that depends on your motivations," she said.

"You really want to talk about my motivations here in the middle of your club?"

Another head shake. "No. Because the show's about to start again and I have to get backstage. So thank you for getting my tires fixed." She held out her hand for the keys.

He didn't hand them over. "How about I just look after these until we have time to discuss my motivations?"

He waited for her to reach for them again. He would have handed them over if she did. But she didn't. Instead she just lifted an eyebrow then shrugged. "Fine." She glanced back over her shoulder at the bar. "Get yourself a drink and watch the show. I'll find you afterward."

Raina spent the show in a half daze. Operating on autopilot, she emceed her way through flirting with the crowd and getting the girls organized backstage. She and Brady had been working on a routine with the pink-and-black wings he'd made for her but she decided not to try it out tonight. Not with Mal in the audience watching her. She couldn't see him, didn't know if he'd stayed up the back at the bar or found another dark spot to lurk, but the stage lights in her eyes meant that she couldn't spot him in the crowd. She could, however, feel him.

Every time she stepped onto the stage, her skin warmed and her breath started to quicken; she had to use all the tricks she'd learned over the years to smile and carry on as if nothing was bothering her. As if she couldn't feel him watching her, feel the weight of his presence in the room.

She'd seen him standing at the bar and felt her heart turn over. She'd gone toward him without thinking. Had found it hard to walk away from him to do her job.

Damn the man. She was trying hard to do the smart thing.

But he kept turning up.

She had a feeling her grip on smart was rapidly loosening. Slipping and sliding as surely as her resistance.

Somehow she made it through the show without falling off the stage or losing her train of thought. When she finally got through the routine of bringing the girls back for a final bow and thanking the band, she might as well have run a marathon. Her breath was coming too fast and her legs felt oddly shaky.

She couldn't stop herself looking for him one last time. And this time she saw him. Standing up by the bar, though on the opposite side of the room from where he had been earlier. Their gazes caught, just for a second, and she thought he tipped the glass he was holding in her direction. Then she made herself look away before she couldn't.

She made herself take her time backstage, for once not going out and mingling with the last of the patrons before they left. She left the task of chasing them all out to Luis and his team while she hung out with the girls as they took off their costumes and wriggled into normal clothes. Some of them would head out to party on awhile longer. Others would be going home to families and bed. While she . . . well, she had to deal with Mal.

What exactly that might involve was something she couldn't quite make her mind focus on. She could play half a dozen scenarios in her head—sending him home, drinking with him, talking to him, finding him gone when she finally emerged from backstage, taking him home with her—but none of it felt quite real. Not when her blood was fizzing and her body was humming and the whole night seemed to have a peculiar sharpness to the air.

One by one the performers left until Raina had no choice but to retreat to her office. Normally she put her makeup on and took it off down in the dressing room with everyone else, but tonight she wasn't quite ready to wipe off the layers of cosmetics. Stage Raina, with her perfectly groomed brows, long black lashes, and bold red lips, always knew what to do. She could tame a song or a crowd or a routine and never miss a beat. Stage Raina could handle Mal Coulter. Real Raina wasn't so sure she could.

So Stage Raina could stay for now. Though she took off the dress and pulled on black jeans and a red sweater and exchanged the four-inch platform heels for boots that were far more comfortable but still gave her height a boost. She was happy enough to run around in flats most of the time—as a dancer, comfort for her feet came first—but tonight she needed those few extra inches.

War paint and battle armor.

Why did she feel like taking on Mal was a fight?

A fight for what, exactly?

It was a question she didn't want to examine too closely.

When she got down to the bar, Mal was still there. The sight of him, standing talking to Luis and Brady, made her pulse kick again. All right. He hadn't left. So she was going to have to deal with him one way or another.

Send him packing or let him come closer.

There wasn't another option and spending any more time dancing around each other was going to shred her nerves.

She pulled her shoulders back and walked into the fray.

The woman was on a mission, that much was clear to Mal as he watched Raina approach. Clear in the

I-mean-business posture of the straight back and the fluid dancer's stride that was tamed from sexy to purposeful. Clear in the sweater that revealed little skin but hugged her body tightly. Clear in the spike-heeled black boots and the flash of red lipstick still turning her mouth into something expressly designed to make a man think the sorts of thoughts he was trying not to think.

Question was, What exactly she was out to achieve? Getting rid of him or . . . no. Better not to think about that.

Though there was probably very little chance of not thinking about it. He'd been thinking about it all night. Ever since he'd climbed into her truck to bring it back to her.

As Raina reached them, Brady and Luis exchanged a look and then Brady said, "All right, we have some stuff to deal with before we go home. Good night." The two of them disappeared through a door to the side of the bar before he had time to respond.

Leaving him alone with Raina.

"You're still here," she said when she reached him. She'd tipped her head into that little head-tilt, challenging thing she did. Nervous.

Good nervous or bad nervous?

"I said I would be."

The angle of her head didn't alter. "So, how did you like the show?"

Definitely nervous. And maybe looking for things to help her make up her mind about him. Like him not liking her show. Well, she was going to have to look for another reason. He'd watched the show for nearly two hours and though, yes, the most sharply focused parts had been those where Raina herself had appeared between each act, he'd found the acts in between surprising. Funny, sexy, thoughtful. And a little bit intriguingly weird. Unexpected. Much like Raina herself. "I thought it was great."

"You—" Her mouth snapped closed.

He waited. Waited for her to say something like *Tell me what your favorite part was.*

But apparently she was too smart to give him that particular opening.

"You're not drinking?" she said looking behind him to the bar. The bartender had taken his glass a good while ago. He'd switched to soda after the whiskey.

"I was waiting for you."

"You want to drink with me?"

"I wanted to see you. If you want to drink, we can drink."

"It's getting late for a nightcap."

He shrugged. She was right. It was close to two a.m. And his body was going to hate him in the morning. He had an early start. But he'd been running on six hours of sleep or less for months now. So another night wasn't going to kill him.

"What's your poison?"

"Scotch usually. Beer. A good Merlot." Ally had drunk tequila by preference. He didn't do tequila anymore. Just the smell of it brought back too many memories.

"And if I don't care to offer you a nightcap?"

"Then I guess I'll walk you to your truck or wherever you need to go and we'll say good night."

"Just like that?"

He blew out a breath. "Raina, I'm not sixteen. Neither

are you. We have something here. Something you're not sure about getting into. I can respect that. I will respect that. But like you said, it's getting late. And I'm too old for long convoluted conversations that dance around the subject."

One side of her mouth lifted. "Convoluted? Now who's using big words?"

"What can I say, I read too. So you decide."

"Drinking or leaving?" she said.

"Or another option. Whatever you want. Tell me to go, I go." He watched indecision and something else—something he hoped was closer to frustration—flicker in her eyes. "Tell me to stay I stay. So tell me to stay."

"That's not letting me decide," she protested.

"I didn't say I wouldn't state my case," he said.

"You want to give me a list of your pros and cons?"

"Preferably just pros for now. So what's it to be?"

"I—" She stopped. Swallowed. "A drink. Just a drink. For the sake of not being convoluted, a drink does not equal sex."

"Thanks for the clarification," he said drily. "But like I said, I'm not sixteen. I don't expect sex in return for the pleasure of my company." He grinned at her, relief pounding his veins. She hadn't sent him home. That was a step in the right direction. He nodded at the bar. "So, do you want to drink here or somewhere else?"

She rolled her shoulders. "Somewhere else. I'll be back here soon enough tomorrow." She rolled her shoulders again. "My place. It's not far from here."

He'd known that vaguely. That she lived close to the club. Which made sense. If you were going to work somewhere that involved long days and late nights, not having a long commute made life easier. He'd found himself wishing a time or two that he'd bought a place on Staten Island but Brooklyn was home, so he was sticking for now. He could always talk Alex into getting a company condo or something for nights when one or more of them needed to crash. Hopefully those nights would get less frequent in a month or so. Once they got into the rhythm of the season itself.

"Earth to Mal," Raina said. "I'm inviting you for a nightcap here, it does a girl's ego no good if you don't answer."

"Well, we can't have that now, can we?" he said. He nodded toward the velvet curtain and the stairs that were going to lead him out of the club and into Raina's more private world. "So lead on."

Chapter Nine

Raina undid the lock on her apartment door and pushed it open with a hand that was relatively steady. She'd been afraid that she might fumble her keys or something. She'd driven them from Madame R to her apartment. Mal had pointed out that leaving her truck on the street was just an invitation if there really was someone out there targeting her. And her apartment building came with a tiny parking lot that she could just squeeze Rose into.

But she didn't really remember much about the actual drive. She'd been far too aware of the man filling the passenger seat to focus on anything else. She was used to driving alone most of the time so it was odd to have someone with her, but it wasn't just the fact that she had a passenger that was making her nervous. No, that was down to who her passenger was.

Mal took up a lot of space. Her truck was big but he made it feel tiny. The cabin smelled like him. Male. Spicy. A hint of the odd mix of alcohol and crowds and greasepaint and candle smoke that she associated with the club still hung around, but mostly the scent of him enveloped her.

The same smell that had surrounded her and soaked into her skin when she'd kissed him.

And now he wasn't just in her truck, he was about to walk into her apartment. For a drink. Not sex. She'd told him that.

But now she had no idea if she was happy with that plan or not.

She held the door as he walked through, keeping an eye out for Wash in case he made one of his infrequent attempts to break for freedom. But no huge gray fuzzball appeared so she followed Mal into the apartment and shut the door, locking it behind them. The apartment was in a slightly nicer part of town than the club—it was strange what the distance of a few blocks could do in a city—but it wasn't all that much better. Still, it was affordable and close to Madame R, so it was fine as far as she was concerned. Plus it was about three times the size of the biggest apartment she'd ever had in Manhattan, so that was a bonus.

She dropped her keys into the vintage soap dish on the console table by the door and hung her bag and coat over the hook next to it.

As she turned back, she heard a thump and a chirrup as Wash jumped down from wherever he'd been sleeping and came to investigate.

He saw Mal and the chirrup changed to a more demanding meow.

Mal's eyebrows rose as he spotted the cat. "Well, he's not the runt of the litter, is he?"

Raina shook her head and bent to scoop Wash up. "He's a Maine Coon, they're big."

"He's bigger than my last dog. Heck, he's almost bigger than you."

She ignored that last part. "You had a little dog?" she asked. Mal seemed more the big-dog type. The kind to own a shepherd or a golden or something.

"Einstein. He was a Boston terrier," Mal said. "I kind of inherited him from a friend. He was a cool little dude."

"Was?"

"He died about a year ago." Mal's face went shuttered for a moment.

Her grip on Wash tightened reflexively, which made him chirrup a protest. "I'm sorry."

"He was fifteen. It's okay."

It wasn't. It never was, she knew that. Thank God Wash was only two. "You don't have a dog now?"

He shook his head. "I'm barely home at the moment. It wouldn't be fair. Maybe one day."

She nodded. And half kicked herself for asking. Dead pets were hardly the sort of thing she'd expected to discuss with Mal. "So," she said. "How about that drink?" She put Wash down. He promptly stalked over to Mal and sat at his feet, peering up at him with golden eyes.

Mal peered down, looking amused. "What's up, cat?"

"His name is Wash," Raina said. Wash sniffed Mal's leg, then rubbed himself quite deliberately across Mal's dark pants, leaving a trail of pale fur before heading for the kitchen. There he took up position beside his bowl with a demanding mrrrrooowwww.

Raina shrugged an apology at Mal and followed Wash. After scooping a suitably Wash-sized portion of food into his bowl, she took out two scotch glasses from the cabinet. One drink. Just one drink. Then she'd send him home.

"Ice?" she asked.

"Yes."

She made the drinks and shepherded him into her living room. Her sofa was small, more a love seat. So she took the spindly-legged pink velvet armchair and waved Mal to the sofa.

Then bounced back up to go to her computer and put on some music.

When she sat back down, Mal was sipping his drink, watching her over the rim of the heavy glass.

"Good scotch," he said.

"Life's too short to drink bad booze." She picked up her glass, took a mouthful, and tried to relax.

"Amen to that." He took another sip, looked around the room. "I like your place."

"It's small." His place, if she was remembering what she'd read about him correctly, was not.

Mal gestured at the room. "This looks like you."

She looked around. It wasn't too messy; despite the hectic last few weeks, she'd managed to spend a few hours here and there keeping the disaster zone to a minimum. But it was a riot of color. And overstuffed with well, stuff. Her tiny desk was disappearing beneath papers. And her plants needed watering. "It's home. For now."

"For now? You're thinking of moving?"

"Eventually, sure."

"Does that mean closing the club?"

"What? Oh. No. It means that one day hopefully the

club will be doing well enough that I can afford somewhere bigger."

"Ah. Somewhere for the giant cat to stretch his legs."

Wash chose that moment to come over and investigate what was happening now that he'd finished his dinner. He looked at Raina sitting in the chair, sent her a why aren't you on the sofa like normal, crazy human look, then sprang onto the sofa. He sniffed at Mal then retreated to the other end of the sofa, sitting watchfully.

"I get the feeling your cat disapproves," Mal said.

"He's a smart cat," she said.

Mal put down his glass. "Okay. Are you going to tell me exactly what about me makes you so nervous?"

How about everything? "That might take another drink or two." She swirled the ice around in her drink, heard the ice clink, then took a swallow. The scotch burned all the way down and set up a warm glow in her stomach. Not enough to distract her, though.

"All right, then who taught you to drink scotch?"

"Taught me?"

"Bad choice of words. Introduced you?"

She shrugged and shifted on the chair. Her legs protested with twinges. What she really needed right now was to stretch. Normally she'd be in the shower or the bath, easing the aches that five hours of too-high heels and performance sentenced her body to. But with Mal here that wasn't going to happen. "I've always danced. Which means paying attention to what I put into my body. When I was younger I was a little obsessed about it and beer was always too many calories. So I drank spirits. And my granddad drank scotch so that's what I drank. By the time I wised up on the diet front and realized I was never going to be a skinny ballerina, I'd acquired the taste for it. Never did go back and learn to love beer."

"Did you want to be a ballerina?"

"For a while. But like I said, wrong body type."

Mal smiled at her over his own glass. There was something wicked about that smile. "It looks pretty good to me."

She shot him a look.

"What? You left that opening a mile wide."

"I thought baseball players were meant to know when not to swing at something."

"Only if you always want to play it safe."

Meaning why not take a risk? On him? She ignored his line. She wasn't ready to step up to the plate. Not just yet. What had she been talking about. Ballet. Right. She looked down. She was hardly built like a bombshell but her proportions—or so her teachers had informed her—were wrong for ballet. "Anyway, ballet and I weren't meant to be. So I switched to other kinds of dance. That was the main thing, that I got to dance." And she'd just kept dancing. No matter what. That had been the one constant thing in her life. Dance. Pushing her body to its limits. Until it started pushing back. Her right calf twinged again and she stretched out her leg with a wince, leaning forward to catch the toe of her boot and pull her foot back to stretch before the twinge could develop into a full-blown cramp.

Mal put his glass down. "Cramp?"

She shook her head. "Not quite."

"Taking off those ridiculous heels might help."

"They're not ridiculous."

"Maybe not. And granted, they're very sexy, but you've been on your feet all day." He leaned forward. "Take them off, then come over here and I'll rub your feet."

Damn. The man played dirty. She loved foot rubs. But letting Mal Coulter put his hands on her bare feet was definitely stepping into dangerous territory. She hesitated.

"Just a foot rub, I swear."

"Dancer's feet aren't pretty," she said. Hers weren't as beaten up as an ex-ballet-dancer's—small mercies—and now that she wasn't performing in eight shows a week, they were starting to look less battered than they used to. But they weren't going to win any beauty contests.

"I'm offering to rub them, not judge them," he said. He patted the sofa. "Come here, Raina Easton."

Good sense told her to stay right where she was. But whiskey and tiredness and the irresistible lure of feet that didn't hurt were outvoting good sense tonight. She unzipped her boots, slipped them off, and then sat beside Mal on the sofa, feeling her heart pound. Her hands gripped the cushions for a second. Stupid body. Why did it react to Mal like he was the most delicious thing ever?

Maybe because he was.

"This is going to be easier if you put your feet in my lap," he said.

She reached for her drink, drained it, then set it on the side table. Telling herself it was the whiskey making her head spin, she scooted back until her spine hit the arm of the sofa where Wash was napping. Which earned her another protesting meow.

"Hush, cat," Mal said. "Captain's orders."

The laugh escaped Raina before she could stop herself.

Mal grinned. "I'm assuming he is named after Wash in *Firefly* then?"

"How did you know?"

He jerked his chin toward her desk. "Well, you have Mal and Inara figurines on top of your computer, for a start."

"You like *Firefly*?" Damn. Points to him.

"What's not to like?" He grinned at her then. "We Mals have to stick together. And I like his style. Though I'm not so big on his stoic repression of his feelings for Inara. But that's a conversation for another time. Now . . ." He patted his lap. "Give me your feet. Captain's orders."

She laughed again. "Sure thing, Captain Tight-pants." She put her feet into his lap.

"My pants aren't tight," he said. "This is a very well-cut suit. Lucas took me to his personal tailor and made me pay a fortune for it."

Given how good he'd looked in the suit back at Deacon, she thought that it had been money well spent. He looked even better now. He'd lost the tie and loosened his collar. Revealing a very distracting strong male throat. "Suit shmoot," she managed as he wrapped his hand around the ball of her foot and pressed his thumb into just the right spot beneath it.

She bit her lip to stifle the moan that rose in her throat.

Good fingers. She was a sucker for good fingers.

Clever hands. Lips that—

No. This was a foot rub.

Nothing more.

And if she believed that then she should probably try

to sell herself a few ownership shares in the bridge that she drove over every other day. Because damn, he had very good fingers.

She bit her lip as he hit another spot that made her muscles shiver in delight and tried to remember all the things that she'd thought were wrong with him.

Right now most of them were escaping her.

Double damn. Triple damn.

Or even, she thought as his fingers pressed and stroked, just a good old-fashioned fu-u-u-ck.

"Better?" Mal asked.

She managed a nod. Her neck felt strangely liquid, as though her head might float right off her body if she weren't careful. "Where did you learn to do that?"

"You can't expect me to give away all my secrets on our first . . . nightcap, can you?" he said. "Or at least, you have to ply me with more liquor first."

She tried to remember where she'd left the scotch. On the kitchen counter. Reaching it would mean getting off this sofa. Which she wasn't doing short of dynamite forcing the issue.

"How about the promise of liquor?" she said.

"I'll think about it." The fingers on her foot were slowly changing their rhythm. Less forceful, less coaxing of the knots and tension from her feet and more stroking every little nerve ending to life.

Who knew her feet had so many nerve endings? Or that the majority of them seemed to have rerouted themselves so they were sending their little spikes of pleasure straight to her groin. Her head dropped back and her eyes drifted close and she was too tired to fight the drugging effect of the sensations he was provoking.

"How about we return to our earlier topic," Mal said. "Tell me what you're afraid of?"

That snapped her eyes open. "Who said I was afraid?"

"Afraid. Concerned. Doubtful. Pick one. Why do you want to run away from this?" His voice was low and soft, the sound of it almost as smooth and targeted as his fingers.

So. The ball, so to speak, had been pitched. The curtain was going up. So was she going to step up to the plate . . . step into the spotlight . . . and tell him the truth or miss her moment?

She'd never been one to shy away from the spotlight. She swallowed. "Would you believe me if I said it's not you, it's me?"

Dark brows lifted. "I might. If you explain it more."

"It . . . it sounds silly. But I just don't trust my instincts with men anymore. Too many mistakes. So when my instincts say *This one*, I'm forced to consider if it's more sensible to do the exact opposite."

He frowned. "Did someone hurt you?"

"I'm thirty. It would be a little strange if I hadn't had my heart broken by now."

"You don't seem the type to let a little heartbreak destroy your confidence," Mal said. "I meant more than that. Did someone—a man—hit you?"

She tried not to shiver as the image of Jeremy, face contorted with anger, sprang to life in her head. But Mal must have noticed something because his expression darkened.

"You don't have to talk about it. Not if you don't want to," he said.

No. It was better to speak up. It had taken time to get

over the sense that it was her fault, the guilt that had gnawed at her and returned with a vengeance when Patrick had stolen from her. Guilt that she hadn't been able to see in advance what their true selves were. But it wasn't her fault. It was theirs. She took a deep breath. Let it out. Met his frowning gaze squarely. "I had one boyfriend. He was . . . difficult. Possessive. He put his fist through a wall a few inches away from my face one night."

"And?" Mal's voice was tense. Disgusted.

"He learned that dancers have plenty of lower-body strength. To the regret of his balls. I kicked him and got out of there and never went back." That wasn't the whole truth. And it left out the sick terror of that night, of running out of the apartment and flagging down the cab to take her to Brady's place, heart pounding in fear, thinking every moment that Jeremy was going to appear. To stop her. To hurt her.

Mal grinned. "Good girl." Then his face turned serious again. "Was that the end of it?"

She shook her head. "He was a problem for a while. Tried to convince me to come back. Turned up at the theater where I was working. Caused trouble. Until some of the guys I worked with dealt with him. He went away after that."

"It's not your fault he was a scumbag," Mal said, voice gentle. "You didn't deserve that."

She sighed. "I know. Logically I know that. But there have been just a couple too many princes who turned into frogs, you know." She looked down at her toes, unwilling to meet his eyes. "The last frog skipped town with most of my bank balance."

Mal frowned again. "Did you find him?"

"I talked to the police. They weren't that interested. Said it would be hard to prove I hadn't given him my passwords, et cetera. We'd been living together about six months. And I didn't have the money for a detective."

"How much?"

"Enough," she said. She didn't want to tell him about her plans for the club and why she was so keen to get her nest egg back up to scratch.

He nodded, obviously happy not to keep pushing the subject for now. "Well, I own a third of a baseball team and I have my own company. I'm not looking to skip town anytime soon and I promise you I don't need your money. And I've never hit a woman in my life."

"I didn't think you had," she said. "But it's not quite that simple."

"I understand being gun-shy," he said. "But you have to take a chance sooner or later."

"Why? My life is complicated enough right now. I'm not sure I even have time for a man. Why complicate it more?"

He ran a finger over her sole and she shivered.

"For one thing, there's that," he said.

"I can pay someone for foot rubs."

"I don't think that shiver was purely due to my foot rub skills."

Was she imagining things or had his eyes gone a shade darker? Was that even possible?

"You mean sex?" She tried to sound casual even though her mouth felt dry. Rookie mistake to bring up sex with a guy. In her experience, talking to guys about sex was best left to those times when you were trying to get said guys to sleep with you. Was that what she was doing? "Last time I checked there was no rule that said single women don't get to have orgasms."

He stilled. He pinned her with those eyes. Which were darker still. Near black. A hot liquid black. She swallowed.

"That may be true," he said. "And maybe one day I'd like to discuss that in more detail—" He stopped. Took a breath. Shook his head as though to clear his mind of something. Something no doubt involving the thought of her naked with her hand between her legs. "But you know, I've always found team sports more enjoyable than solo ones."

So had she. And now she was the one with pictures in her head. Naked pictures. Of Mal with *his* hand between her legs. Much more fun. Though far more dangerous. She tried to pull her foot back. He didn't let go.

"I think we've strayed from the subject," she said, trying to ignore the throaty note in her voice.

"You brought it up."

"And I'm shutting it down."

His fingers released. "If you say so. Which brings us back to bad choices. And why I'm not one."

"I only have your word for that."

He smiled. "You want references? I can call Alex right now."

"Alex knows that you're a good boyfriend?" She tilted her head at him, glad to ease the conversation back to lighter territory. "Is there something you're not telling me, Mr. Coulter?"

"Alex has known me since I was eighteen," he said. "And good looking as he is, he's never tried to convince me to bat for the other team. Mostly because he's pretty firmly entrenched in the same team I am. Team Girls Are Good. Now, stop changing the subject."

She sighed. "I don't know. It's just kind of hard to forget all the wrong choices, sometimes."

"I've made wrong choices, too," he said. "Everyone does."

"Not like mine,"

"You might be surprised. But that's a conversation for another time. You don't have to be perfect, Raina. No one does."

"Maybe. But you know what they say. Two wrongs don't make a right."

"I've never really cared what 'they' have to say about things. Two wrongs might not make a right. But maybe they make a good enough."

"A right for now?" She wanted him to be right. But she was horribly afraid he wasn't. "I'm not sure I have another right for now left in me."

"Raina." His hand grazed her cheek, and she couldn't stop herself leaning into his touch. "How about we just start from here and see what happens?"

Chapter Ten

"Define start from here?" Raina said.

His thumb brushed her lip, then he lifted his hand. "How about we start with another drink?"

He was giving her space. Time to think. Everything she needed. Which made it hard for her do the smart thing and climb off the sofa. She wanted to lean in. Get closer. Touch him back. Instead, she swung her feet off his lap and pushed to her feet, wincing a little at the pull in her legs.

"Okay?" he asked.

"Yes." She smiled. "Just a dancer who's getting older."

"You're barely thirty."

"That's ancient in dance years," she said. Rising to her toes, she stretched briefly then padded into the kitchen to retrieve the scotch.

"Is that why you have the club now instead of doing Broadway?"

She nodded. "That and the fact that no one ever got

rich in a Broadway chorus." She carried the scotch back with her and refilled their glasses.

"You want to be rich?" Mal asked as she passed him his drink.

"I want to be comfortable," she said. "To not be at the mercy of a landlord and the whims of others."

"And burlesque can give you that?"

She shrugged. "It's a start. If I can, I'll buy the building eventually. Have the club. Have some equity. I can build from there."

"Brooklyn real estate is expensive."

"No kidding." She sipped scotch. "But we'll see. I have four years left on the lease." At least she hoped she did. If Phil didn't change his mind and sell. "That gives me time to put money away, to build up a track record that would convince a bank to lend to me."

"It's a good plan. And if you ever want advice on real estate, Alex is your man."

She almost choked on her scotch. "I'm sure Alex Winters is too busy to worry about my investment portfolio or lack thereof."

Mal grinned. "Maybe. But he knows the ins and outs of the market and he knows a hell of a lot of talented people."

"I'll think about it." She took another sip and eyed the armchair and then the sofa. Wash, for once, hadn't woken from his napping position on the sofa arm to jump into the warm spot she'd vacated. That space was still there. If she wanted to sit back down so close to Mal.

Where was the harm? Mal had made it perfectly clear he wasn't going to do any jumping or lunging for her unless she invited him to. Perfectly safe.

And she wanted to be near him even if she didn't yet want to give in to the desire for more. She slipped back onto the sofa, curling her legs up beneath her. Her calves and feet still ached slightly but she wasn't ready to ask Mal to put his hands on her again. Not yet.

"So, Mr. Coulter," she said. "We keep talking about me. Tell me something about you."

Another glass and a half of scotch later and Raina's eyes were growing heavy, weighted down just enough by scotch to relax her. It was late. Too late for everything she needed to do in the morning. But it turned out that talking to Mal was easy, and the deep rumble of his voice was soothing, and it was tempting to just keep on talking. See in the sunrise. Something she hadn't done from this side in quite some time.

But before she could stop herself, a yawn stole across her face. She tried to hide it but to no avail.

"You're tired," Mal said.

"I am," she admitted. The yawn hadn't relieved the sleepiness stealing over her.

"Me too," he said. He glanced toward the window. Rain had been pouring down for the last hour or so. She realized that he didn't actually have a car with him. They'd driven her pickup. Of course, he had a driver or could call a cab. Though it seemed kind of heartless to throw the man out into the weather at three a.m. So. Go or . . .

Or what, exactly? Six feet plus of Malachi Coulter wouldn't fit on her couch. But she had a perfectly decadent king-sized bed.

"It's late," she said.

"It is," he agreed. His eyes had gone intent again, though he hadn't moved from his position slouched against the arm of the couch, body turned to face her.

"You don't have a car."

"Also true."

The ball was obviously in her court. "I have a bed," she said after swallowing. "You could stay. Sleep, I mean. That's all that's on the table."

"You want me to keep one foot on the floor at all times?" he asked.

"That sounds uncomfortable. No." She shook her head. "No, I trust you to be a gentleman."

He smiled then, that delighted heart-stopping smile, and she wondered if she had completely lost her mind. "In that case, Ms. Easton, I accept."

There was an arm around her. Raina's eyes snapped open. Malachi Coulter's arm. Heavy and warm and just as weirdly comforting as it had been when they'd fallen asleep.

She had no desire to free herself of that weight. Not just yet. The clock on her nightstand told her it was a little after five. Which meant she'd only been asleep a few hours.

But somehow she felt wide awake. As though she'd slept soundly for eight hours rather than a quarter of that.

Maybe Mal gave off magic sleeping fumes?

She wouldn't put it past him. The man did everything well.

He even slept well. No snoring. No thrashing around. No, he'd just put his arm around her waist, pulled her close back against him, and promptly fallen asleep. A skill learned in the army, perhaps? In a war zone, it was probably pretty handy to be able to sleep wherever you found yourself. She'd lain there for a minute or two, not really believing that he really did want to sleep and trying to make up her mind exactly how she felt about the fact that he could just fall asleep with her lying next to him—and then, to her surprise, she'd drifted off, too.

But now she was awake.

Awake and humming with awareness of Mal warm and solid behind her.

The room smelled like him. Smelled like male and good things and suddenly she was achingly aware that she wasn't happy with him just *sleeping* beside her.

But was that fair?

Most guys she knew wouldn't say no to sex if it was offered, but Mal was more complicated than just sex. Because she didn't know if it could be just sex with him. And didn't know if she wanted it to be anything more than that.

But even as she was trying to figure out what she should do—what she wanted to do—she couldn't help pressing a little closer against him.

Which led to the discovery that parts of him were wide awake. And very . . . tempting. She took a breath, which somehow pressed them closer still

"If you keep doing that then I'm going to have to assume that we might be redefining 'see what happens.'" Mal's voice rumbled in her ear.

She froze. "You're awake."

"Light sleeper," he said. "Particularly when a gorgeous woman starts wriggling around in bed with me."

"I didn't wriggle."

"It felt wriggly to me," he said with a chuckle that sent his breath dancing warmly across the back of her neck. She shivered from the sensation. "So did that," he added. "Do it again."

"I don't know," she said. "It might inflame your imagination."

"Darlin', I think we've already gone beyond my imagination being inflamed."

So the pleasingly hard erection pressing against her butt was informing her.

All that just waiting there for her. The thought of it sent a pulse of heat to her crotch. The warmth spread and bloomed across her skin from there. Mal had been the perfect gentleman all night. He was still being the perfect gentleman. Erection or no erection he'd made no move to take the lead.

Which left it up to her. She swallowed, throat suddenly dry. She knew what her body wanted. But was she ready for the consequences? "Do you want to 'redefine'?" she asked.

"I think the answer to that question is pretty obvious. The real question is whether you want to."

"And if I don't?"

"Then I guess it's a cold shower for me this morning."

"You'd just walk away?"

"You say no and that's the only option. Unless your version of redefining includes the sorts of things that might be too complicated to discuss this early in the morning."

"Are you asking me if I'm kinky?" She wasn't. Or at least, no more than the average woman. Right now she could think of quite a few interesting scenarios involving Malachi Coulter and some of her silk scarves. And then there was her lingerie collection . . . she shivered again thinking about what color Mal's eyes might turn if he saw her in some of the lace-and-silk confections that lived in her dresser.

"Only if you're telling me you're into something that's some sort of lifestyle level of serious. Otherwise I'm asking if you can either stop talking and let me kiss you or let me get up and have that cold shower."

She twisted then, bringing herself around and scooting up slightly so they were face-to-face. That was the problem with tall men. She wasn't. Which took some managing of logistics. Mal watched her, his brown eyes once again that hot dark shade she was starting to like a lot. "You'd really just get up and walk away?"

"I wouldn't be happy about it, but yes."

That answer made her unreasonably happy. All over.

She slid closer to him, hooked a leg over his waist. He didn't wait for another invitation. His mouth came down on hers, hot and sure and demanding, and she let him take her down to that place of heat and darkness and wildness that drove everything else away.

He tasted better than anyone had a right to first thing in the morning. He'd stolen some toothpaste and her spare toothbrush while she'd removed her makeup before they'd gone to sleep and he still somehow tasted like mint and deliciousness.

But she didn't get to wonder just how he'd managed that minor miracle for too long because his hand was sliding up her back, the worn cotton of the big old T-shirt she'd worn to bed to avoid giving him any message other than *sleep* coming with it.

She lifted her arm from around his neck, suddenly sure. She wanted him. Wanted him hot and hard.

Mal whisked the T-shirt over her head, leaving her in just cotton panties. Then he rolled so she was under him, his hips, still clad in boxers, pressed into hers in just the right place.

She almost screamed. Instead she just pressed up into him, writhing a little so that he rubbed against her.

Damn. So damned good.

His mouth came down on hers again for another of those sublime kisses and then he moved lower. Which, given their height difference, meant she lost contact with the part of him she wanted most.

She was about to protest when his mouth closed over her nipple, teeth dragging over sensitized skin just slightly. Just right. Things went hot and dark again as the slick of his tongue and the heat of his mouth and the suction and tiny nips of teeth and strokes of fingers made her forget where she was for a few long minutes.

He had a very, very talented mouth. She had to remember to compliment him.

If she ever regained the ability to speak.

She wasn't sure she would. Not while he was touching her at least. He rolled to the side, bringing her with him so they were face-to-face again. His mouth didn't leave her breast but his fingers moved down, tracing a spiraling path that made each inch he touched light up until she was convinced she must be glowing.

Her stomach muscles tensed as he reached the edge

of her underwear. He traced the line of the elastic, which made her shiver, and then one talented finger slid under the narrow band and parted her lips to land on her clit with unerring instinct.

This time she did scream. Or moan at least. It wasn't a coherent noise but it made him lift his head.

"I like that noise," he said.

"I like your fingers," she managed to reply.

"I'm just getting started," he said with a wicked grin. Another finger slid in to join the first.

"Promises, promises."

His eyebrows lifted and his fingers did a sort of rolling shimmy on either side of her clit that made her moan again.

"I never make a promise I can't keep," he said and then he tugged her panties down. She lifted her hips and let him free her legs.

His hand came back to her, teasing her again. She rolled onto her back and let her legs fall open, wanting more.

Mal made an approving noise and slid two fingers inside her. The shock of it—of how good it felt—made her clench around him, and this time he was the one making noises.

"Damn," he said softly. "I wish you knew how good that feels."

"Feels pretty good on my end," she said.

"It'll feel better in a minute."

"There are condoms in the top drawer of the nightstand on your side of the bed." At least she hoped there were. She tried to remember if she'd bought condoms recently.

"We don't need a condom yet," he said.

"We don't?" She tried to keep the disappointment out of her voice. "Because I was really hoping you were going to take off those boxers and fuck me."

"Oh I will," Mal said. "But I'm going to make you come first."

"I'm in favor of that plan." In fact, she was going to scream if he didn't stop talking and get on with it. His fingers were still sliding slowly in and out of her and she could feel herself getting wetter with every stroke but she needed more than fingers. No matter how skilled they were.

His fingers crooked inside her and a pulse of sheer pleasure suddenly shot through her. Maybe she was wrong about the fingers thing, maybe—

But she should have known that Malachi Coulter was not the kind of guy who needed instructions. Because somehow he was between her legs and his mouth came down on her clit and his tongue hit her exactly where she needed pressure.

She gave up any pretense of trying to think. Trying to work out what he was going to do next. She just gave herself up to it. It didn't take very long. Between his tongue and his fingers and the fact that it had been too long since someone else had given her an orgasm, she felt herself start to tense and shiver and felt the rush of it building in her blood only a second or so before she came with a shriek that was probably loud enough to wake up half the building.

She drifted for a moment, reveling in the sensations floating through her. She was vaguely aware that the weight of Mal's body moved away from her; if she could have moved, she would have grabbed for him to bring him back, but it was all she could do to just lie there and enjoy.

The man had skills.

"You still with me?" Mal asked as he lay back beside her.

She opened her eyes. There he was. Smiling at her with those delicious eyes. Her gaze drifted lower.

He'd lost the boxer shorts. And the sight of Mal naked was just as spectacular as she'd imagined.

She reached down and curled her fingers around him. "Hello," she said with a smile of her own.

Mal breathed out. Hard. And then held out a condom. "I believe you requested one of these."

"Oh goody." She took the condom while he laughed.

She liked a man who could laugh in bed. Sex was fantastic but also sometimes ridiculous. Though, as she peeled the condom wrapper open and felt him flex under her hand, hot skin so smooth over hardness, she felt pretty serious about what was about to happen.

Too impatient for tricks, she put the condom on him the old-fashioned way and pushed him onto his back. He didn't resist, which was a plus. Men who didn't need to be in charge all the time were another thing she liked.

She swung a leg over Mal and he wrapped his hands around her waist. She bent down and kissed him and then lifted her hips, found the right angle, and pushed down onto him.

Oh. God.

He was large but not too large. Enough to stretch and push against her as she moved, and she made herself take it slowly. Until he was deep inside her.

She opened her eyes and smiled.

"Christ," he muttered fervently.

"No, Raina," she said and leaned forward to brace her arms on his shoulders so that she could move against him and feel that slide inside all over again.

Mal let her set the pace for a minute or so, and she watched as his stomach muscles tightened and his face went all intent while he did. He was so obviously holding himself back that it made her stomach flutter to think what he might do when she finally pushed him over the edge. She increased the pace. His hands tightened around her sides, moving with her, keeping her steady.

Keeping her safe.

Oh. God.

She moaned then and he smiled. One hand let go of her, found her clit again, and pressed hard, which made her lose all sense of what she was doing as the pleasure blasted through her.

Then somehow—God, the man had good abs—he sat up, coming up to kiss her while he lifted her so that she was sitting in his lap, legs wrapped around his waist.

She'd dated strong guys before—dancers tended to be pretty powerful—but never one as strong and tall as Mal. He made her feel tiny. But not smaller. How did that even work? She couldn't figure it out. Just kissed him back when he kissed her. Wrapped herself around him as tightly as she could. Because right in that moment, she couldn't imagine letting him go.

Not that she had to. He moved again, bringing her with him, so that he stayed inside her. Now he was on top and he started to move, slow and sure at first, finding a rhythm as steady as a drumbeat.

One that made her stop thinking, boneless with it, unable to do anything but find the movement that matched his, that turned this into a dance. A dance with no music other than the beat she felt in her head and through her body. Fierce and hungry and not gentle as he picked up the pace and she moved to meet him and there was nothing but the slide and the heat and the weight of him above her and his fingers tangled in hers above her head and the pleasure that grew darker and hotter until she let it take her over a second time and she shuddered around him, calling his name as he didn't stop, didn't pause, just kept driving into her, dancing with her until he came, too, and the world stopped a moment.

Mal rolled to one side and Raina felt the loss of him, but he reached out and pulled her close against his chest. She rested her forehead on it and felt how fast his heart was pounding. She'd done that. It made her smile. She tipped her head back.

"Hello," she said.

She saw his mouth curve up though his eyes remained closed. "You know it's kind of cruel to expect a guy to talk straight after sex, right?"

She laughed and snuggled back down. "I'm sure it's good for your brain. Take advantage of all that extra post-exertion oxygen surging around."

"I'm pretty sure that all the oxygen left my body a way back there." His arms tightened around her and they lay still for a moment. Then she heard a rustle as he turned his head.

"Crap."

She blinked. "That's not exactly the reaction I was expecting."

"It's after six," he said.

She yawned. "Probably." Then her brain started working. "Crap. You have to go. You have a flight." Her instinct was to grab him, tell him he couldn't go. She made herself stay still. This was Mal. They'd slept together exactly once and he owned a baseball team. Which meant he had to travel.

"I have a debriefing with my team and then a flight," he said.

"When are you back?" she asked. She was proud of herself for sounding casual.

"Thursday. Our next home game is Friday night."

She knew that. Because she knew the schedule of days the Angels had to work. But she hadn't previously figured out the implications. That the team being away meant Mal being away. Damn. She wanted him again already.

Which maybe meant it was just as well he was going.

"Are you going to travel with the team whenever they go?" she asked. She pulled herself out of his arms. Made herself sit up and look around for her robe. It was usually draped over the end of her bed but they'd obviously dislodged it.

Mal looked regretful as he watched her. "Not every time but as many as I can for the start of the season. I want to get a feel for the other stadiums. See how they do things. Let the team settle into their routine."

Well, that was something. He wouldn't be gone all the time.

But he was leaving now. And despite all the logical

arguments, she wasn't happy about it. She ducked down to pick up the robe. "You grab a shower, I'll make coffee. There are clean towels in the cupboard in the hall." She slipped into the robe and out of the bedroom before she could do something stupid like ask him not to go. He had to go.

Wash made a sleepy meow as she passed through the living room on the way to the kitchen. Then he jumped down from the sofa and trailed behind her, making his usual eager-for-breakfast noises. She wasn't usually up this early, but that didn't seem to bother him. Nothing bothered Wash when it came to food.

She started coffee, heard the shower start, and fed Wash while she tried to figure out how she felt. Physically fantastic. She should have been exhausted but apparently sex with Mal was as good as a few hours of sleep.

But emotionally, she wasn't so pleased with things. First nights were meant to end in breakfast in bed and sleeping in and more sex.

"Suck it up, princess," she muttered to herself. She got out mugs and found the sugar. She drank her coffee straight black. She had no idea how Mal drank his.

Damn. She'd slept with him and she didn't even know that. Which was exactly the sort of thing she'd told herself she wasn't going to do. No leaping into things too fast without thinking.

The sound of the water died and a minute or so later, Mal emerged, dressed with his hair wet around his face. He smiled at her. "I called Ned. He'll pick me up in about ten minutes."

Ten minutes wasn't long enough to figure this out.

Then again, right now, she wasn't sure ten days would be. Or ten weeks.

"How do you like your coffee?" she asked.

"Black. One sugar." He came over to where she stood. Looked down at her a moment. "Everything okay?"

She nodded. "All good."

His eyes narrowed. "Not the most convincing delivery of that line." He stepped closer then, before she could argue, lifted her up so she was sitting on the counter. He leaned in, kissed her nose. "Stop thinking so hard," he said. "If I didn't have to get on a plane today then we'd still be in that bedroom. I'm not making a quick getaway, I promise. I don't want to go." He kissed her then, softly. Coaxing with his mouth until her lips parted and things went wild again. He pulled back, rested his forehead on hers. "Damn."

She waited a few second while her breathing slowed. "I think we screwed up the timing on this one."

"It's only until Thursday," he said. "Time will fly."

"It had better," she said. She didn't think it would, though. She was going to be counting the hours until he got back. And that was worrying. She kissed him again. Just one more time. And then she did the sensible thing and let him drink his coffee and walk out her front door.

Chapter Eleven

Mal made it to Deacon by eight, skinning into the meeting of his security team just on time. To his surprise, Alex and Lucas were sitting with the rest of the guys.

Alex lifted an eyebrow as Mal put his coffee—Ned, thank goodness, had brought coffee when he'd picked Mal up and had, even better, brought a whole thermos full—down on the conference room table.

Mal ignored Alex. He wasn't going to explain why he was the last one to arrive at his own meeting.

Because that would only lead to inconvenient questions about the reasons. And he was in no way ready to talk to Alex and Lucas about Raina.

Too soon.

Not when he could still feel her hands around him, feel her nails digging into his shoulders and the strength of her body, sleek with dancer's muscle, moving with his.

Good God.

He'd never found it so hard to drag himself out of a woman's bed before.

When he'd walked into the kitchen to see her standing there wearing nothing but a short silky robe as red as her hair, it had taken an inhuman amount of effort not to grab her and haul her straight back to the bedroom. Or even just down onto the nearest flat surface.

Eyes on the prize.

He had a job to do.

Thinking about Raina wouldn't help. Of course, there wasn't a chance in hell that he'd be able to stop thinking about her, so what he had to do was shunt those thoughts off to one side for now. Think about Deacon and the Saints. Get the job done.

Situation normal.

He hoped.

He cleared his throat and turned on the tablet he'd brought into the room with his coffee.

"Okay, guys," he said as the buzz of conversation died and his team focused on him. "Good job yesterday. So let's go through it and figure out what we can do better next time. Chen, why don't you start?" He nodded at the wiry dark-haired man sitting next to Alex. He'd seconded Chen Sung from MC Shield to run the crew here at Deacon for a few months. They'd met in the army. Good man in a fight. And a brilliant mind for spotting trouble before it started.

Which reminded him, he needed to get Chen's report on Raina's truck. He'd asked him to go over the tapes from the parking garage last night. See if Chen could spot the knife-happy perp anywhere.

But business first. Get through the meeting; then there would be time for tapes and tires before he had to leave for Baltimore.

Chen started talking and Mal made himself pay attention. He nodded when Chen suggested a change in the security patrol patterns and times to better match the key movements in the crowd at change of innings and the end of the game. Then Chen passed the ball to Lee Reynolds, who went over the couple of problems they'd had with gates and security scanners.

Mal signed off on the expenditure Lee asked for to fix those problems—God, he was going to be happy when they had time and cash flow to rip all the bloody gates and scanners out and put in state-of-the-art systems, but that wasn't this season—and made a note in his tablet to double check the pricing on the scanners via his company contacts. He might be able to get a better deal.

The rest of the meeting went smoothly. No one had any major issues to report. They'd thrown out one guy who'd managed to get drunk by the end of the third inning and a few others who were pushing the line later in the game. There'd been the usual crop of contraband in people's bags coming into the game. Booze mostly, which was confiscated. A few knives. Those guys didn't get into the game. Or so he'd thought. But then there were Raina's tires. Of course, you didn't have to get into the game to get into the parking garage. That would explain how the security team hadn't found a knife on whoever had done it. But hopefully he'd find out exactly how the guy had gotten in when he talked to Chen.

Hopefully the zero-tolerance message would get through to the fans pretty quickly. Tom Jameson had had good security screening but Mal had upped the number of people searching bags and the stations to do it, which meant they could search more thoroughly.

There would always be macho assholes who thought they needed a weapon at a baseball game but they weren't getting into his damned park.

He dismissed the team, thanking them again for a good job. For a team so newly pulled together they'd done well, even the couple of guys who were relative newbies hired to beef up the numbers. He asked Chen to meet him in his office in fifteen minutes.

Then he turned to Alex and Lucas. "Not bad for a first run."

Alex nodded. "They did well."

"Running late this morning?" Lucas asked, his blue eyes amused. "Too much champagne at the party?"

"Something like that," Mal said. His whereabouts last night weren't up for discussion. "Now. There's one more thing that happened yesterday. I asked Chen to look into it before we discussed it with the rest of the security team and then everyone else."

Lucas's eyes narrowed. "What happened?"

"Someone slashed Raina Easton's tires in the underground lot," Mal said.

"Excuse me?" Alex said. His voice had gone cool. Pissed. Good. Mal was pissed, too. "How the fuck did that happen?"

"That's what Chen's looking into. Her truck is bright pink, so it might just have been the most obvious target."

"Might?" Alex said.

"She's had a few incidents at her club. Vandalism, mostly."

"You think someone has a problem with her?"

He shrugged. "I don't know. I've spoken to her club manager and the guy who does security there. Given them some suggestions."

"Anyone looked at the reaction to the Angels yet?" Lucas said.

Mal shook his head. "Haven't had a chance. Have you?"

"No. Alex?"

Alex scowled. "I asked the media team to do a sweep of articles and social media and have the report for us when we get to Baltimore. But I haven't looked myself. Do you think this is because of the Angels?"

"From what I can gather, the incidents at the club started before this. But if there's someone who has a problem with her, it could spill over onto the Angels."

"Not too mention the Angels are likely to attract some nuts anyway," Lucas said.

Alex nodded. "We knew that would happen. So Mal will make sure the security around them is increased. We'll deal with Raina first."

"Deal with her?" Mal said, trying to keep the edge out of his tone.

"Make sure she's okay," Alex said. "Maybe get her a driver for game days as a start. She really has a pink truck?"

"Yeah," Mal said. "Big old Ford. Great truck, actually. If you like pink."

"Well, she is a girl," Lucas said. "I hear some of them like pink."

"Maybe you can buy Sara a pink helo," Mal said.

"Not sure Sara's the pink type," Lucas said. "She likes blue."

"I think we've strayed from the subject, "Alex said. "Mal, talk to Raina about a driver."

He grimaced. "She's not going to like it."

That earned him a look from Alex. "Oh?"

"I already talked to her last night. She wasn't that keen to have me interfering."

"She works for us. So we have a right to interfere when it comes to anything to do with the Saints."

"Well, I'm happy for you to try explaining that to her," Mal said. "She's got a mind of her own."

"You seem to know a lot about her," Lucas said. "Where were you last night, exactly?"

"No comment," Mal said. "Now I suggest we go see what Chen has to say so none of us miss our damn plane."

Chen's report didn't do anything to improve any of their moods. The security tape showed a guy in dark pants and dark hoodie for a few minutes during the seventh inning, but there wasn't a feed that had directly covered Raina's truck. Because someone had tilted the camera that should have been pointed at the spot where she was parked.

Fuck.

Messing with the camera suggested that this wasn't a random incident. Not just teenagers daring each other or some guy who'd drunk too much Bud and taken exception to a pink Ford. Someone had gone after Raina's truck specifically. Their hooded friend, perhaps. Mal scowled at the screen. Chen had already written the work order to rectify the camera gap. But that didn't help them identify the guy. Or figure out how he'd gotten in.

"The place is a rabbit warren, Mal," Chen said. "You know that. We'll increase the parking garage staff and make sure we're covering all the entrances and exits but this guy knew how to mess with a camera, so he's not an idiot."

"Fix the problem," Alex said. "I don't want anyone getting in or out of the underground lot that we don't know about. And tell Raina she's won herself a brand-new escort to games. I don't care if she doesn't like it. Tell her to come yell at me if she has to."

"I will," Mal said.

"Chen, you'll put all this in a report for the police?" Lucas asked.

Chen nodded. "Already done."

"And we fixed her tires, I assume?" Alex said.

Mal nodded. "Taken care of. Tuck did them. He checked the truck over but I haven't had a chance to talk to him this morning to see if he found anything. I'll call him next."

"Okay." Alex still didn't look happy but he'd obviously decided that everything that could have been done since last night had been done. "Then let's get on with the rest of the day."

Raina contemplated going back to bed when Mal left but she was still buzzing from sex and the hastily gulped cup of coffee she'd shared with him before he'd gone.

So she played with Wash, tossing his favorite catnip toy for him to chase around and occasionally return to her for fifteen minutes or so. Then she brushed him when he finally flopped down on the sofa next to her.

Grooming Wash always led to her being covered in cat fur, so next stop was the bathroom.

Her bathroom where Mal had recently been naked.

Nope. Don't think about the naked man.

He wasn't going to be naked again anywhere near her for days so thinking about it was just self-inflicted mental cruelty.

She sighed and made sure the shower was a few degrees cooler than she usually liked.

After she'd showered, and pulled on yoga pants and a sweatshirt, she made herself breakfast, poured more coffee, and settled down at her computer to check her email.

When she opened the mail program, a cascade of messages started downloading. Twitter notifications. Facebook mentions. Emails from the email loop the girls at the club used and another burlesque loop she belonged to. All of them seemed to have Fallen Angels somewhere in the subject or the message.

Yikes.

Had the press savaged the girls or something?

She flicked her browser open and did a quick Google search.

There were many, many, many hits. The top ones all coming from news or baseball or sports sites. She was fairly sure there was going to be a lot of flak on the baseball sites so she ignored those and clicked on the top newspaper result. Which was the Staten Island paper. Wow. Had everyone on Staten Island clicked on the story?

The link brought up the front page of the paper, which was half filled with a full color shot of Marly in all her blond Valkyrie glory, white wings gleaming behind her and a shit-eating grin pasted across her face.

SAINTS SEEK DIVINE INTERVENTION, the headline screamed, and Raina rolled her eyes. Still, she'd expected the Angels' name to give the headline writers of the world an excuse to roll out their punning mojo. It wasn't the worst it could have been. She scanned the story. It was a mix of praise for the girls and the journalist speculating why the heck the new owners of the Saints thought they needed cheerleaders. On the whole it seemed to be slightly in favor of the idea. So that was good. The article had about four hundred comments.

She never read the comments. Nothing good came of newspaper article comments. She'd learned that on Broadway. You couldn't please everyone and there was little point trying. She closed the tab resolutely.

Back to the search results. She waded through a few more news links, which all seemed to be the same sort of story. Hot girls. Good dancers. Why did we need cheerleaders in baseball but well done Alex Winters for finding a way to generate some interest in the team.

Not as bad as expected. She sipped coffee, finished her toast and apricot jam, and stared at the list of sporting site links in the search results. Should she or shouldn't she?

While she was trying to decide, her phone started to ring.

Brady. She pressed the speakerphone button.

"Hey, you," she said.

"Oh good, you're up," Brady said cheerfully. "I thought you might still be in bed. Wait, why aren't you still in bed? Didn't you take that lovely man home with you last night?"

"We had a nightcap," she said.

"Is that what you're calling it these days? Seriously,

Rai, if you didn't do that man there is something very, very wrong with you."

"No comment," she said.

"No comment means guilty as charged," Brady crowed. "Well done. Luis and I are very proud. It's been too long."

"Did you call just to dissect what goes on in my bedroom or was there another reason?" she asked hastily before he could go into chapter and verse on exactly how long it had been. Because the answer was a little sad. It was over a year since Patrick had done his vanishing act. A year was too long. Her body, which was aching in a pleasant way in some of those unused places, agreed with her. It was keen to get back into fighting shape in that department. She needed daily workouts.

Damn Malachi and his stupid baseball team.

She sighed.

Brady laughed. "Damn, that must have been good sex. Which again forces me to ask why you're not still in bed?"

"Because baseball is stupid," she muttered.

"Ah. Away game, is it?"

"The next three or four games are away," she said. "What kind of stupid sport is that?"

"I take it he's traveling with the team then? My sympathies."

"I'll survive," Raina said.

"Let's hope so. But hey, I have something that will cheer you up."

"What?"

"Are you at your computer?"

"Yes."

"Take a look at the club's Facebook page."

She opened the page. For a moment, she couldn't see what was different; then the number next to the LIKES button registered. "Three thousand likes? We got two thousand likes overnight?" Holy crap. Brady had been good at working social media for them but burlesque was kind of a niche market and they'd thought they'd been doing well to build to a thousand.

"Yup," Brady said. "And that's not the best part. Luis just finished going through the reservation system. All the reserved tables are booked out for two months solid."

"You're kidding." They often sold out the reserved tables on Saturday nights, but most nights only a few of them were booked in advance. Given that there was an extra charge for the prime position of the reserved seats, having them all booked out for months was a nice chunk of extra change. If everyone ended up turning up, of course. The club scene anywhere around New York was pretty fickle.

"Not kidding. I think we're going to be turning people away at the door," Brady said. "I called Paolo. He said he's going to put in a booze order today. And bump up the catering."

"Huh," Raina said. She'd taken the job at the Saints hoping that it might lead to some extra choreography gigs here and there. That and a bit of publicity for the club. Turned out she'd underestimated that part. "But how do they even know about us?"

"You haven't read your email, have you?"

"I read a couple of the news stories but that's it so far."

"You got mentioned as the choreographer in a few of the stories. And some of them talked a little about you. Including the *New York Times* and *USA Today*."

"*USA Today*?" She blinked, wondering if she was still asleep. But apparently not. "That's crazy." She paused. "Have you read any of the stuff on the sports sites? I didn't start those yet."

"Luis is looking now."

"What's he saying."

"Mixed reactions. Some liked it. Some raving about the end of baseball and society as we know it. About what we expected. Lots of pictures of the squad. Even the ones who were complaining seemed to manage to include lots of those."

"No such thing as bad publicity, I guess," she said.

"Nope," Brady agreed. "So you need to get all the girls in here early today so we can run some extra numbers. If we're going to be packing them in then we need some new stuff. More things to throw into the mix."

"I take it you have some ideas?" she said.

"Well, there's a baseball number to start with. What's a good song for a baseball number?"

"I don't know. Who sings about baseball? 'Take Me Out to the Ballgame' isn't exactly sexy."

"Agreed. I'll have a look. There must be something."

"There's that song from *Smash*. Didn't the Marilyn musical in that show have a number about baseball?"

"It did," Brady said. "So that's an idea."

"Or Pat Benatar," Raina mused. " 'Hit Me With Your Best Shot.' Only don't go getting ideas about unison baseball bat swinging or anything. That stuff is hard to pull off. Too much practice required." Having been on the wrong end of a fumbled cane or two in various dance routines in her time, she had no trouble picturing disaster scenarios involving baseball bats.

She started scrolling through her email again, looking to see if anything looked like it was about something besides the Angels.

"Not even one?"

"We'll see. Surely someone makes inflatable bats or something. Use one of those."

"No one needs to see a deflated baseball bat mid-routine," Brady countered. "Speaking of equipment, how was—"

"No comment," Raina said firmly.

Brady laughed and she started to say "Shut up" but the second word never made it out of her mouth as she stared at the email address on her screen. Jman@supermail.com. Fuck. Jeremy.

Her heart started pounding.

"Raina? Raina, what's wrong?" Brady's voice sounded like it was coming from a distance.

"I got an email from Jeremy," she managed.

Brady swore. "Don't open it. We'll be right there," he said and left Raina staring at the screen with silence in her ear as he hung up.

It only took fifteen minutes before Brady and Luis arrived. Raina let them in, and Brady headed straight for her computer.

"What did it say?" he demanded.

She shook her head. "I didn't read it."

Brady fixed her with his bright-blue eyes. Which were suddenly a very steely shade of bright blue. "Honestly?"

"Yes. I don't want to know."

"You can't just ignore him," Luis said.

"Why not?"

"Well, for one thing, someone slashed your tires. And now your crazy ex is back in the picture. You need to tell Mal."

"Oh no. There's no telling Mal."

That earned her identical exasperated looks from both men.

"If you don't tell Mal," Brady said, "I will." Luis backed up this statement with an emphatic nod, as if to say *And if he doesn't, I will.*

Crap. See, this was why she should have listened to reason when it came to Mal and kept things professional. If he was merely her boss then she wouldn't hesitate to tell him about Jeremy. But now, now that he'd been in her bed, she didn't want to dump the crazy of her past life on him any more than she already had. She wanted uncomplicated. Mal in white-knight mode—and she had no doubt that he would want to charge in and fix things, take control of the situation—would only make things complicated.

"Mal has more important things on his mind than Jeremy. Besides, he's in Baltimore with the team."

"They have these devices that let you communicate with people far away now," Luis said, deadpan. "You may have heard of them? They're called phones."

"Ha ha. Okay, how about this. We read the email. If it's anything alarming—my definition of alarming—I'll call Mal. If it's not, then I'll wait and tell him when he gets back from Baltimore."

They frowned at her.

"Are you two practicing how to make expressions in unison now that you're married?" she said, trying to lighten the mood a little. "I didn't say I wouldn't tell Mal. Just that if what's in the email isn't—"

"The fact that he's emailing at all is alarming," Brady said.

"He wants me to be alarmed," Raina said. "If we react like the sky is falling, if he thinks he's freaked me out, then he wins." She produced a frown of her own. "And he's not going to win."

"So tell Mal. He's got a security company. He must eat jerks like Jeremy for breakfast. Tell him and he'll take care of it. Simple," Brady said.

"I don't need saving," Raina snapped.

"No, but nothing wrong with asking for a little help," Brady said mildly.

She bit back the mixture of fury and panic rising in her throat. Brady and Luis were here to help. They meant well. They weren't trying to take over. But still, she was going to deal with this problem her way. She took a deep breath and went to the computer to open the damned email.

It was short.

Looking good, R. Nice gig you scored.

On the face of it, that was a perfectly polite message. But she knew Jeremy. This was his way of telling her that he had his eye on her again. And the *nice gig* was the sort of subtle putdown he used to use on her all the time. Implying she couldn't have gotten the job without sleeping with someone. Because he couldn't imagine anyone getting ahead just because they worked hard and earned things. But she knew the truth.

Brady and Luis were leaning over her shoulders, reading along.

"See," she said, sitting straighter. "Nothing terrible. I'll tell Mal when he gets back."

"If Jeremy sends anything else, you'll let us know?"

"Yes. I'm not an idiot." She knew if Jeremy did send anything else and she told them, they'd be beating down Mal's door with the news. And she would be hot on their heels. But she wasn't going to run scared from one email. She would ignore him, as she had ignored his existence for several years, and not let him turn her life into fear again.

She shut down the mail program and put the computer to sleep. "Enough of dickheads past. We have a club to run."

Chapter Twelve

The day passed in a blur of work and a nap to make up for her lost night's sleep and then rehearsal. She'd emailed all of the Angels to congratulate them on the job they'd done and to remind them that there was practice the next morning. She'd received an excited text from Marly, who announced that she had ten thousand new Twitter followers. And an annoyed message from Ana about why it was Marly's picture that all the papers had used. And then, more pleasingly, a call from Mal in Baltimore. She'd managed to avoid telling him about Jeremy. He didn't have long to talk but somehow, in a few short minutes, he managed to make an innocent-seeming request for her email address seem like a proposition.

By the time she'd hung up the phone she'd been turned on and missing him all over again. Which was when she'd decided to go to the club and try to work him and everything else out of her system with four hours of dance rehearsal.

It had helped a little but now it was Sunday night, the club was opening its doors, and she was sitting in front of the mirror in the dressing room and still couldn't manage to focus all her attention on the performance and emceeing. It took her three attempts to get her false eyelashes on, and that was something she could do in her sleep.

Brady wandered past her mirror while she was finally getting the lashes into position. He stopped and studied her face. "More glitter," he pronounced. "If you're wearing the black dress, go for more glitter on the cheeks and eyes and dark-red lips. And the peacock earrings."

"Really? With the black?" The new black dress he'd made her was alternating bands of black satin and lace. Some of the lace was backed by not-so-sheer fabric the same color as her skin. Some of it wasn't. Which made watching her wearing it an exercise in guessing which bits of her body you were really seeing. Exactly the effect they had been aiming for. Sexy but mysterious.

The lace bands had tiny black crystals sewn over them, picking out some of the flowers and flourishes of the fine fabric.

"The crystals throw off peacock shades in the light," Brady pointed out. He leaned over and lifted the peacock earrings from the rack they were hanging on. Shaped like a male peacock sitting in a silver hoop, the colors of his feathers picked out by crystals and enamel, they were extravagant to say the least. Large even before taking into account the chains of crystals that fell from the bottom of the hoop, fanning out to form the tails of the birds.

The earrings had originally been designed for the outfit—such as it was—she'd worn for a peacock-themed fan dance she used to perform, but she hadn't done that routine for over a year now. One of the other girls had reused the feathers in the fan for another routine but Raina had never quite been able to give up the earrings. They were too gorgeous.

They also weighed a ton.

"Maybe just for the first half," she said. "Then I'll change the look." Otherwise her ears might fall off. Brady was a genius costume designer but he hadn't ever experienced the peculiar pain of earrings that weighted your ears down like lead.

He shrugged. "Your call. Are you going to sing tonight?"

"Probably not. We have enough going on, don't we?" She didn't perform an actual routine or sing more than a few times a week these days. And without enough sleep, she didn't want to push her voice.

"If everyone gets back here, we do." Brady said.

"Who's missing?" She frowned at him—or his reflection—as she picked up a vial of fine silver glitter powder and a brush.

"Glynna went to go check on her kids for an hour or so," Brady said. "Her sitter rang, said the little one—what's his name?"

"Ty," Raina said, patting glitter over her eye shadow.

"Right, Ty. He's got a fever or something. So she wanted to check on him."

"Well, she'll come back. She always does." Glynna was a few years older than Raina. A retired Broadway dancer, too, she had settled down with the guy and had babies, and then found herself with an irresistible urge to perform again. Which had led her to burlesque. She was one of Raina's star solo performers who came up with wicked routines with ingenious regularity. The audiences loved her. So she needed to make it back.

"She does," Brady agreed. "Okay. I'll go finalize the run sheet. Luis told me to tell you there's a queue at the door already."

"Really?" She blinked in surprise, causing glitter to flutter down onto her cheeks. Which saved her putting it there later. "It's not even eight." Madame R's opened its doors at eight but the show didn't start until nine. And there were rarely more than a few people through the door before eight.

"Gotta love baseball," Brady said. "Now get glittering and I'll bring you back tea with the run sheet. And don't worry. Luis has all the exits covered. Jeremy wouldn't get in even if he was dumb enough to turn up here. Which he won't be."

She summoned a smile, trying to convince both Brady and herself that she believed him. She mostly succeeded. "What would I do without you?" she said. "Now go while I finish my sparkle." Brady kissed her cheek and hugged her with one arm before heading out of the room. Raina turned her attention back to the mirror and picked up her vampiest red lipstick. Full house, huh? Stage Raina was needed for a full house, so real-life Raina and her obsession with Malachi and worries about anything else were going to have to just take a back seat for the next five hours.

Of course, forgetting about Mal would have been easier if the first people Raina spotted when she stepped out onto the stage to open the show hadn't been Maggie

Jameson and Sara Charles, sitting with a couple of friends at one of the very front tables. What the heck were they doing here? Sure, she'd offered to leave Maggie's name at the door—and she had—but she hadn't thought that Maggie would actually come down here. Besides which, shouldn't she be in Baltimore?

Maggie and her friends whooped and clapped when they saw her. Raina sent a smile in their direction and then got on with the show.

During the first intermission, curiosity burning, she worked her way around the room, greeting regulars and saying hello to first-timers—so many first-timers—until she ended up by Maggie's table.

Maggie jumped out of her chair and hugged her quickly. "Raina, this place is fabulous. And the show is even better." She sounded extra revved up, even for Maggie. Raina shot a quick glance at the table. There were tall glasses in front of each woman. Filled with bright-pink liquid. Which meant they were drinking the killer Madam R cosmopolitans that Brady had invented. Cranberry juice and three different kinds of flavored vodka and a kick of St-Germain for extra oomph.

She grinned as Maggie let go. The four women were going to be sorry about this in the morning. She knew from experience. Brady had invented the killer Cosmo for one of her birthday parties. She'd felt far far older than her years when she'd woken up with the hangover from hell the morning after. "I thought you'd be in Baltimore," she said as Maggie stepped back.

Maggie shook her head, her long dark hair, which was tamed into perfectly blow-dried waves tonight bouncing with the movement. "It was my birthday during the week and my dad wasn't home. He got home last night so he wanted to do birthday lunch today. It's our tradition. And then the girls decided we should go out tonight to keep the celebration going."

"Well then, happy birthday," Raina said. "Drinks are on me."

Maggie started to protest and Raina cut her off. "No arguments. How about you introduce me to your friends instead?"

Maggie turned back to the table. "Sure. You know Sara, right?"

Raina nodded.

"Well, this is Hana Tuckerson—she's Brett's wife." Maggie was nodding at a slender woman who had chin-length black hair and dark eyes. Raina tried to remember if she'd learned anything about Hana in her time studying the Saints. Brett's wife. Right. Now she remembered. "You're the tae kwan do champ. Very cool."

"I'm retired," Hana said. "These days I save my round-house for special occasions. Like when Brett annoys me." She grinned at Raina and lifted one of the pink drinks. "Nice to meet you. You do good cocktails."

Raina laughed. "Those have a kick to them. Fair warning."

"Hana can drink the rest of us under the table," Maggie said. "It's not fair."

Hana snorted. "You need more training. You spend too many early nights tucked up with Alex."

"Well, do you blame her?" said the other woman at the table. She was a cool-looking blonde, her long hair spilling down past her shoulder blades, looking very pale over a severe black dress that seemed conservative until she moved and Raina realized that the front was slashed almost down to her navel.

"Hi, I'm Shelly Finch," the blonde said, holding out her hand with a friendly smile.

"Shelly's an entertainment reporter," Maggie said. "She can give you a great write-up."

"She's also engaged to Hector," Sara added helpfully. "They're getting married as soon as the season's over. In Hawaii."

"Sounds fantastic," Raina said. Hector Moreno was the team's catcher, she knew that much. It made sense that Maggie's best friends were all involved in baseball. After all, hers were all dancers.

"I insisted on it being somewhere warm," Shelley said. "If I have to work around his ridiculous baseball schedule, then he can pony up for a tropical location. I didn't want to have to wear a fur wedding dress, and New York in November is kind of dismal."

Raina grinned approvingly. "My kind of thinking. I've never liked the cold. If I'm ever old and rich I'd like to live somewhere that's warm all the time. It'll be easier on my worn-out old bones."

"Tell me about it," Hana said. "I have a few places where I had fractures during my career and they ache half the winter. Must be worse for dancers. That stuff is hard on the body."

"I like the cold," Maggie said. "Maybe because I associate it with free time. No baseball. It's when all the fun things happened when I grew up. And Dad was home most of the time. Not that baseball isn't fun," she added.

"Baseball is fine by me," Raina said. "We've had a lot of interest in the club since yesterday."

"I thought the Angels' routine was great," Sara said. "Those wings were amazing."

"Those were Brady's idea. He's does a lot of the design work here. Makes most of my costumes."

Shelly was eyeing her dress with a speculative expression. "If he made that dress then he's missed his calling. He should have been a fashion designer."

"He has the dance bug," Raina said. "It's kind of incurable." She caught sight of Brady out of the corner of an eye. He tapped his watch, meaning she had about two minutes before they were supposed to start again. "Now, excuse me, I have to get back to work. Happy birthday again, Maggie."

She made her getaway and got backstage before Brady's head exploded.

She reapplied her lipstick, changed her earrings to a pair made from jet that didn't weigh half a ton, and smiled at him. "Don't panic, I hear the boss here is pretty relaxed about starting on time."

"That's because she's the one who is making us late," Brady said. "Who were you talking to out there?"

"The tall brunette is Maggie Jameson," Raina said. "You know, her dad used to own the Saints."

"Yes, I know who Maggie Jameson is," Brady said. "Baseball fan, remember?"

"Well, that's her. It was her birthday last week, so make sure the bar guys know to comp their table. They're drinking killer cosmos so they're going to hate themselves in the morning. No big credit card bill will ease some of the pain. See if the kitchen can rustle up some cupcakes or something." Paolo usually made sure there was something in the tiny cool room that could be used if any of the customers with a reserved table sprang an "It's my birthday" surprise without organizing their own cake. "The usual. Glynna can sing her Happy Birthday number."

Brady nodded. "Got it." He smoothed his hand over her hair, tweaking how it lay. "Okay. Perfect. Out you go."

The show started again and was running smoothly. Crowded as the room was, those in the audience were getting into the groove of the burlesque acts and the group routines and the odd torch song that Brady liked to throw into the mix.

Raina came offstage after doing a quick fill-in while a costume emergency—a busted heel on one of Glynna's shoes—was taken care of and almost ran into Luis. She came to a halt just in time, teetering on the spiked heels of her boots, which weren't designed for fast stops. Luis steadied her by catching her arm. After an ungraceful wobble, she righted herself.

"Thanks." Then she frowned. "What are you doing back here?" Luis rarely came backstage during a performance. "Is there a problem?"

He nodded. "You need to come up to your office for a while."

"I'm in the middle of a show here."

"I know. But someone just drove by and threw a bunch of firecrackers at the door. Luckily there isn't a queue anymore but one of them went off right against the door and Tallie's arm got burned. We're lucky the place didn't catch fire."

"Shit." Raina looked around for Brady, caught his eye. He saw Luis and was by their side in the next second.

"What's up?" he demanded.

"Something I need to deal with," Raina said. "Can you get Glynna to do the next few breaks, please? Or you can do it if you're in the mood."

Brady was brilliant at working the crowd when the mood struck him. But these days, he stayed mostly behind the scenes.

Brady nodded. "You go. We'll figure it out."

"Thanks, I'll be back as soon as I can."

She followed Luis back to her office and dropped into the nearest chair. "Is Tallie okay?" she asked.

"I sent Rick with her to the ER to get the burn looked at," Luis said. "And I sent Benji up to take the door with Eli. The cops will be here soon to take a look."

"You called the cops?" Raina asked. Then nodded. "Good. It's your call, of course, but if Tallie got hurt then they need to know." She studied him a moment. "Who else did you call?"

Luis's expression went flat. "I let Mal know, if that's what you're asking. He asked me to let him know if anything else happened."

"It's not exactly his business," she said.

"It is," Luis said. He ran his hand over his head. "For one thing you're working for him, and for another you're sleeping with him. So he has a right to know if you're in danger."

"I'm not in danger," she protested. "And Brady has a big mouth."

"I have eyes in my head. You two were practically setting each other on fire the other day. Brady didn't need to tell me anything. And you don't know if you're in danger. This is an escalation. It's one thing to spray-paint a door when the club is closed. Trying to set fire to the place when it's open is another category altogether. And then there's the email—"

"You didn't tell him about that, too, did you?" Raina asked.

Luis shook his head. "No. But you should." He paused for a moment, and Raina heard the faint crackle of his earpiece. "Cops are here. You stay. I'll bring them up. And yes, I'll be discreet about it."

He vanished and Raina fidgeted while she waited for him to return with the police. Who were perfectly polite and listened to Luis's description of what had happened tonight and before. Including her car.

"Ma'am." The older of the two cops, a woman with calm gray eyes and dark-brown hair pulled back into a neat bun at the back of her head, turned to Raina. "Do you agree with what he's just told us?"

"Yes," Raina said. "I didn't see what happened to-night, I was inside. But I saw the graffiti. And my truck obviously."

"The truck incident happened on Staten Island? Was a report filed there?"

She nodded. "I know the Saints' security team filed a report. I'm meant to file one, too, but I didn't have a chance to get to Staten Island today. I'm going tomorrow and I'll do it then."

"All right." The woman—Officer Banks according to her name badge—nodded. "Make sure you file that re-port. I'm not sure there's a lot we can do about tonight. Once you get a clearer look at the vehicle on your secu-rity tapes, let us know. But there's not much left of the firecrackers apart from ashes. We'll take some pictures and go talk to the woman in the ER. But please let us know if anything more happens." She pulled out a card, handed it to Raina. "That's my number. Call me direct if you need to."

"Thank you," Raina said. "I appreciate that."

"Can't stand creeps who target women," Banks said. "We can't get them all, more's the pity, but maybe we can stop this one. Hopefully this was another stupid prank, but please, be sensible. You've had a lot of publicity with this Saints thing—yes, I know about that—and that can bring out the crazies. Be safe."

"I will," Raina said. "I don't want anyone, me or my staff, getting hurt." She hesitated. Then decided that the police needed the whole picture. "I had an email today from an ex who, well, let's just say we didn't part on good terms." She saw the younger cop stiffen.

"He hit you?" he asked.

"It didn't get quite that far. But he was aggressive. I left and I haven't heard from him in several years."

"Nothing after any of the other incidents?" Office Banks asked.

Raina shook her head.

"Well, without any evidence he was anywhere near here, I can't do much, I'm afraid. Do you have an address or phone number?"

"Only where he was when we were together. I have no idea if he's still there. I have the email, of course."

"Forward that to me. And let me know if you hear from him again.

"I will."

"Good." The woman turned to Luis. "I suggest you close the doors, don't let anyone else in tonight. This place looks pretty full anyway."

"We're under code," Luis said.

"I'm sure you are. But if there's someone out there with a grudge, why risk letting him or her in?"

"We're only open until one a.m. anyway," Raina said. "We'll close the doors, it's fine. Now, if you'll excuse me, Officers, I have to get back to the show. If there's anything else Luis can get for you—including coffee or something—just ask."

Mal knocked on Alex's door a little harder than he intended. Fury burned his gut, not dying down since the first hot hard flare of anger had hit him when Luis had called him to tell him what had happened at Madame R. When Alex didn't answer the door, Mal pounded again.

"Calm down, I'm coming," Alex shouted from inside. A few seconds later the door swung open, revealing Alex in jeans and a T-shirt that was inside out.

"What's—" he started. Then his eyes narrowed as he spotted the roller case at Mal's feet. "Going somewhere?"

"Back to New York," Mal said.

"We have a game tomorrow."

"I know, I'll be back."

"What happened?" Alex asked. "Is there a problem at the stadium?"

Mal shook his head. "No. At Raina's club."

"Something serious? Was someone hurt?"

"Not badly."

Alex yawned then, scrubbing his hand over his chin,

and Mal realized he'd woken him up. Shit. Still, he'd wanted to come tell him he was going in person.

"So if I ask you why you're charging off back to New York in the middle of the night when it's not serious, are you going to tell me?" Alex asked.

Mal shrugged. "You're a smart guy. You can join the dots."

"You and Raina?" Alex asked.

"Maybe," Mal said. "I like her."

"Okay then," Alex said. And then he grinned. "Shit. I'm starting to think there's something in the water at Deacon. We've barely been there four months and all three of us suddenly have girlfriends."

"I'm not sure we're quite at the girlfriend stage," Mal said.

"Are you about to travel for several hours in the middle of the night to see her before you have to turn around and fly back here in the morning?" Alex asked.

"Yes," Mal said. Then. "Shit."

"If she isn't your girlfriend, then you're inclined in that direction, I'd say," Alex said. "Good." He nodded. "I'm happy for you. It's been a . . ."

"I know," Mal said. Alex and Lucas had only met Ally a few times but they'd both been there for him when she'd died, trying to bring him through the grief.

"And you're going now because you think it's a good idea, not because you're . . ." Alex trailed off but Mal knew what he was asking. Was he being overprotective? Trying to fix things he couldn't fix. Protect things that didn't want or need to be protected. Like he had with Ally.

Ally who'd died anyway.

"I don't know," he said honestly. "But I need to go."

Alex nodded. "Then go."

"Don't tell anyone what I said about Raina. I haven't asked her if she's ready for everyone to know."

"It's in the vault. Don't worry. Did you get a flight?"

"Charter job," Mal admitted. "Old friend of mine."

"You and your old friends. You could run for president one day. Get elected just by activating your super-secret ex-army-buddy network."

"Go back to bed," Mal said. "You're not making any sense."

Alex gave him the finger and shut the door.

Chapter Thirteen

The rest of the show passed in a blur. Once again instinct and autopilot got Raina through as she rode the wave of adrenaline, shock and anger churning her stomach. Whoever was messing with her, she was going to kick their ass if she ever got hold of them. This was her damned club and her damned people and no one fucked with them.

After the show, she skipped her usual post-performance mingling and stomped up to her office. Brady knocked on the door about two minutes later.

"What?" she demanded.

"Maggie Jameson asked if she can talk to you a moment."

Raina sighed. She wasn't exactly in the mood for a chat but Maggie was the Saints in a way, and the Saints were paying her. She wondered if Mal had called Maggie. Raina had half expected him to call her but so far, nothing. So maybe he was, like a sensible person, asleep in Baltimore.

Brady reappeared with Maggie in tow. He showed her in before pulling the door closed and leaving them to it.

"I saw the police," Maggie said as she took a seat. "Did something happen? Mal told me about your truck. I'm sorry about that."

"It's not your fault," Raina said. "And yes, there was a little incident with some idiots and some fireworks out the front of the building. But everything is okay now."

"You need to tell Mal," Maggie said. "He can help you if someone is giving you trouble. It's what he does."

Raina regarded her for a moment, unsure of the best approach to this. For all she knew, Mal had called Maggie even if she hadn't said so. In which case Maggie already knew that Mal had talked to Luis and this might be a test to see exactly what Raina was going to say.

The muscles in her neck tightened as she thought about it. She decided that it was simpler just to tell the truth. Only maybe not the whole truth. "Luis—he's my security guy—he already talked to Mal."

"Good," Maggie said. Then she paused. "How does your security guy know Mal?"

"Mal had a chat with him after the truck thing," Raina said. "Made some suggestions." There. Mostly the truth. Slightly out of order. But she wasn't about to tell Maggie Jameson that she'd slept with Mal without asking Mal if he was okay with his friends knowing about that first.

"I see," Maggie said. "Well, good. Mal can help. He's a good guy."

"Yes," Raina said. "He is. All three of them are from what I've seen."

Maggie rose, nodding. "We're going to grab some pizza. Soak up some of that vodka. Do you want to come with us?"

"I should talk to the staff here," Raina said. "Tell them what happened and what we're doing about it."

"We can wait," Maggie offered. "Alex's driver is coming to get us. We're not going to be too late. Hana and I are going to Baltimore in the morning and Shelly and Sara have to work."

Pizza and some girl talk sounded pretty good. She hung out with the gals from the club but when it came right down to it, she was their boss, so apart from Glynna and Tallie, who'd been there the longest, she couldn't really let her hair down around them. "Let me go see how everyone is doing and then I'll let you know," Raina said. "Sorry about this, normally I'd love to but it's been an odd night and I need—"

"You need to make sure your people are okay. I get that," Maggie said. "I grew up with a baseball team. I understand what it's like."

It was nearly two thirty when Raina arrived home suitably stuffed full of pizza and the glass of scotch that Maggie had insisted of buying her at the pizza place. The food and the spirits had taken the edge off the night. She'd talked all the Madame R staff through what had happened to Tallie and sent everyone home with the promise they'd discuss it more on Monday if anyone wanted to.

She really wanted a long hot bath but wasn't sure she'd stay awake if she indulged. So instead, she took a ten-minute steaming-hot shower, climbed into an old *Rent*

T-shirt she wore to sleep in and her red robe, and then
wandered back out to feed Wash. While he was chomp-
ing through his food with his usual enthusiasm, she
boiled water to make peppermint tea. That would finish
the wind-down process. Help her sleep, hopefully. She
almost dropped the teacup in her hand when her intercom buzzer sounded. Catching it just before it got away
from her, she swore as she stalked over to the phone. If
some idiot kid was playing games, she was going to give
them a mouthful.

"What do you want?" she said into the speaker.

"You," Mal's voice replied.

She pushed the button to let him in so hard and fast
she wondered if she'd broken it.

Apparently not. And apparently Mal could levitate because she'd barely finished unlocking the door when
he knocked.

"What are you doing here?" she asked in wonder as
she threw open the door. He looked tired, stubble dark-
ening his jaw, hair wild. The gray Henley underneath his
leather jacket was creased. He'd never looked better to
her.

"Are you okay?" he asked roughly.

"I'm fine," she said, feeling a smile spread across her
face. "But you're supposed to be in Baltimore."

"Do you want to talk about where I'm supposed to be
or do you want to get naked with me?" He pushed the
door shut behind him then reached for her.

"I'll take door number two, please," she said, and
laughed as he picked her up. She wrapped her legs around
his waist and started kissing him wildly. Mal bumped his
way through the kitchen then stopped at the sofa. Wash

protested and bolted as they descended onto it in a tangle of limbs. Mal's hand slid up her leg. "No panties. That makes things easier."

"Speak for yourself, you're wearing far too many clothes." Raina said, then gasped as Mal pulled her T-shirt up and fastened his mouth over a nipple, drawing it into his mouth and making her shiver.

"Actually, I take that back. Keep your clothes on."

"I can multitask," Mal mumbled, and she heard the sound of a zipper being lowered.

Raina giggled. "Condom?" she suggested.

"Wallet. Back pocket," Mal said. His fingers slid into her and she lost track of what she was supposed to be doing. Wallet. Condom. Mal inside her. Right.

She tried to reach around but given the angle and the sheer size of Mal, she couldn't reach. "Wait," she muttered. "Let me up."

Mal looked up, frowning. That didn't stop him driving her crazy with those long clever fingers, she noted.

"Something wrong?"

"My arms are short and your body is long," she said. "If you want that condom, you're going to have to let me up."

His face cleared. "Ah." He looked down the sofa. "This is never going to work. You need a sofa for normal-sized people." He sat up and she pushed him off onto the floor.

"The floor is flat," she said.

He grinned then. "So it is." He raised a hip, pulled his wallet free of the offending pocket, and passed it to her. She found the condom and then found herself pulled down on top of Mal. Who'd managed to lose the jeans and his boxers while she was condom hunting. He didn't mess around, her Malachi.

She decided to follow his lead, tore open the condom packet, and then sat up.

"Hello again," she said and wrapped her hand around the lovely erection that she'd spent all day trying not to think about. God, had it only been this morning that he'd left? It felt like forever.

But that didn't matter because he was here now. Here and naked and waiting for her watching with those sin-dark eyes. So maybe there was time to take a little time. She wriggled farther down on his legs and bent forward to taste him.

"Are you trying to kill me?" Mal asked as she closed her mouth over the head of his cock.

She let him go again and smiled up at him. "I can answer that question or I can keep doing what I'm doing. Your choice."

"I'm shutting up now," Mal said.

"Not for long, I hope," she muttered and then she took him again. Took him slowly, learning the contours and taste of him. Experimenting with fingers and tongue to find out what he liked and what he didn't until he was panting and groaning and his hands fisted in her hair, guiding her to take him deeper.

She did so. Slowly at first and then more feeding, sucking harder and faster and deeper until she felt his stomach muscles start to tremble. Then she stopped and he groaned. She rolled the condom into place and slid back up his body, groaning a little herself as she slid over the hard length of him. It felt so damned good she slid back down, taking her weight on her arms to enjoy the sensation all over again. And again. And a fourth time.

Apparently that was about the limit of his tolerance. Because he grabbed her and rolled her and then slid inside her with a fierceness that made her clench around him. She closed her eyes and let him take her, needing him to drive away the day and the fear and the anger. Letting him use her to drive away whatever demons were driving him, too. Faster and harder until there was only flesh meeting flesh. Pure sensation. Pure delight. No idea what was her and what was him. Until the orgasm exploded through her and dissolved her completely.

"That was lovely," Raina said some unknown time later when they were both lying in her bed, naked and sweaty and boneless. Mal was pretty sure he'd melted completely. He'd come twice already and he was fairly sure Raina was one or two ahead of him. Either that or she was a better actress than he'd thought.

"Thanks," he managed.

"You want to tell me what it was about?" she asked.

He came back into his body with a thud. "What do you mean?"

"You just flew for about three hours in the wrong direction in the middle of the night to land on my doorstep. Don't get me wrong, I'm very, very happy you're here, but it's a little . . . unexpected."

Odd was what she really meant. He felt himself stiffen. Had he screwed up coming here?

Raina's lips brushed against his shoulder and he relaxed

a little. Even if she thought he was odd, it didn't seem to have put her off.

"You don't have to tell me and I really do appreciate you coming to make sure I'm all right," she said. "But I feel like maybe I've tripped and hit a button of yours. Something to do with some of those wrong choices you keep telling me you've made, maybe? So if you tell me, maybe I can avoid tripping over it again." She pressed another kiss against his skin. "But it's up to you. Your secrets are yours."

His secrets. Not so much secrets as failures. The dead he carried with him like any soldier did. Friends he hadn't been able to save. And then there was Ally.

Raina needed to know about Ally sooner or later. "I lost someone," he said softly. "I mean, I've lost plenty of people. Kind of hard to avoid in my old line of work."

"But this one was different? Who was she?"

"How do you know it was a she?"

"Call it a lucky guess," she said and snuggled closer.

He tightened his arm around her, breathing in the smell of her.

"Do you want to tell me?"

Ally. How did he start with Ally? How to describe who she was? Who she had been. Who she'd become. The fierce wildness of her. Though the woman in his arms, though smaller and very different, had her own flavor of fierce and wild. So maybe she'd understand. Ally would have liked Raina. Probably would have gotten up on stage and demanded to learn how to dance in a corset and four-inch heels if she'd had the chance. But she never would.

"Ally was a soldier," he said. "Kind of wild. I was kind

of wild back then, too. We got each other through some tough times."

"You loved her?" Raina's voice was very quiet.

"Yes," he said and even now, it made his breath go rough for a minute. "Very much."

"What happened?"

"She got out of the army a few months before I did," he said. "And by the time I got home, she wasn't doing so well. Finding the transition hard. Stay in long enough and some people get addicted to the adrenaline rush."

"I get that," Raina said. "Performers get addicted to the high of it, too."

"I thought she'd settle down," Mal said. "I got her to talk to a counselor, thought that would help. Thought she just needed time. But she kept taking risks. Rock climbing. Parachuting." Too much alcohol and other things. But he didn't need to tell Raina that part. "One day she went ultragliding and things went wrong. She died."

Raina didn't say anything for a moment. Her arms tightened around him. "I'm sorry. That sucks. You must have been pretty mad at her."

It felt like she'd just pitched a fastball straight through his defenses. No one close to him had ever said that to him. Recognized that, tangled up with the grief, there was a healthy dose of *Why the hell did you have to go and fuck this up?* The therapist he'd seen a few times had. And now Raina. Damn.

"Yeah, I was. Mad that I couldn't help her. But you can spend a long time being mad about things that will never change. So I had to let her go."

"And have you?"

She didn't sound mad or offended. She sounded curious.

He nodded. "She's gone. I loved her. Part of me will always love her. But she's gone and I'm still here. And she'd kick my butt if I spent the rest of my life moping."

Raina laughed. "I think I would have liked her."

"I think she would have liked you." He sighed. "I'm over her. But sometimes I get a little . . ."

"Overprotective?" Raina said. She rolled herself over and pushed up so that she was looking down at him.

"Yeah. Lucas says I want to save the world."

"You already did that part in the army, didn't you?"

"I like to think I helped make things better but that's a hard thing to know. War isn't that simple."

"Nothing's that simple. So you want to save the world. Slay the dragons and keep the princesses safe?"

"Something like that."

She smiled. "Well, as much as I like a good knight, I have to tell you, I'm not a princess. I don't need to be locked up in a tower. I won't be locked up in a tower."

"I don't need to lock you up."

Her face went pensive. "Not literally. That would be weird. And really creepy and I'd have to call the cops on your ass. But there are things I want to do in my life. And some of them aren't the safest things on earth. I want to learn to ski and maybe bungee-jump and some other stuff that I never got to do when I was dancing because I couldn't afford to injure myself. I don't live my life within the lines. Not all the time."

He sucked in a breath. "I know that."

"Yeah, but can you live with it? Because my choices

are mine. No one else gets to choose for me. Or control what I do. So if you already know that the answer is no, we should cut our losses. Before anyone gets hurt."

It might already be too late for that. But saying that would probably just scare her off.

"And if I don't know?"

"Then I need to know if you can try to be okay with it. Otherwise, it's that cutting-our-losses thing again. I know this is early. And maybe we'll do this for a few weeks or months and get sick of the sight of each other but like I said, I've made bad choices before. You might be a knight—even a slightly rusty one—but that doesn't mean you're not a bad choice. Not if you want to change who I am or what I do." She put her hand on his chest. Right on the scar that cut across under his right pec where he'd been sliced open by a flying piece of glass in an explosion. "You've got scars. I do, too. Maybe we're both sliced up into puzzle pieces. But that doesn't mean we're the right fit, no matter how well we do this"—she waved her hand at his body and hers—"together."

"I know," he said. "You're right."

"But?" she said.

"But I'd like to see if we could fit. See what happens. I promise to try not to be a douche and try to wrap you up in bubble wrap."

She laughed "Bubble wrap? Isn't it usually cotton wool?"

"You're not the cotton wool type. Bubble wrap. Fun. Addictive. Like you."

That earned him an eye-roll. "Are you trying to charm me?"

"I'm trying to picture you wrapped in bubble wrap. Maybe you could meet me at the door like that next time."

"Sounds sweaty."

"Sounds fun." He grinned at her. "So what do you think? You have permission to call me out when I'm being ridiculous. I'll do the same for you if you refuse to listen to perfectly reasonable suggestions. And we'll see what happens."

Her head was tilted, her wild red hair sticking up in all directions. She smoothed it down and studied him. "I think . . . I think there's something else I need to tell you."

He felt himself go alert, tried to still the reaction. "Okay."

"I had an email from my ex. The wall-punching one." Her expression was wary.

He kept his voice calm, with an effort. "Does he email you often?"

"No. No, I haven't heard from him in a long time. I think he must have seen one of the news stories about the Angels."

"And what did he have to say?" He didn't like coincidences. Someone was harassing Raina and here was her ex popping up. Then again, he didn't like solutions that were too neat.

She shook her head, looking frustrated. "It wasn't anything bad. Not overtly. More like he was just letting me know that he was still out there."

"That doesn't sound good," he said. "When was this?"

"Earlier today."

"Before I called?" Why hadn't she told him?

"Yes. And before you get mad, I didn't tell you because I didn't want to distract you from Baltimore. And there's nothing really to tell."

"A potentially violent ex is not *nothing*." This time his voice wasn't quite as calm as he would have liked.

"I was going to tell you when you got back. And if he'd emailed again I would have told you straightaway." She studied him, green eyes serious. "I was handling it."

Her definition of handling it was apparently different from his. But he remembered what she'd said. About not wanting to be controlled. So he couldn't just take over and do things his way. Not if he wanted to keep waking up next to her. He took a breath. Pushed back the worry and anger. She was safe. And she had told him. She'd given him that much. He could respect her boundaries in return. "Okay." He nodded once. "Okay. Let's see what happens."

A delighted smile spread across her face. "Really? You're okay with it?"

He shrugged. "I'll deal."

"Good." She leaned forward, kissed him.

Relief made him go boneless again. He hadn't screwed it up. Then he remembered there was something he needed to tell her. "While we're sharing, there's something else you need to know."

Raina drew back. "Oh?"

"Yeah. I told Alex that we were . . . considering our options."

"You did?"

"I had to tell him I was leaving," Mal said. "It was pretty hard to explain why without that part."

She chewed her lip. "Did he—"

"He was fine. It's fine. He's happy about it. And he won't tell anybody else until I say it's okay. Okay?"

"Okay. I just wasn't expecting it."

"Well, your friends know. Or suspect. So it's fair that mine do, too. Eventually." He smiled and pressed a kiss to her hand. "So what do you think?"

She bent forward to kiss him again. Longer this time. Slower. "I think it's okay. And I think you're about to get lucky."

Chapter Fourteen

The next week passed far too quickly for Raina's liking. Mal left again and then came back and left again. The footage from outside Madame R's showed a dark truck driving past, but whoever had thrown the firecrackers had been clever enough to cover up their plates first, so other than the make and model, it wasn't much help. She hoped that it meant that the firecrackers had been unrelated to anything else but she knew that Mal—even though he wasn't pushing the issue—wasn't ready to let it go. He'd had another conversation with Luis, and the club was now practically bristling with security cameras. Even a cunning one that scanned the IDs they were checking to record them.

The Saints lost their second home game but not by much, and they'd won two of their away games.

And even though the team had lost the second game at Deacon, the Angels had continued to get plenty of press, most of it positive. There'd been a minor hiccup when Chen's team had done some work in their locker room to replace one of the security feeds and a spark from a drill had somehow set off a sprinkler. Which in turn had soaked the contents of several of the girls' lockers. Marly had been on of the unlucky ones but her good humor about it and the way she'd received Chen's awkward apology had apparently set the standard for the other girls and no one had thrown a tantrum. Thankfully Ana's locker had stayed dry. Everything had dried out with minimal damage and Maggie had brought down a batch of Shonda's cookies so everyone had been happy. Well, the dancers who allowed themselves carbs had been. Ana had looked at the cookies like they were made from arsenic and entrails and stomped off.

Best of all, there had been no further contact from Jeremy.

So she was in a pretty good mood when she headed to rehearsals for the Angels on Tuesday afternoon.

She had just about reached the Angels' locker room when she heard Maggie calling her name. Spinning on her heels, she stopped and waiting for Maggie to catch up with her.

"Hey, Raina," Maggie said.

"Hi. Nice shirt," Raina said. Maggie was wearing a scarlet silk shirt tucked into a black pencil skirt. She'd make a good sexy librarian, Raina decided, wondering if she could come up with a burlesque version of that outfit. The guys would eat it up. Maggie had legs that went on forever. And good boobs. And hell, she was going off on a tangent. Her head was so stuffed with rehearsals for the Angels and the club and her stolen nights with Mal, she found her brain wandering off on strange tangents at very odd moments.

"Thanks." Maggie smiled. "So can I grab you for a few minutes?"

Raina checked her watch. She was already cutting it fine. "I've got rehearsal, can I come see you after? It's just a quick one today, so I'll be about ninety minutes?"

Maggie nodded. "That's fine. Maybe I'll sneak out and watch you for a bit. Alex has me analyzing attendance statistics going back practically to when baseball was invented. It's not the most riveting thing ever."

"Don't tell me there's something about baseball that's not riveting," Raina teased. "Won't you get kicked out of the Jameson family for that?"

"Probably," Maggie said. "But the good stuff outweighs the bad. Now get going. I've got fresh cookies in my office. They'll all vanish once the guys get back later, so get them while they're there."

"What time are they arriving?" Raina asked, trying to sound casual. Mal had told her he'd be back today but not what time.

"I think the flight gets in at three," Maggie said. "Sara's picking them up at JFK, so they'll be here sometime around four. They took a later flight because Mal wanted to look at something at the Twins' field. Why? Did Mal need to talk to you about something? Has something else happened at the club?"

Raina shook her head. "No, nothing like that. Just curious. Okay. I will come and find you and claim my cookie reward after I put these Angels through their paces. We're trying a new routine tonight."

"You're still doing the wings at the start though, right?" Maggie said. "I love the wings."

"Wings are in," Raina confirmed. She wasn't going to mess with that opening routine until she had to. Someone had filmed the entire thing at Friday's game and put it up on YouTube and even though the footage was pretty crappy it had gotten something like five hundred thousand hits already. Which only went to prove the power of wings. When wielded by her lean mean dancing machine. Who were waiting for her to tune them up a little. Maybe they could get even more hits if she tweaked things just a fraction.

Raina knocked on Maggie's door about two hours later. One of the dancers had twisted her ankle slightly at practice so there'd been some running around finding ice and getting the team doctor—Steven "Indy" (as everyone called him) Jones—to take a look at it. That was a perk of working for a baseball team. Medical staff on premises. At least when the team was at home. Dr. Jones had strapped Haylee's ankle and ordered her to rest it for a few hours and come back to get it checked before the performance. They had two extra girls on the squad to cover injuries, so it wasn't a big deal. Just making her late.

"Come in," Maggie said.

Raina poked her head through the door. Oliver Shields, the Saints' first baseman, was perched on the edge of Maggie's desk. Raina hadn't really met many of the players yet but she knew what most of them looked like thanks to her research and the dancers' tendency to show her pictures of the team hotties despite her repeated lectures on the ban on getting mixed up with players. Ollie Shields was a favorite with them. She couldn't blame them. He was tall and had dark hair and olive skin like Maggie. They looked like a matched set. As she walked in he smiled at her, revealing killer dimples to round out the package.

She kept her answering smile strictly polite. "Hey, Maggie," she said. "Sorry I'm late."

"Everything okay?" Maggie asked. She reached down and pulled out a plastic tub from her desk drawer. "Come get a cookie before Ollie tries to eat them all."

"I don't eat them all," Ollie said. "You won't give them to me."

"You can go sweet-talk Shonda for your own damned cookies," Maggie said. "Besides, you don't want to get too fat for your uniform, do you?"

Ollie stuck his tongue out her. Raina studied him out of the corner of her eyes as she went over to collect her cookie. Ollie Shields was in no danger of busting out of his uniform anytime soon. He was lean and muscled, the long-sleeved blue T- shirt and dark jeans he had on out-lining his body quite nicely. If she hadn't had Mal, she might have been tempted. Except for the baseball player part. He had to have women throwing themselves at him every five seconds. Not her thing.

"Raina, this is Ollie," Maggie said. "He was just leaving."

"You don't really want to get rid of me, do you?" Ollie asked. "Your life will be bereft of meaning and purpose once I leave."

"I'll take my chances," Maggie retorted. "Run away and go do whatever you should be doing before a game. Raina and I have important business things to discuss."

That was news to Raina. But as she bit into the truly excellent chocolate chip and pecan cookie, she decided she was happy to be blindsided by something if she got more cookies as a reward.

Ollie reached for the cookie container. "Just one more for the road."

Maggie shook her head. "Don't blame me if Dan makes you do extra laps or something."

"I'll bribe him with cookies if he tries," Ollie said.

"That only works for me. He likes me," Maggie said. "You're the problem child."

"I'm a model citizen."

"A model citizen who is *leaving*," Maggie stressed.

Ollie snapped a salute. "Yes, ma'am, boss lady." He nodded at Raina. "Nice to meet you. Those dancers of yours are doing a good job." He got to his feet in a graceful sort of flow that told Raina that, yup, he was an athlete who knew what to do with his body. She made a mental note to give another speech to the Angels about the wisdom—or lack thereof—of getting tangled up with any of the players. If they were dealing with temptations like Oliver, frequent reminders couldn't hurt.

Ollie closed the door behind him and Maggie waved at the seat in front of desk. "Sorry about Ollie, he gets bored easily. He needs a hobby."

"Professional baseball isn't enough?"

"He needs to use his brain. He's gotten by on his body all his life but that can't last forever," Maggie said.

"You sound like you've known him a long time," Raina said. Maggie offered the cookies again and she took another one. She would spend some time on her treadmill to make up for it. The curse of being short and built the way she was was that she gained weight fast. And Brady's costumes were unforgiving. Though she could always just order him to make her new ones.

"Since I was fifteen," Maggie said. "He was a rookie here. We kind of grew up together." Her expression turned a little nostalgic.

"Did you two . . . ?"

"Yeah. But we work better as friends. He drives me crazy sometimes. He needs someone who'll—Well, I've never figured that part out. But someone who isn't me."

"I'm sure Alex is happy about that."

"Ollie and I were over long before Alex appeared on the scene," Maggie said. "But I didn't ask you here to talk about Ollie. Unless you want to take a shot at him? He really is a good guy under the nonsense."

Raina blinked. Apparently Alex really hadn't told anyone what Mal had told him about their relationship. That was unexpected. But good. So best not to give herself away. Without ending up having to go on a blind date with Oliver Shields. That one would be hard to explain. She shook her head. "Sounds like hard work. He's cute but no real . . . twinkle."

"Twinkle?"

"You know. When you look at a guy and he's got that look about him, that little spark in his eyes that means you know he's got some game?"

"You don't get twinkle from Ollie?"

"Not my type. He looks like a dancer, kind of. That long, lean thing. Been there, done that. I like my men a little more filled out. Grown up. Or something."

"Grown up has a definite appeal," Maggie agreed.

"Okay, no Ollie. He can find his own dates without any help from us. So let's talk business. Your Angels have been getting lots of press, yes?"

"I think they're kind of your Angels," Raina said.

"Nope. I couldn't choreograph a dance routine if you paid me. And it was Alex's idea. But you've turned it into something more than he could have anticipated," Maggie said. "So all the excellent free publicity is your doing."

"It's not all excellent."

"No, but we knew some of the old school weren't going to like it. They don't matter. Neither do the weirdos. Let's focus on the good. Which is that people like your Angels and they're interested in you. The media office has had some interview requests. Would that be something you'd be interested in doing?"

Interviews. Ugh. She'd done a few when Madame R had opened and of course, pieces here and there in various theater magazines and for blogs and the burlesque scene, but it wasn't her favorite thing in the world. "What kind of interviews?"

"Some print. Some TV. *Good Morning America* has made some nibbles about getting the Angels to do something on their show. And maybe interview you."

TV. Her stomach clenched. Yikes.

"We can organize some media training for you. And whichever of the girls you think would make a good impression. We don't have to say yes to anything just yet."

Saying no would be wimpy. And hey, free media training couldn't be a bad thing. If nothing else, it was bound to be useful down the track. It was just another kind of performance, right? She could handle that. "Training would be great," she said. "And there are a few of the girls who would be good at this, I think." Marly and Leanna and maybe even Char. The three of them were bubbly and friendly and had brains to go with their dance skills. Not Ana. She was photogenic but Raina couldn't trust her to not throw a fit in public.

Maggie nodded and reached for her mouse. "Okay. I'll get the media gals to email you with some possible times and we'll see what we can come up with. Bet you didn't think you were going to be on *GMA* when you took this job."

"To be honest, I kind of expected that we'd last about two performances before Alex changed his mind."

"Well, so far so good. Just keep doing what you're doing."

"Sure," Raina said. "As long as I keep getting cookies."

"Deal," Maggie said.

There was a knock on the door and it opened.

"Hey, Mags, are you—"

Mal's voice. Mal's voice breaking off at the sight of her. She made herself stay still. Then turn casually.

There he was. He'd only been gone two days but damn, it was good to see him. She bit her lip so she wouldn't grin at him.

"Oh, sorry," Mal said. "Didn't realize you were busy. Hi, Raina."

He made the words sound so casual. So why did they make her want to rip his clothes off? Damn the man. He'd bewitched her somehow.

"Mal," she said. "Hello."

"We were just finishing up," Maggie said. "I was talking to Raina about doing some press."

Mal frowned. "Press?"

"We've had some interview requests. People find our Angels interesting, apparently."

"That might not be the best idea," Mal said.

Maggie lifted an eyebrow. "Oh?"

"You know what's been going on with Raina's club," Mal said. "She might not want to draw attention to herself right now."

"Drawing attention to myself is kind of what I do for a living," Raina interjected.

"Besides which, I doubt anyone's going to try anything in a TV studio," Maggie said. "They have pretty good security."

"I think I'm the best judge of that," Mal said.

"Fine, then I'll let you sort out that side of things. But we're not passing up free publicity when it's offered. The less money we have to spend on the promotion, the more you have to play with the stadium and make it all Space Age," Maggie said. "Okay?"

He shrugged and Raina didn't think he was all that okay at all. But that was a conversation best had with just the two of them alone. Unless they wanted Maggie to know what was going on between them.

"Okay," Mal said. "In that case, can I borrow Raina a minute? We've changed a few security things the Angels need to know about."

"Sure," Maggie said. "We're done." She frowned. "Wait, didn't you want something for me?"

"I'll come back," Mal said. "Raina has to get ready

for the performance soon. You, on the other hand, just have to get to the owners' box on time."

"I have to have time to make with the pretty," Maggie said with a grin.

Mal lifted his eyebrows. "In that shirt, you have plenty of pretty. Are you trying to give Alex a heart attack or something?"

"No, just remind him of what he's missing when he goes away and leaves me all alone."

"I think that'll do it," Mal said. "So I'll come back. Raina? You all set? We'll go to my office."

Chapter Fifteen

Raina said good-bye to Maggie and followed Mal to his office. Not the security office where he hung out most often but his actual office where she'd had her very first meeting with him. When he'd been all cranky and adorable. Now he was just adorable. She wondered if everyone she passed could hear her heart pounding as she walked next to him and made inane small talk. Or if they knew she was counting the seconds until they were alone.

Mal closed the office door behind them with a firm click that suggested he'd locked it. Then he reached for her and proceeded to kiss the living daylights out of her for several long and delicious minutes.

"Someone will see us," she squeaked when he let her up for air.

"Nope. Trust me, I know where every camera in this place is and only I have the code that activates the one in here."

"Still," she said. "You go sit over at your desk. You're going to rumple me and then people will know."

"You're wearing workout clothes. They don't rumple."

"Hair does. Makeup does." She pointed at the desk. "Get thee behind it, Satan."

"Satan? I thought I was a knight."

"Knights don't kiss like that. Devils do."

Mal laughed but backed away to the desk and sat. "Happy?"

"Very. Good kiss by the way. Just in case you were wondering."

That earned her a grin. "Thought it was better to start with that."

"Before we fight, you mean?"

"Fight?"

"You know, argue. Discuss. Disagree. The part where you tell me that you don't want me to do any press and then I say that maybe that's a little extreme and we go a few rounds before we work things out." She hoped that he was going to be able to work it out. After all, he'd said he would try to let her do things her way.

"Ah, that part. Sounds like you've got it all worked out," he said.

"There's the part where we can have really hot makeup sex after I'm done tonight."

His eyebrows lifted. "Trying to bribe me, Ms. Easton?"

"Is it working? Can I distract you from the fight part by offering up my body as a sacrifice to the dark lord?" She tried to look like that wasn't a very appealing prospect. Office. They were in Mal's office. In the middle of a building filled with many, many people. She couldn't lose her head and let him kiss her—or do anything else to her—again.

"You said no to the body part just a few minutes ago."

"So I did." She sighed. Her past self was sensible. She should listen to her. "Okay, then, dark lord. On to the arguing."

"You make it difficult to remember what I wanted to argue about," Mal said. "I keep thinking about what's under those workout clothes."

"A body in desperate need of a shower," she said. "Not sexy at all. So mind out of the gutter. Let's get this discussion going. There's this thing called a baseball game happening tonight."

"So I hear. All right then, discussion it is. I don't think that you doing any interviews right now is a good idea."

"Why not?"

"Because, like I said to Maggie, stuff has been happening. Stuff that suggests there is someone unpleasant out there with a bone to pick with you. I'd rather you didn't give him a clear shot, so to speak."

"So far there's been graffiti, flat tires, and some fireworks. Hardly life threatening."

"Getting worse."

"Yes. And believe me, that thought doesn't exactly make me happy. But I'm not going to let some loser run my life and make me run scared. So I'm not agreeing to do no press at all."

He folded his arms and gave her a very annoyed dark lord look. Kind of sexy really. Probably not the effect he was aiming for. She stifled a grin. She liked a man who fought fair. No sulking. No pouting. No getting huffy when she tried to lighten the situation. At least, not so far. Maybe he really was a grown-up.

The kind of guy she could trust.

She squelched that thought. Too soon. After all, he wasn't perfect. There was the dead girlfriend for one thing. She still wasn't sure how she felt about that. Not jealous, well, no more than reasonable. But . . . there was something there. It was pretty hard to compete with a memory after all. Someone frozen in time with their faults fading every day and only the good stuff remaining.

And then there were those buttons that this Ally, and for this part Raina did want to smack her, had installed in Mal. Sure, the guy had possibly had a good slab of *Must save the world* in his personality to begin with. Joining the army was a good indication of that. But then Ally had gone and made him fail at saving someone precious to him. Raina had enough buttons of her own to recognize a good one when she saw it. Mal wasn't perfect. He came with issues.

The question was, Did those issues make him knight in slightly battered armor or a real dark lord? One who was beyond finding the light again?

And how far she would be willing to go to find out? To see if he crossed a line. That was the part that scared her. Would she recognize the point where she needed to let go or not?

But that was her button. And right now, this was about Mal's.

"So somewhere between zero press and appearing on every show the media office can dig up," she offered. "That seems to be the range we're dealing with. What's the easy stuff, print? Print seems safe enough. Reporters can come here to Deacon. They'll probably dig up some of my burlesque pictures but there's nothing out there that I don't already know about. Nothing that should worry the Saints given that you vetted me before you hired me. Sound about right?"

Mal nodded. "Yes."

"Right. So print is okay. But TV gets to more people. So TV is good. TV equals butts on seats at your games and all that good stuff. Now, I'm no press expert, but I'm hazarding a guess that the TV shows might be more inter-ested in my tall leggy dancer girls than in me, so we can probably keep me behind the scenes for most of those."

"That would be good," Mal said. His shoulders low-ered slightly and Raina felt her stomach muscles loosen in response. "Better would be keeping you behind the scenes entirely."

She shrugged. "Maggie was right about TV studios having good security."

"Not all the morning shows. They do those segments right out on the street. Any idiot could be in the crowd."

"Okay, so no location shoots. Studio only. Unless they want to come here and shoot something to play later. How about that? That way you can vet everyone to your little dark security lord heart's content and control the whole shebang."

"You're enjoying this, aren't you?" he said.

"My parents always taught me to use my words. And my gran said life was too short to spend wheedling folks to do what you want with the indirect approach. She was more the face things head-on and just say what the hell you want type."

"I like the sound of her," Mal said.

"She was awesome," Raina said. "She was two inches shorter than me and no one ever crossed her. Ruled the whole damned family." She smiled crookedly, the old familiar pang hitting her as she pictured Violet's face. "So I learned at the feet of a master, mister. I can do this all day. Or at least for another thirty minutes or so. Then I have to go Angel wrangling instead of dark lord wrangling."

"You're wrangling me?"

"Trying to? Is it working?" She batted her eyelashes at him and he laughed.

"I think it might be. Okay. Yes to print. Yes to some TV. Limited TV. Let the reporters wrangle the Angels for a change."

She resisted the urge to do a fist pump. They'd done it. A nice mature compromise. Sure, Mal might still have an issue or two when push came to shove about her going on camera but he hadn't tried to just lay down the law and ride over what she wanted. Good dark lord. Nice dark lord.

Freakin' hot dark lord.

"You're sure there are no cameras running in here?" she asked.

"One hundred percent certain."

"In that case, come here and kiss me. My gran taught me to get what I want and right now that's what I want." And she laughed again as he came over and did just that.

When Raina emerged from the locker rooms after the game, Alex was waiting for her in the corridor outside. She stopped, coming to an awkward halt with her gear bag on one shoulder. Her giant supplies case whacked the back of her ankle when it didn't stop as fast as she did.

"Ow. Alex. Hi. Congratulations on the game," she said, trying not wince. The Saints had won again. Just. But it was a win. And she'd managed to keep the squad from getting too excited about the prospect of interviews and media.

Alex smiled. "Thanks. Are you okay?"

"This case has a mind of its own." She bent down to rub her ankle, trying not to feel like she was making an idiot of herself in front of her boss. She really should spring for a new case sometime soon. One that actually steered. Alex probably had expensive luggage that never misbehaved. Made by teams of Swiss engineers or something.

Alex waited for her to straighten. "Attack luggage. I get that. We could get you a team-branded case. Something less deadly. Call it a bonus. Your Angels seem to be inspiring the team to great things."

She nodded, not wanting him to think she was mooching for free stuff. "Happy to oblige. Did you need something? I have to get back to Brooklyn for the second half of my show."

Alex held out a hand. "I came to walk you to your truck. Let me take that case for you. We can walk and talk."

She let go of the handle and stepped away. They headed toward the parking lot. "What did you want to talk to me about?"

"Do you ever rent out Madame R for private functions?" Alex asked.

She nodded. "Sometimes. For the right price. Not

weekends preferably or it would have to be a really, really right price. Why? What were you thinking?"

"Maggie said her dad used to throw team parties sometimes. In about a month we have a good run of games here again. The Yankees on Sunday then Monday off then the Yankees again for the next two days."

"No travel," she said.

"No. So that's a window to do something for the team. Let them blow off a little steam. Not too much steam but they're professionals. They know they have to play the next day."

"Sounds like a good idea," Raina said. "But why my club?"

"Maggie keeps talking about how much fun it was. Said your show was great. So I thought maybe you could do a shorter version of that and then we'd bring in caterers to do food and you can do the beverages. Would that work?"

She nodded. A fat fee for a private function was just another welcome addition to her nest egg. She wasn't going to say no.

Alex smiled again. Which made him even more ridiculously handsome.

"Great. I want to do something special for Maggie. Things were crazy this year around her birthday so a bit of belated fuss can't hurt."

"I approve of men wanting to spoil their girlfriends." They'd reached Rose and Alex hauled the case into the back of the truck. "Let me talk to Brady and Luis and Paolo—they manage Madame R with me. We'll price some options for you if you send me the date you're thinking of. The Monday?" She fished in her bag for her keys, then paused as something occurred to her. "When you say something special, you do just mean a party, don't you? You're not planning any grand gestures?"

"Grand gestures?"

"Putting a rock on Maggie's finger as big as that blue iceberg Sara wears? We get people proposing every so often at the club and I have to say, if it were me, I'd rather my proposal be private. It always feels a bit . . . aggressive. Puts the girl on the spot. Of course, I'm not Maggie, and I'm sure she'd love a rock as big as an iceberg, so tell me to go soak my head if you want."

"No head soaking. I agree. When I propose to Maggie, I don't want an audience."

The look on his face—half eager, half awed—made her smile. "Awwww, you said when."

His expression turned startled. "What?"

"Just now. You said when you propose. Not if." She grinned at him. "Don't worry, your secret is safe with me. I know you two haven't been dating all that long. Though Lucas and Sara are engaged."

"Lucas doesn't mess around," Alex said.

"And you do?"

"No, but Maggie and I are different. Maggie is invested in this place. She wants the Saints to do really well this season. Her head's not in the right spot for anything else right now. I want her full attention when the time comes."

She smiled at him approvingly. Definitely grown up. Which boded well for his friends being grown-ups, too. She could get used to this. The thought kept her smiling all the way back to Brooklyn.

* * *

Two weeks later Mal watched Raina turn on the charm for the way-too-polished host of a cable news morning show and tried not to get too annoyed.

It was the third TV interview she'd done but the first without any of the Angels with her. Raina had apparently had to deal with some tensions in the squad about who was getting more press exposure, so she'd decided to do this one solo. Mal had tried to dig out of her who was causing trouble—if he had to guess he'd pick Ana, who always seemed a little too fond of herself and a little too keen on talking to the players rather than her fellow Angels at club events. She was, admittedly, gorgeous, but he'd come across her type before. Not a team player. But Raina had said it was her problem to deal with and that she wasn't going to tell him who was involved until she had to. He was respecting that.

The host was asking the same inane questions as they had at the other stations but he kept smiling at Raina a little too broadly for Mal's liking.

Raina didn't seem fazed by it, though, and she smiled back and gave answers that were smart and charming. He wasn't so sure about the charming part. The host seemed to like it a little too much.

But it was all going smoothly and he made himself relax. Then the host—Blair, that was the idiot's name—said, "So Raina, you're a burlesque dancer. Isn't that like being a stripper?" A picture of Raina in black leather corset and fishnets and bright-red shoes—a shot Mal recognized from the Madame R website—appeared on the screen behind the host. "I mean, that outfit is pretty risqué, isn't it?"

What the fuck? Mal bristled and grabbed the arm of the floor manager standing beside him. "Shut this down. *Now*," he growled. "Before I shut him down."

The man nodded and hurried off. Mal watched Raina. She had blinked when Blair had proved himself to be a complete moron by asking that question but she hadn't answered. Yet.

"Strippers take their clothes off and give men lap dances. There are lots of great dancers who strip out there but that's not what I do, Blair. Burlesque is about sexual tension, not sex. And the way it's done at my club, it's about a lot more than that. Like female empowerment. And respect for women. The kind you apparently weren't taught very well. Now, did you have another question?" Raina said in a steely voice.

Mal bit back a laugh as Blair's face went red. Which didn't mean he wouldn't still have a thing or two to say to the guy about how to talk to women after the show. But Raina had taken him down quite nicely on air, and that was a good start.

Abruptly Blair put his hand on his ear and then nodded and turned to the camera. "And we'll back right after this break. This is Blair Hansen and I've been talking to Raina Easton, choreographer for the Fallen Angels, the new dance squad that has been making waves over at Deacon Field. Don't go away, your great morning is just getting started."

Mal waited a few seconds until the movement of the crew told him that they were off air. He learned the signs in the previous two interviews. He started to walk onto the floor of the small studio but Raina met him before he could get too far.

She wrapped a hand around his arm. "Mal," she said warningly. "You can't punch out a journalist."

"I'm not going to punch him," Mal said. "Just explain to him that there are some questions that come with a price tag."

He looked over her head at Blair, who was being fussed over by a makeup man. But he was looking at Mal and he must have got the message that Mal was trying to convey with his glare because he went pale under the heavy makeup he wore.

"Mal," Raina said again. "Let's go. We have to get back to Deacon. Game day, remember? He's not worth the trouble. I took care of it. He was just trying to score a point and if you go and do something dumb, then he will have. So shake it off, big boy. He's not the last guy you'll hear call me a stripper, if you and I keep going."

"Maybe not. And if he isn't then he's not going to be the only one who's going to regret saying it."

"Not a damsel in distress here," she said. "Remember?" She tugged on his arm again. "Let's go."

Mal looked down at her. She didn't look upset. Concerned maybe, but not upset. Concerned about him. Which meant that if he kept going, she was going to move to upset. Because of something he'd done. Which would make him the dickhead in this scenario. He took a deep breath and sent one last glare in Blair's direction. "You're right. Let's go."

Chapter Sixteen

"I'll walk you down to the locker room," Mal said as Raina pulled into the underground parking lot at Deacon. She had a space nearer the elevator now; Mal had insisted, claiming it was easier for the security team to keep their eyes on Rose if she had a prime position.

"You don't have to. I'm going by the wardrobe room to do wing check first. Brady gave me a bunch of spare feathers in case any have come loose," Raina said, killing the ignition and tugging her keys free. The wings, effective as they were, were a little high-maintenance, shedding feathers with alarming ease. Not wanting moth-eaten Angels, Raina had added feather-sewing skills to her arsenal. She glanced at Mal as she undid her seat belt. He seemed to have calmed down on the drive back to Staten Island but she wasn't sure if he had really forgotten about that idiot TV host—who, she had to confess, she would have been quite happy to let Mal punch in the nose—or whether he was just acting that way to make her feel better.

"I'm going to the security office, it's on my way," Mal said.

Only if your definition of *on his way* was "one floor up and on the opposite side of the stadium." But she didn't think that arguing with him was the best approach right now. So she waited while he grabbed her bags—no point trying to dissuade him from that, either, right this second—and then she locked Rose.

"What do you think our chances are today?" she asked as they walked. Surely that was a suitable change of subject? Baseball. He liked baseball. He owned the damned team.

Mal looked down at her. "It's okay, I'm over Blair the prick. You don't have to cheer me up by talking about sports."

"Hey, I like baseball, too," she said, a little indignant. And a little annoyed that he'd seen through her ploy so easily. "And I work hard for this team."

"Yes, you do. Okay, then, if you really want to know." He started to talk baseball statistics at her. Comparing the performances of the Saints versus the Orioles and who was injured and who was in form. She nodded and smiled and pretended she understood all of it. Some of it made sense, but statistics ignored the heart of the game. The magic when a team gelled and started to play like many bodies with one mind. At least, she assumed that happened for sports teams just like it did for dancers or theater companies. And given she'd never been able to figure out why some nights were magical and every movement was easy and it all just worked until the air fairly shimmered with light when she was dancing, she had to also assume that no one had yet worked out what combination of chemistry and work and luck turned a baseball team into an unstoppable run machine.

The players were superstitious; she'd seen them tapping bats in the dugout or working rosary beads or carrying good-luck charms in the bullpen when she'd watched the Angels from the sidelines during the last match. On game days, Ollie Shields always wore his cap backward until he stepped onto the field. Then he turned it right-way around. And immediately back again when he stepped off.

Habit as a way of evoking performance. Which turned into superstition. She understood that.

Mal's flow of information came to a halt as they reached the storage room where the wings were kept. Raina pulled out the swipe card that opened the door, but the reader beeped and the two little lights stayed obstinately red.

"That's weird," she said.

Mal took the card from her and swiped it again. Another beep. Then he tried his own. Another beep.

Frowning, he tugged at the steel handle on the door. Which swung open.

Raina's stomach dropped. "That's not good."

"No," Mal said. "It's not." He pulled out his phone and punched a button. "Chen, get down here, wing room. Stat." He shoved the phone back in his pocket. "Stay here." The door came fully open as he yanked at it.

The room inside was dark and no one came running out wielding a chain saw or something equally deadly.

"Turn on the lights," Raina suggested.

"They should be on. The storeroom lights all have motion sensors. Saves power when no one's in them." He waved his hand inside the door, then, when no lights came on, slid his hand down the wall, feeling for the switch. He found it and light spilled out into the hallway. Mal started swearing.

"What?" Raina demanded.

"Stay there," he repeated.

"Is there a dead body?" she asked.

"No."

"Then let me see." She ducked under his arm and then froze in place when she saw what Mal had seen.

The floor was covered in feathers. Fluffy white feathers. Or *bits of feathers* might have been the more accurate description. The lockers that held each pair of wings were all open and the wings themselves—the bare stripped frames—lay in the piles of feathers. Some of them had been broken, not just stripped.

"Fuck," she breathed. She shut her eyes briefly but when she reopened them, the carnage still lay before her. "Who did this?"

"Trust me, I'm going to find out," Mal said. She felt him step closer, so her back was against his chest. Solid. Warm. Safe.

Safe was good. Suddenly the world didn't feel so safe. "Is this because of me? Did someone do that because of me?"

"I don't know," Mal said. "It's possible."

"Someone hates me that much?" She heard the crack in her voice and swallowed. Hard. Took a breath, then another. "I need to call Brady. We can fix these."

"Not by tonight, you can't," Mal said. "And we need to get the police here before you can even touch anything."

"But—"

"But nothing." He took her hand and pulled her gently back out into the corridor. Chen was just rounding the curve, coming toward them at a jog.

He slowed when he reached them. "What's up?"

Mal waved a hand at the door. "Have a look. But don't step over the threshold."

Chen looked. Then spun back to Mal, dark eyes fierce. "How?"

"That's what I was just about to ask," Mal said. "What happened here today?" He looked back at Raina. "When did you last check on the wings?"

"We had some of them out for the TV spot on Sunday," Raina said. "They were fine then."

"So sometime between then and now," Mal said. "And I'm assuming no one saw this on the tapes; otherwise we wouldn't just be finding out about it now. So the question is, how the hell did someone get in here?"

"Fuck, Mal," Chen said. "I don't know. But whoever is must know what he's doing."

"There's been nothing odd going on?"

Chen frowned. Then his face cleared. "They were doing work on one of the lighting towers this morning. The power had to be cycled on and off a couple of times on the side of the stadium. But it was only out a minute tops at any one time."

"Long enough for someone to bugger the lock and override the motion sensor. If they were good."

"Very good," Chen agreed.

Raina's stomach went cold. Very good. What exactly did that mean coming from two guys who were probably ex-special-forces. A professional? Did someone hate her enough to hire a professional burglar or whatever it was you'd call someone who could do this to screw with her?

"Go back to the office. Start running the tapes and checking the system. Everything gets checked before anyone comes through the gates tonight. Including that lighting tower. Get the police in here. Also go back over the records of any of the contractors and subcontractors we've had in here this week."

Chen nodded. "On it." He started walking back the way he'd come then broke into a jog. Raina didn't blame him. She kind of felt like running away herself.

"And what are we going to do?" she asked.

"Well, the first step is telling Lucas and Alex."

They met in Alex's office. Raina hadn't been in it since the day Alex had first brought her in for an interview. Maybe she should have said no right back then and none of this would be happening now.

Mal made her sit down.

"I'm fine," she said. It was a lie. She felt hot and clammy, stomach rolling queasily. All that work. Brady's beautiful work. Destroyed. Savaged. Did someone want to do that to her?

"Just sit," he said.

"I'm not a dog, Malachi." She wasn't going to cringe like one.

Maggie, who was in the chair to Raina's right, put a hand on her arm. "That must have been a shock, seeing those wings."

"It was. But I'm not going to fall over." Well, she didn't think she was going to. She hoped. She sucked in a breath, locking down the fear. Working on focusing on the anger. Who the hell was doing this and what the hell gave him the right? All that hard work that Brady had put in. All the work the girls had put in. All the hard work she'd put in, goddamn it, and now someone was trying to scare them all away.

Make them scared.

Make them hurt.

Well screw that. She scowled. Her expression pretty much matched that on the faces of Alex, Mal, and Lucas. Alex was sitting at his desk, Lucas was standing in front of it, and Mal was standing on Raina's left ignoring the chair right behind his legs.

"I should have brought the cookies," Maggie said.

Raina smiled. The guys didn't.

"Definitely cookies," Maggie said. "C'mon, guys, this is serious but do you have to stand there looking like you want to burn the place down?"

"What I want to know is how this happened?" Alex said.

"I'm working on that," Mal growled. "It might be that whoever did this used the power outages from the lighting work to at least get into the storeroom. How he—"

"It could be a she," Maggie said.

A she. Raina blinked. She hadn't thought about that. Someone on the squad? Someone who was pissed off about not getting her due? Ana? Surely not.

"I don't know," Mal said. "Those wings are pretty big. To tear them up like that, just one person. That takes some strength."

"Maybe they used a knife or something," Lucas said. "Blades can do plenty of damage."

Lucas would know. He was the surgeon, after all. Raina didn't want to think about someone slashing up the wings. Knife or otherwise.

Maggie turned to Raina. "What do you think? You told me Ana was pretty mad about missing out on the interviews. Would she do something like this?"

"I . . . don't know. I think she's pretty ruthless and wants her own way. But I'm not sure she's crazy enough to sabotage the whole team. I can see her doing sneaky things to individual girls, maybe. But this, this risks having the whole team not get to perform. Which means she wouldn't get to perform. I don't know."

"We'd better talk to her," Maggie said. "See what she has to say."

Mal nodded. "Can't hurt. Though Raina's right, it seems like shooting yourself in the foot, to risk benching the squad. I think it's more likely to be someone else."

"Well, the police will be able to tell us more about that, maybe," Alex said. "And Mal's team is combing through all the security data. So that brings us to the more immediate problem."

Raina watched Mal's jaw tighten at the mention of his team. She wouldn't want to be whoever had fucked this up. If someone had fucked up.

"Which is?" Maggie asked.

"Whether the Angels are going to perform tonight," Alex said.

Raina's head snapped around. "What? Of course we're going on."

"That might not be the smartest thing," Mal said. "If someone is targeting you or the squad, then you're just giving them a clear shot."

"Someone is trying to scare us. If we don't go on, then they've succeeded." Raina protested. "That's just giving in."

"She has a point there, Mal," Alex said.

"We don't even know if the girls will want to go on," Mal said. "You have to tell them about this. You can't send them out there without them knowing what's happened. For one thing, you'll need to explain why they can't wear their wings tonight."

"Do you have another routine?" Maggie asked. "You usually do three. The opening one with the wings and then the two between innings."

"Yeah, we have a few we've been working on," Raina said. "And we can work out a costume change easily enough. We'll just swap things around. It won't be as dramatic as the wings but it will do."

"You tell Brady to get started on a new set. Wherever he got them done," Alex said. "Tell him we'll pay a big bonus if they're ready for Friday night. That way you can do tonight and tomorrow with the new routine and come back with the wings for the weekend before we go to Toronto. Send the guys off with some team spirit."

"The guys are going to be pissed about this," Lucas added. "Most of them seem to like having the girls here."

"They're baseball players, of course they like having eighteen—nineteen, sorry, Raina—gorgeous women around," Maggie said.

"They won't like them being messed with," Lucas said.

"Good. Then they can channel that mad into winning the games," Raina said. "They can come out swinging. And so will we. Don't worry, I'll talk to the girls. Dancers believe in *The show must go on*. Even if some of them don't want to do it, we can do the routines with a reduced number."

"If you're sure," Alex said. "If you don't want to, then that's okay, Raina."

"I'm sure. Mal's team is good. They're not going to let anything happen to us. And it's not like they went after one of us anyway. They went for the costumes. Easy target. It's creepy as fuck but screw them. Oops, sorry," she added. "Not professional."

"Accurate, though," Alex said. "Okay, then that's the plan. Raina and Maggie and I will go talk to the Angels. Lucas, you can talk to the team, and Mal will work with his people and the police."

"And tonight we can all go home and collapse into bed," Maggie said. "I swear, I don't need this much adrenaline. Baseball is plenty exciting enough without weird shit."

"I hear you," Raina said. She stood and stretched, trying to convince herself she wasn't as tired as she felt. She was grateful that she wasn't going to have to go out and perform tonight like the Angels. Though if too many of them balked at the idea, she might have to. "I have a date with my comforter, my cat, and half my weight in chocolate."

"No you don't," Mal said. The growl had come back into his voice.

"Excuse me?"

"You're not going home. You can come stay with me for a while."

Maggie's face broke into a grin at the same time as Lucas's eyebrows shot up. Alex just looked at Mal and shook his head. Raina felt her face get hot. "Don't be stupid, I'm going home."

"Not going to happen. We don't know if this is the same guy pulling shit at your club. but if it is, then he's stepping things up another level. Your apartment has security that a clown could get through. My place is safe."

"That may be true," Raina said. "But it also comes with you. Right now, I'm not sure that's a bonus. You have a big mouth."

Mal crossed his arms and looked stony. "Alex already knew. He probably already told Maggie."

"Nope," Alex said. "Don't dig me a hole along with your own there, Mal."

Mal ignored him. "And I would have told Lucas soon. No one cares that we're sleeping together, Raina. Except me. I care. I care about you and I'm not going to let you put yourself in danger when there's a simple fix. I can't stop you and the Angels doing your thing. I won't stop you doing what you do. But I can stop you going home to somewhere that's not safe.

"It's my home. And there's Wash."

"You can bring the monster cat to my place," Mal said. "There's plenty of space for him to run around and plenty of furniture for him to scratch."

"Mal's place is kind of like Fort Knox," Maggie said. "He's right, you would be safe."

"Maybe we should give Raina and Mal some time to talk about this for a few minutes," Lucas suggested.

Maggie stood. "Raina? Is that what you want?"

"I'm fine," Raina said. "And yes, Malachi and I have a discussion to have."

Alex was the last to leave. He closed the door softly. Raina half suspected that Maggie, Alex, and Lucas were standing outside the door eavesdropping. But even if they were, it didn't change the fact that she and Mal had to talk about this.

"I'm not going to change my mind," Mal said abruptly. "I want you to stay at my place. If you're pissed at me, fine. I'll stay somewhere else. But you're going to be somewhere safe."

"I am pissed at you," Raina said. "But the living arrangements aren't the main problem. The problem is you ambushing me. This is a relationship. At least I hope it's a relationship and that means communication. Compromise. Remember compromise?"

"I'm not compromising on your safety," he said.

She sighed and rubbed her neck. "And I think we're firmly back in button-pushing territory for both of us. I don't like being controlled and treated like property. You don't like giving up control. This is a problem, Mal."

"This isn't exactly situation normal," Mal said. "Once we catch whoever did this, then you can move back to your place. Everything will be fine."

"Until the next time you want to be in charge," Raina said. "Like in the next ten seconds when I tell you I'm still going to Madame R's tonight unless you or the police can give me a concrete reason not to."

She could practically hear his teeth grinding.

"I figured as much," Mal said. "So go. I'll talk to Luis

and there will be extra security. There, that's a compromise."

It was. Much to her surprise. The squirmy stress knots in her stomach loosened a little. "Okay. Good."

"That's me giving a little," Mal said. "So are you going to give a little, too?"

"You mean by staying with you?"

His brow lifted. "Yes. You and the giant cat somewhere nice and impenetrable until this is sorted out."

"You know, most guys make an invitation to move in with them sound a little more romantic," she muttered.

"And when I do that," Mal said, "it will be romantic. But I didn't think we were there yet. Are we?"

She shook her head. "No. Maybe we need to see if we can get through the next few days without driving each other crazy first."

He grinned at her then. "Not much chance of that."

"Not that kind of crazy."

"I like that kind of crazy."

"I know you do. You dark lords have sex on the brain."

He snorted. "Maybe. But generic sex on the brain isn't the same thing as very specific sex on the brain. With one specific person."

His eyes had gone hot again and she felt her annoyance start to melt. "Don't look at me like that," she said. "That's not fighting fair."

His smile broadened. "Well, you know what they say. All's fair in love and war."

"I always hated that saying," she muttered.

"Yeah, but you like me," Mal said and pulled her in to kiss her.

Chapter Seventeen

"Did you find anything yet?" Mal stopped by the bank of monitors where the guys from the team were studying the security feeds for the last forty-eight hours, taking up point position next to Chen.

Chen looked up. He'd worked his black hair into a series of rumpled spikes, and there were several empty energy drink cans next to his monitor. The red and gold koi tattooed on his forearm twitched as he drummed his fingers on his trackpad. Frustrated then. So mostly likely the answer to his question was going to be no.

"Done with the police?" Chen asked.

"Yes. They dusted for prints but there are way too many of them. They'll have to fingerprint all the Angels and the maintenance guys and anyone else around here who's been in that room for a start. But if he's good, he will have worn gloves anyway. They didn't find anything else except some scratches around one of the vent covers."

Chen started. "They think he came in through the vent system?"

The thought of someone crawling around in the ventilation system, which went on for miles, was Mal's worst nightmare. "They don't know. Maybe. The vent looks pretty clean but we had them all cleaned when we were doing the refit. So there wasn't much dirt to start with. But get Spike to get in there and have a look. He's the skinniest."

"He'll love that."

"That's why I pay him the big bucks," Mal said. "Did you call in the other teams? I want as many extra bodies on the ground as we can get tonight. But only guys known to us. No outsiders."

"Yup, all the Saints' teams are coming in and I called Em back at the office to see who she could rustle up as well. And I'm running background on the contractors again. Don't worry, boss. No one will get through us."

"That's what we thought yesterday," Mal said.

Chen shot him a look.

Mal held up his hands. "I'm not blaming anyone unless we can prove that someone fucked up. This guy is obviously good. But we're better. So move over so I can help you run this damned tape."

It took about an hour but they finally found something. "There," Mal said, pointing at the screen where a lighting crew was entering. "Six of them, then that other one by the truck. His cap looks like it's a bit darker than the others'. And there's only six at the bottom of the tower there. So where's the other one? Our dark-hatted friend."

"Maybe he's gone inside, or taking a leak or something," Chen said.

"I want to talk to that crew," Mal said. "Double-check. And then start looking through the tapes for anyone who looks like our odd man out."

"If he took off the cap and the overalls after he broke away from them, then he could be anyone."

"Yup. So start playing with the recognition software you like so much. Get it to find me a match. Maybe start at the lower levels. If he did go in through the ventilation system, that would be easier to access from a lower level. Fewer people around than in the office tower. And he'd stand out on the stadium levels."

"Will do," Chen said.

"Call me when you find it," Mal said. "He's good but no one's perfect. He will have fucked up somewhere. We just need a good look at his face."

"Home sweet home," Mal said about eight hours later when he unlocked the front door to his apartment and turned back to take the cat carrier from Raina.

Wash squawked indignantly, as he'd been doing on and off since Raina had wrestled him into the carrier, but he weighed a ton so she handed him over without protesting. She was too tired to protest. She just wanted a flat surface to lie down on and eight hours' sleep. She couldn't remember the last time she'd had eight hours' sleep.

"Come on in," Mal said.

Lights came on as Raina stepped over the threshold, pulling her suitcase in behind her. She'd only brought a small one because she just couldn't face trying to work out what to bring to fill more than one tonight, and she was still hoping that this was all going to blow over in a few days. So that she could go home again. Wash's stuff, his bed and bowls and food and the carrier, took up more space than her suitcase.

The sudden illumination revealed a semicircular entry hall that was empty except for a battered-looking square wooden table to the right of the door they'd come through and a couple of huge black-and-white photos of mountains on either side of the double doors opposite. Mal opened those and she followed him into his apartment. Though it was hardly an apartment. *Penthouse* was the word she was looking for. They'd come up the elevator right to the top of the building. That meant penthouse.

The double doors opened onto a huge room. Big enough to fit Raina's entire apartment plus probably all of Madame R's twice over. The walls were bare red brick; iron girders ran the length of the roof. Warehouse conversion chic. Or something.

There were several groupings of big brown leather sofas in various parts of the vast space, either facing the row of windows that ran the length of the left side of the room or in squared formations to create the illusion of closeness.

"Cozy," she said drily.

"I like space," Mal said.

"You could play baseball in here," Raina said.

He shrugged. "Basketball, maybe. Baseballs and windows don't mix. Come on, the bedrooms are this way. Do you want me to let Wash out or do you want to keep him in one room for a day or two? Isn't that what you do with cats?"

"Something like that," Raina said. "He's fairly relaxed as cats go but one room might be a better idea if you're attached to your sofas."

"If he can shred leather, then I'm impressed," Mal said. "I can buy more sofas." He kept walking and Raina walked behind him, head turning from side to side as she tried to form an impression other than "big." Polished floors. Reds and browns and dark grays with flashes of white. An eclectic mix of art. Big photos, black-and-white and color of both baseball scenes and nature. Five guitars hung on one section of wall.

"You play guitar?" Raina said.

"Not very well," Mal said. "But I like the way they look."

They reached the far end of the room and a door made of red-brown wood that toned with the bricks.

Beyond that was another corridor. She was starting to feel like she'd stepped into the TARDIS. Bigger on the inside.

"My room's the door at the far end," Mal said. "Kitchen's this one." He pushed the first door on the right open and Raina caught a glimpse of stainless steel and gleaming glass and more reddish wood in the cabinets.

Mal ignored the next few doors and Raina restrained her curiosity. He finally stopped just before the end of the corridor where the door he'd indicated was his dead in front of them and then opened the last door on the left before the corridor ended. "This can be you," he said. "Make yourself at home. I'll get the rest of Wash's stuff from your truck." He put Wash's carrier down on the carpet just inside the door and smiled at her. "I'll be right back."

"You might want to take a snack for the hike," she said.

"I'm used to it. Keeps me fit."

She suspected that one of the other doors would reveal a home gym of some sort. Mal would want to work out in a way that suited in him and when it suited him. He'd have his own setup.

But she could explore the rest of the doors later. Right now she wanted to get Wash settled and then sleep.

She bent down and opened the carrier. Wash stalked out with an angry-sounding "Mrrrooowwwww." He looked up at her and then around the room. Then promptly sat down and gave a much more curious chirp of inquiry as his head swiveled from side to side, surveying the room again.

Mal didn't skimp on guest bedrooms apparently. The bed was a king size, piled with pillows and a comforter in shades of light gray, black, and red. A bank of low drawers stood against the wall opposite the bed, with a giant TV on the wall above them. The windows were hidden by a floor-to-ceiling fall of curtains in a shimmery shade of one of the deeper grays in the bed linen. The fourth wall was shiny black. She could just make out the outlines of doors in the gleaming expanse. Wardrobe, she assumed. Not that she really needed a wardrobe. The nightstands were the same lacquered black with low silver lamps with black shades. There was a matching black door in the same wall as the bed.

"Hey cat, I think we got an en suite," she said. Wash looked at her suspiciously. "Don't blame me. I didn't choose the change in location. You need to chew on something of Mal's to get even for that." She wandered over to the door, opened it, and stuck her head into the room. Which made the lights come on. Definite fan of motion sensors, her Mal. The bathroom held a very long, very deep-black bath and a shower and a toilet. Nice. Plus having an en suite made figuring out where to put Wash's litter tray easy. She would investigate more when Mal came back.

She backed up and sat on the bed, toeing off the ratty beat-up Nikes she'd put on at the club after the show. She was wearing jeans and her oldest sweatshirt and she'd scrubbed her face clean of makeup. Glamour at its finest.

She flopped back on the bed and heard Wash land beside her. He butted her cheek with his head then climbed onto her stomach, sat down, and started grooming a paw. The slurping sound was kind of soothing and she let herself drift for a while.

"Someone's feeling at home."

She raised her head and peered around Wash. Mal stood in the doorway with the box full of cat paraphernalia. "He always does." She sat up, lifting Wash onto the comforter.

"Don't get up. I'll put this stuff in the bathroom," Mal said.

She lay back down. Just for a minute. She needed a minute.

Somewhere in the distance she vaguely recognized the sound of water running. But she couldn't quite make herself get off the bed to investigate. Mal had exceptional taste in mattresses, she decided. It was firm but somehow soft at the same time. Like lying in a supportive cloud. It made her brain go blank and cloudy, too. Just what the doctor had ordered. She felt a weight on the bed beside her.

"Don't bother me, Wash, I'll feed you in a minute," she murmured.

"Not Wash, Mal," Mal said with a soft laugh.

She opened her eyes. "Big," she said. Then ran her hand over his chin and the stubble that had sprung up as it did at the end of every long day. "Furry. Same same."

"Can Wash do this?" he said and kissed her. Softly. Sweetly. It made her sink back down into the cloudy bliss.

"Mmmm," she sighed. "Probably not. His breath usually smells like cat food."

"I know you were looking forward to angry makeup sex," Mal said. "But I have another idea."

"You do? Does it involve sleeping?"

His hand slid up under her sweatshirt, found her breast. He brushed a thumb over her nipple. "You can sleep if you want." His thumb moved again and the cloud dissolved then re-formed into a whole different kind of pleasant.

She opened her eyes. "You have my attention."

Mal stood, scooped her up.

"Show-off," she said.

"It's not my fault you didn't eat enough spinach growing up."

"I come from a long line of short women," she said. "There isn't enough spinach in the world."

"Good things come in small packages."

"Only some things," she said with a giggle. "In some things, size is an . . . advantage."

They were in the bathroom now. The bath was full and the steam rising from it smelled like spices and flowers.

Three white candles flickered in the niche in the tiled wall, making the dark water shimmer. Mal put her down and then pulled her sweatshirt over her head.

"Why, Mr. Coulter, are you trying to entice me to sin in a bathroom?"

"That was the plan," Mal said. Her T-shirt joined the sweatshirt on the floor. And then he pulled his own shirt over his head.

She let herself watch for a moment. It was a sight that hadn't gotten old, Mal without all his clothes on. All that tanned skin and muscle and dark hair. A definite enticement to sin. She shimmied out of her jeans and underwear and dipped her hand into the water. Perfect temperature. She climbed in and sat down. The level came nearly to her chin. A sigh of delight escaped her as the perfumed heat surrounded her and she ducked under the water to wet her hair. When she resurfaced, Mal was naked.

"Hello." She smiled up at him. "Are you going to join me?"

"Just enjoying the view," he said.

Raina looked down. In the darkened room, against the black stone of the bath, her skin was very pale. And very visible. "It's even better close up."

"I know." He climbed in, making the water slosh. "Come here." He crooked a finger at her and she waded her way up the bath and tangled her legs around his waist.

They kissed again, long and slow. The water lapped around her body and Mal's hand stroked wet skin and everything shivered and shimmered around her as he teased and caressed.

"I want you," she managed to say on the end of a gasp.

"You've got me," he said. And then somehow he was standing and she was wrapped in a towel and then they were back in the bedroom. He laid her down and dried her off and then proceeded to get her wet all over again with fingers and tongue until she had to say it again.

"I want you. Now. Please, Mal."

"Whatever you say." He was over her then, and then inside her and the world clicked into place as she felt that connection. Mal. Buttons and all, he was there and hers and that was what she needed. She hung on, wanting to be closer, pulling him down to her and into her with each of his thrusts. Wanting to wrap him around her until they became one person. Until eventually she reached the point where the pleasure spilled over and took her away with it, melting her into him with one last repetition of his name. One that sounded suspiciously like "I love you, Mal."

"Okay, ladies," Raina said, standing in the middle of the Angels locker room on Saturday before the game. "We've got our wings back. So you're going to go out there and kick some Angel butt, right?"

There was a smattering of laughter and clapping. Even Ana managed a smile. She was apparently turning over a new leaf since she'd had to face Mal and Alex and Raina asking her whether or not she'd been involved in damaging the wings. Her hotly indignant denial had rung true, but it seemed that the fact that she'd been pulled up had made her stop and think about what impression her attitude might be giving.

Raina didn't know whether her change of heart was

going to stick but she was happy to have one less problem for now.

"Shouldn't that be help the Saints kick butt? Kicking Angel butt sounds kind of wrong," Marly said from her spot on the nearest bench. Her makeup and hair were immaculate and show-ready, but she still looked kind of tense. Nervous. They all were. Mal had provided extra security for the squad since the wings incident—which was why Raina was giving her pep talk with Chen in the room, his dark eyes watchful as he covered the door.

"You get the general idea," Raina said. "The guys have been winning all week and you've heard what some of them said in the press about what happened to the wings." Several of the players, Brett Tuckerson and Ollie Shields included, had sent some pretty clear messages about what they thought about losers who messed with their squad. Politely worded—probably more politely than any of them would have liked if Maggie hadn't been riding herd on their public behavior—but perfectly clear.

"They've had your back, so it's time for us to have theirs again. Anyone got any questions about the routines or anything else? We're about twenty minutes out, so speak now or don't expect mercy if you screw up." She grinned at the group. "At the very least, you will be last in the cookie line all week."

That made them groan. Shonda's cookies were rapidly assuming legend status in the squad after Maggie had brought another batch to the locker room the day after the wings had been wrecked. They'd vanished before anyone could blink, eaten to the last crumb. Even Ana had devoured one.

Raina was starting to think that Shonda should go into business and become a cookie entrepreneur. After all, she was working with Alex and had spent twenty-odd years before that as Tom Jameson's executive assistant. She had a lightning-quick brain to go with her mad cookie skills. She'd make a mint.

But right now Raina needed to think about cheerleading, not cookies.

She looked around the squad, giving them time. Marly's wasn't the only faintly nervous face, but no one had pulled out of the performance. They had guts, these girls. "No questions? All right. Two minutes to finish whatever needs spraying or pinning or touching up. Then we're going to wing up and go put on a show."

The Angels started peeling off from their seats and heading back toward the mirrors and dressing tables. Marly stayed put.

"You all set?" Raina asked. Across the room, Chen lifted an eyebrow, as though asking if everything was okay. Raina gave a tiny shrug then focused back on Marly. "Marly?"

The blonde nodded but stayed where she was.

"Everything okay?" Raina persisted.

Marly smiled. To Raina's eye, it looked a little stagy.

"I'm fine," Marly said.

"Are you sure about that? If anything's happening, you need to let me know. You heard Mal earlier in the week, any weird messages or anything, you have to tell us. They have a couple of pictures of the guy going into the store-room but nothing with his whole face. So any info to help out is good.

"I know," Marly said. She shrugged. "There's this one

thing I got on Twitter about two hours ago. I mean, I get plenty of shitty sexist drivel and come-ons every day but this one. Something about it bothered me more than usual. And it's no worse than the others, so I'm not sure why."

"Show me," Raina said firmly.

Marly found her phone and brought up the offending message. She passed the phone to Raina. "This. I took a screen cap of the message and then the guy's profile, like Mal said. Then I blocked him of course. That's the message."

Raina looked down at the screen. "Angel Slut. For fuck's sake, what is wrong with people?"

She'd hardly finished the sentence when Chen was by her side, looking ominous.

"What's the problem?" he asked.

Raina handed him the phone and watched his expression go even stonier as he read the tweet. He looked at Marly, anger flaring in his eyes.

He handed her back the phone. "Is that the first message from this guy?"

Marly nodded. "Yes. But it's not the message, I mean, yes, it's pathetic and disgusting, but it's not the first time someone's used that word to me. But have a look at the next one. His profile page."

A flick of her finger brought up the next picture and she tilted the phone so Raina and Chen could both see it. The profile name was *TomSmith*. Hello, fake name. There was no profile picture to go with the name, just a generic Twitter egg. But the header picture was of a long white feather.

"Is that one of our feathers?" Raina asked.

"I don't know. It could just be a feather. But it's . . ."

"Creepy," Raina supplied. "And definitely the sort of thing Mal needs to know about."

"Agreed," Chen said. He held out his hand for the phone. "I'll mail the pics to him."

"And I'll go talk to him," Raina said.

Chen looked like he wanted to argue.

"You have to stay with the squad. You're the muscle." She flashed Chen a smile. "More useful than me if anything happens."

"Yes, stay, please," Marly said to him and Raina thought she saw him redden faintly. Interesting. But she had no time to figure out if Chen was just maybe, crushing on one of her squad. She needed to talk to Mal.

Chapter Eighteen

Two weeks later, Raina found herself the host of an impromptu late-Sunday-night pizza-and-party-planning dinner with Maggie and Sara. They'd shown up at Madame R again for the second half of the show and then, claiming boredom with the guys away, had somehow strong-armed her into inviting them back to Mal's place as it was "the closest."

She had a hunch it was something more like curiosity because both of them claimed they'd never been to Mal's before, and who was she to argue? With Mal gone, the huge apartment made her feel like a very small fish swimming endlessly round and round in a blue-whale-sized aquarium. Even Wash's big paws couldn't fill the space.

Which was why the three of them were currently sitting along the stainless-steel counter in Mal's kitchen and eating far too many calories while Wash wound his way around their legs, begging for pepperoni.

"He's worse than Dougal," Sara said. "Maybe he's part Labrador and that's why he's so big?"

Raina grinned. "Maybe. But he doesn't need more pizza. He always gets cheese in his fur and then that's a whole other problem. So ignore him."

Sara peeled a slice of pepperoni from her pizza, tore off a tiny piece, and offered it to Wash, who slurped it off her finger with a swipe of his tongue and then looked smug.

"Don't blame me if you're now stalked by a Maine Coon for the rest of the night," Raina said. "Now, back to the party. Maggie, did Alex look at that final menu?"

Maggie nodded, mouth half full, and then swallowed. "Yup. He's good with it. So that's one more thing off the list."

"How often do you throw these parties?" Raina asked. All the players, their various partners, the Angels and their other halves, Saints' staff, and a few other people added up to a big number.

Maggie shrugged. "A few times a year."

"Plus the odd fund-raiser for our community programs," Sara added. "Those are the really huge ones. I wish you'd been at the one at the Paragon, Raina. It was very cool."

She and Maggie exchanged a look that Raina didn't quite know how to interpret.

"Well, maybe I'll get to come to the next one." She'd seen pictures of the Paragon party courtesy of Maggie. It had looked amazing. If she scored an invite to the next Saints ball, wild horses wouldn't keep her away.

"Seems like a shoe-in to me. Alex isn't going to get rid of the Angels now. The guys haven't lost a game since your wings got wrecked. No messing with that. It's their longest winning streak in about ten years." Maggie bounced on her stool. "If it keeps up, we have a shot at the play-offs. A long shot, true, but a shot."

Raina took another piece of pizza. "Fingers crossed."

"All available parts crossed," Maggie agreed. "I'm not getting my hopes up. There are still lots of games between now and the end of the season. And there are lots of teams out there that are stronger than us on paper."

"Yes," Sara said solemnly. "All of them."

"Hey." Maggie balled up a paper napkin and threw it at her. "Is that any way for the future wife of one of the owners to talk?"

Sara caught the napkin and threw it straight back, laughing. "You're the future wife of one of the owners, too. You tell me."

Raina lifted an eyebrow. "Maggie, something you're not telling me? Did Alex . . ."

"No." Maggie shook her dark curls decisively. "It's too soon. Some of us don't do romance quite so whirlwind as Sara and Lucas."

Sara laughed. "You say that now but if Alex asked you, you'd say yes in a heartbeat."

"Sure," Maggie agreed. "I'm not an idiot."

"And here Raina is living with Mal already," Sara added.

"Not living with," Raina said firmly. "*Staying* with. Temporarily."

Maggie tilted her head at her. "But it's going okay? You and Mal? He doesn't say much, he's spending every spare second with the security team. I swear they've been over every inch of Deacon three times now."

"I know," Raina said. "I get the summary reports every night from him. Don't get me wrong, we're getting along fine and he does remember to loosen up occasionally, but he's definitely a little . . . intense right now."

"He's the save-the-world type," Maggie said. "That's why he joined the army after that bombing at their college."

"The what?" Raina said.

Maggie looked guilty. "He didn't tell you that part? About why he joined the army?"

Raina shook her head. "No. He told me about Ally."

"Well, that's a good sign," Maggie said.

"But he didn't mention a bombing."

Sara and Maggie looked at each other again. But then Sara shrugged. "It's not a secret. It's on the Internet if you go digging far enough in their backgrounds. Mal and Alex and Lucas met at college. They were all baseball players. Freshmen at the University of Texas."

"Mal played baseball?" Raina said. "I mean, obviously he loves it, and I figured he played in high school or something, but college ball? He was that good?"

"He's a great batter," Maggie said. "His swing is a thing of beauty. All three of them were good. Lucas was a pitcher and Alex was the catcher. All of them wanted to play in the major leagues."

"But there was a bomb? What happened?"

"One of the white-supremacist, anti-government-type groups thought it would make a point to bomb a college baseball game," Maggie said, with a grimace. "God knows what that point was supposed to be. The three of them were on the field and they went back into the stand that got hit worst by the bomb—which was on fire by the way—and dragged a bunch of people free. Lucas's shoulder got screwed up and he decided to become a doctor. Alex decided he wanted to be able to make a difference in the world and switched to business and building his empire and Mal . . ."

"Mal joined the army," Raina said. "He really *is* trying to save the world."

"Well, he was," Maggie said. "He's mellowed a bit now, from what Alex tells me. But stuff like this, people he cares about in danger, people messing with his team, well, that's got to—"

"Push some buttons," Raina broke in. "Yes. I've figured that part out. The part I'm still trying to work out is how to switch them back off before he drives himself— and me—crazy."

"Just be there for him," Sara said. "I'm not saying agree to everything he wants. Guys like the terrible trio, they're way too used to getting their own way and you have to stand up for yourself or they'll roll right over you. But they're still human. They need things. And it looks like Mal's decided one of those things is you. So, as the future wife of one of his best friends, I'm in favor of you working things out."

"Me too," Maggie added. "Well, just because I think Mal's a great guy and Alex is happy when the other two are happy, so win–win. Not the wife part. There will be no more wife talk."

"Agreed," Raina said. "So let's finish the pizza and talk about something else. Mal is my problem right now." She smiled, thinking about the little ways that Mal had been making her stay here fun. Sending her random gifts when he was out of town. Stealing moments so they

could just hang out and watch old movies. Arranging for
the Taj Mahal of cat towers to be delivered and installed
in the main room for Wash to entertain himself. And then
there was all the sex. Which kept getting better and better. She was worried she might actually spontaneously
combust from sheer lust one day if it kept getting better.
"As problems go, it's a nice one to have."

"They seem to be enjoying themselves," Brady said as
he helped Raina zip up her sparkly silver dress backstage.

"Are you kidding? This party kills." She grinned at
him over her shoulder. "We rock."

"Yes, we do. But we already knew that. So now that
you've got all our new baseball friends liquored up and
fed, are you ready to put on a show?"

"When am I not ready?" Raina said. Nerves twisted
in her stomach despite her bravado. This felt like a big
deal. This was Mal and Alex and Lucas and Maggie and
the Angels and everyone else who'd been so good to her
since she'd taken on this crazy project. Not strangers.
Friends. Some of whom were about to see a side of her
they didn't know about. Mal and Maggie and Sara had
seen the show before, and the shortened version she and
Brady had put together erred on the side of less confront-
ing and less skin . . . but it was still sexy and a little out
there. She took a breath. Fuck it. This was who she was.
This was what made her heart pound and her blood sing,
just like baseball did for all of them. Maybe some of them
wouldn't like it, but it wouldn't be the first time that had
happened.

You can't please everyone. That was another of her gran's lessons. One that was her mantra these days. Other people's hang-ups and fears were their problems.

"Not my circus, not my monkeys," she muttered under her breath and straightened her shoulders. Brady handed her the microphone—covered in silver crystals to match her dress—and then the band kicked in, and she stepped through the curtain to put on a hell of a show.

It all went smoothly for the first hour. The Saints people whooped and hollered and clapped in the right places. And went silent in that good way during some of the acts. The way that meant they were enthralled and thinking. Just what she wanted. And now they had two numbers left. The finale with everyone but before that, just her. And her black-and-pink wings. A far more wicked version of the white Angels.

Brady had paired the wings with a corset made of black leather that curved around her body like a second skin. It went with very short shorts made of the same leather. A collar of black crystals circled her throat, and matching bands wrapped her wrists. Fishnets and thigh-high black leather boots finished the look off.

She looked like the kind of angel who made the others fall. Very, very hot. But somehow not slutty. She was never sure how Brady managed to pull that off in his costumes. He pushed things right up to the line but never pushed them over.

And she had to admit she was looking forward to finding out whether everyone else appreciated his talents.

Brady hooked a wireless headset mike over her ear. She couldn't hold a mike and work the wings easily.

"Ready?" he asked.

She nodded. "Time to show them how it's done in our world."

He kissed her cheek and left the stage.

Breathe, she thought, and then the music started and the curtain whizzed away, leaving her standing in the spotlight, arms raised, wings spread.

She heard the audience gasp and smiled. "Who wants to get bad with me?" she purred into the mike and then started to dance.

The bank of lights above her came on, shedding enough light to let her see into the crowd. She spotted Mal at one of the front tables. He looked . . . arrested. She sent him a smile meant just for him before she spun around to start the next series of moves as the music slowed.

As she came full circle, there a shockingly loud pop above her and a shower of sparks as one of the lights exploded. Instinctively she ducked, throwing an arm up to protect her face from hot glass, waiting for Brady to hit the switch to kill the row of lights before any others could flare and overload as well. But before he could, Mal was on stage with her. On stage and sweeping her off her feet, cradling her too him, though how he managed that with the wings, she couldn't quite understand. He had her off the stage almost before the rest of the lights went down.

"Mal," she hissed as they got backstage. "Put me down."

He didn't seem to hear her. Just kept heading in a direction she knew led to one of the exits. "Mal!" she yelled a little louder. "Mal, it was just a light going. It happens. Put me *down*."

He didn't stop. She hauled a hand back and socked his arm as they reached the exit. "PUT. ME. DOWN," she repeated as he reached for the door. She stretched out her leg and planted her boot against the door, bracing so he couldn't open it.

That seemed to stop him. Behind them, she could hear the sounds of alarm. Too many voices. No one was screaming but she knew the sound of a crowd about to freak out. "Mal, it was just a light. Let go of me." She waved a hand in front of his face. "Earth to Mal. We need to go back and make sure everyone knows things are under control."

He shook his head. "Nope. You don't know what's happening back there." He moved away from the door so her foot couldn't reach it, then twisted to throw it open. And carried her out into the night.

They were in the back alley behind the club. Rose was parked at the far end, and that's the direction Mal headed.

Raina socked his arm again. "Mal, if you don't put me down, I will start screaming my head off."

He stopped. "It's not safe."

"It's perfectly safe," she said. "You're overreacting." She hoped he was overreacting. But she couldn't see anyone running past the other end of the alley where Madame R's front door was so she had to assume that it had just been the lights and nothing else had happened after Mal had carted her off. She wanted to know for sure.

Which meant she needed him to let go of her. He wasn't hurting her but she needed to snap him out of whatever was happening in his head. To stop when she said stop. To hear her. To stay in control. She could feel the tension in his arms, locking around her so tightly it was almost painful. His breathing was heavy, eyes scanning the alley for God knows what danger he was imagining.

"Please, Mal," she said softly. "I'm okay. Let me go."

His eyes locked onto hers, his mouth set.

"Let me go," she repeated.

That seemed to register. He set her on her feet. She stepped back, just a little.

"Mal? Do you know where we are?" she asked.

"Outside the club," he said.

Well, that was good. She'd been half worried he was having a true flashback. But he sounded rational, not like someone having a panic attack.

"We should go back," she said. "Get everything calmed down."

"You don't know what's back there."

"Neither do you," she shot back. "And that's my club. I'm responsible for my staff and everyone else inside that building. I'm not going to leave them all there. You wouldn't in my place."

He shook his head.

"I'm not asking you," she said. Anger was starting to build now, mixing with the adrenaline and worry. "I'm telling you. I'm going to go back inside. Are you coming with me?"

He stepped toward her. She moved back. "Mal, if you try and pick me up again, I will do something unpleasant to you."

He stopped, mouth twisting. "I want you to be safe."

"I'm standing right here. Perfectly well. I don't think any glass got on me." She suspected her wings might be a bit mangled from Mal's manhandling but Brady could fix those. "I'm okay. I'm not so sure about you, though."

"I'm not going to apologize for trying to keep you safe."

"I'm not asking you to apologize. I'm asking you to stop for a minute and see if you can see that what you just did was an overreaction. You just grabbed me and forced me to go with you. And you didn't listen to me when I said stop."

"I needed to get you out of there." His voice was rough. Almost impatient. Like he couldn't understand why she was angry. She needed him to understand.

"I understand that you thought that." She made an effort to sound calm. "And I know you're trained to act and get the job done but you scared me."

He winced as though she had punched him. "Raina—"

She held out a hand. "No. Sorry. I need some time with this. You didn't hurt me, I know you wouldn't hurt me and I know what you were trying to do but you did scare me. And I'm not okay with that. A protective streak is one thing. But this went beyond that. I've had guys who wanted to control me before. Who wanted to tell me what to do. To make me do things their way. Who wouldn't listen when I said no. I'm not going there again. It's not love. It's control."

He stayed silent. Watching her. Every muscle in his body tensed. She could see the struggle in him. To not do what his instincts were telling him to do.

To take over. To take her away.

"I'm going to go back inside," she said.

His hand shot out, then halted just before he grabbed her wrist.

She looked down at the hand then back at its owner then took two steps back again. Distance. Out of reach. She hated that she was doing that calculation in her head. The way she had, she'd realized in the days after she'd first left Jeremy, been doing with Jeremy for quite some time before he finally cracked that night. The thought made her breath catch and her stomach twist. "I'm glad you didn't do what you almost just did. But I think we need a break here, Mal. You need to figure some things out. I'm going back inside. Maybe you should go back to Deacon for a few hours so I can get Wash and my things from your place."

"Raina." The words were a plea.

"No," she said. "I've told you what I want and right now you get no say in anything to do with what I do."

"Fine." His eyes looked almost black in the weird lighting of the alley. Black and unfriendly. Pissed off. Well, that made two of them.

She wheeled and stalked back down the alley, aware that one of her wings felt weird, its weight unbalanced. As she reached the back exit, it opened and Luis stuck his head out. "Raina. There you are." He looked past her and his face went still. "Is Mal coming back in? I got things calmed down and we fixed the light. Brady wanted to know if you want to do the finale."

She refused to turn around and look back at Mal. To see what she was walking away from. Because it would be too easy for him to convince her that everything was okay. And it wasn't. And if she stood here in the alley and thought about that hard, she was going to burst into tears all over Luis. She took a shaky breath and walked past Luis into the opening doorway. Back where she belonged. Her world. Not Mal's. "No," she said. "Show's over."

Chapter Nineteen

It took every ounce of Raina's willpower—and a few gallons of coffee to make up for her lack of sleep—to walk into Deacon the next afternoon. She painted her face and donned an all-black outfit apart from the blue-and-silver scarf—her concession to the Saints' colors—wrapped around her neck. The skinny jeans and spiked heels and her favorite battered leather jacket weren't making her feel any better. Not even the nearly Stage-Raina makeup was working. But she hoped they might at least convince everyone else that she felt better. Doubtful when almost everyone she was going to see today had been at Madame R last night. Had seen Mal sweep her off the stage.

And by now, unless the Saints grapevine had failed spectacularly, a lot of them would know that he hadn't come back into the club.

For which she was grateful. It had been hard enough to hold herself together while she apologized to Alex for the drama and then overseen the post-party cleanup. Luis and Brady had gone with her to Mal's but he hadn't been there. They'd scooped up Wash and Raina's things and taken her back to their house. She'd tried to argue and get them to take her to her apartment but Luis had put his foot down.

"Mal overreacted," he said. "I'm not arguing with that. I get why you're upset. But they haven't found whoever it was who went to town on your wings, so until then you're not staying alone."

By that point she was too tired to fight. She'd used up all her fight on Mal. She'd cried in the shower and then crawled into bed with Wash, who'd slept far more soundly than she had.

Mal hadn't called or texted or contacted her in any way. She was fighting not to check her phone every five seconds. But she'd told him to leave her alone and apparently that was one order he was taking seriously.

Careful what you wish for.

Or something.

They needed space: That much was clear. But that didn't mean space was easy.

Maggie was standing outside the Angels' locker room.

She gave Raina a quick hug. "I just came to see if you're okay."

"I am," Raina said. "And I'll stay okay as long as you don't add in some sort of plea on Mal's behalf."

"I haven't seen him," Maggie said. "I gather from Alex and Lucas that he's holed up down in the security office. But no, I won't argue his case. I think he's a good guy but he has to realize he's not Superman sooner or later. I hope it's sooner."

So do I.

"I have to go in and talk to the girls," Raina said. "Thanks for checking on me but I'm okay. Mal and I— well, maybe we're just not a good fit. I can't be what he needs if he needs someone who'll stay inside where he can see her every second of the day."

"Just don't write him off too fast," Maggie said. "And now I'll leave you before I break my promise and start defending him. See you after the game."

"Go Saints," Raina said. Then she walked into the locker room to rev up her Angels and try and forget about her demon for a few hours.

"You know, we thought you might be joining us," Lucas said. "Being one of the owners of a team that just won another game."

Mal looked up from his computer monitor. Lucas stood in the door to his office, beer in hand. He wore a Saints jacket over a white polo shirt that looked brand new and unwrinkled despite the fact Lucas must have been wearing it for hours. "Busy," he said shortly. He rubbed his hand along his jaw and looked back at the computer, feeling the stiffness in his body from sitting too long. His own clothes were definitely not unrumpled. He'd been down here since last night, which made it the seventh night in a row he'd worked through the night at Deacon since the party. He desperately needed a shower, some clothes that he hadn't dug out of the duffel he kept stashed in his office, and some sleep in a real bed. But he couldn't bring himself to leave.

That would mean going home to his apartment. Where Raina wasn't.

"Do you mind if I ask what you're doing?"

"Looking at the Angels' social media reports," Mal said. "Another one of those feather accounts popped up."

"Feather accounts?" Lucas asked, walking around behind Mal to peer over his shoulder. "Does this have something to do with Marly? Is she still getting crap online?"

"They all do," Mal said. "A depressing percentage of men seem to think that 'come sit on my face' is the Twitter equivalent of hello. But no, she hasn't had anything specific. Not that I can figure out. The first account that tweeted at her was shut down by the time I got to look at it. But every so often, I get a ping on that feather image it used. So far, about ninety percent of the time, it's people just using similar feather pics. But there have been a couple of accounts that appear, tweet something at one of the Angels—Marly twice—and then close down again."

"Can you trace the users?"

"I have some of the guys at MC looking into it. It's not easy unless whoever it is fucks up and forgets to hide his identity. And so far this guy is being very, very careful. But they're digging."

"Well, if anyone can do it, your guys can," Lucas said. "So why don't you come downstairs and join in the celebration?"

Mal shook his head.

"C'mon, Mal, you've been holed up down here since the party," Lucas said.

"It's not like I have anything else to occupy my time," Mal said. "And we kind of have a lot going on."

Lucas walked back around the desk. "Have you talked to Raina?"

"She made it fairly clear she didn't want to talk to me," Mal said.

"Well, she was freaked out," Lucas said. "You did go a little overboard. But that was a week ago. She's had some space. You should give it a go. Unless you're determined to be an idiot and lose the best thing that's happened to you for several years."

"I thought buying the Saints was the best thing we'd done in several years," Mal said.

"It's very cool but a baseball team isn't going to keep you warm at night. Won't build a life with you. Won't love you," Lucas said. "If you want all that, of course."

"I scared her," Mal said. That was the part that was killing him. The fact that he'd scared her. Made her feel unsafe. She was too strong to be scared. And she'd been through plenty of crap without him adding to it.

"Yes, I imagine you did," Lucas said. "But you know, in the medical world, we have this thing about symptoms and causes. If you ask me, what you did at the club is a symptom. Remove the cause, lose the symptom."

"I'm not sure it's that simple."

"Didn't say it was simple. It might be that this has all triggered some of the stuff you thought you'd dealt with when you first got out. And after Ally's death. Maybe you'll need to talk to someone about that some more. Or maybe if you find the fucker who's messing with Raina and the Angels, you'll be fine. Neither of which is an easy fix. But it's worth thinking about."

"You think she'd talk to me?" Mal asked.

"You can at least try an apology," Lucas said. "Start from there and work up to some world-class groveling. Give her the moon. Or whatever the Raina equivalent of that is. That usually works. But only if you're ready to listen to her and curb those instincts of yours. Otherwise you're just going to set up the cycle all over again. And that won't be doing anyone any favors. So think about it, but think hard before you decide." He drained his beer, set the empty bottle on Mal's desk. "Now, it's my professional opinion that you are in desperate need of a few of these and eight solid hours' sleep. But you're a big boy and I'm not going to force you to come join the party."

"That's because you know you couldn't," Mal said, feeling a flash of humor for the first time in a week.

"You keep telling yourself that, big guy," Lucas said. "Brains win over brawn any day."

"You wish. Now stop bothering me. I can't do anything until I've finished looking at this, so if you want me to stop working, then leave me alone."

"Sad, sad, sad," Lucas said, but he left. Mal shook himself and got back to work.

In the end he didn't go to the party but he did shut down his system at midnight and call Ned to drive him home. When he got there, he showered, changed and made himself a sandwich, feeling hungry for the first time in days. He was eating it standing over the counter in his kitchen, trying to ignore the fact he missed Wash prowling around trying to steal his food, when his phone beeped to tell him he had an email.

Lucas.

Apparently midnight was the perfect time to take another swing at him. He almost ignored the message but changed his mind and checked it.

Something to think about, the subject line read.

Then the message was just: *Better than a baseball team. L.*

There was a video file attached.

Damn.

He switched to the computer in his study and pulled up the file there. Two quick clicks and it started to play.

Home video from the quality. And somewhere dark. Lots of voices. The screen was a wobbly blur but then it settled and Mal recognized what he was looking at. Madame R's. The night of the party. He could tell from all the Saints colored balloons being bounced around the room.

What the hell, Lucas?

He stared at the screen listening to the sounds of the crowd. Laughter and chatter. And then music started pounding through the room.

His heart nearly stopped. He knew that song. And he knew what he was about to see.

On the screen, the video zoomed in, focusing on the shimmering black curtain drawn across the stage. Which suddenly flew apart and revealed Raina in all her black-and-pink-angel glory.

The sight of her had nearly stopped his heart at the party. He'd wanted to leap onto the stage and carry her off as soon as she'd appeared.

Carry her off to somewhere dark and private with a big bed where he could remove some of that leather and maybe work out how to tie her down with those wings and do the sorts of things she liked him doing to her until she came about a thousand times.

"*Breathe*," Maggie had said in his ear on the night, and he'd taken that advice. Had stayed there, mesmerized, watching Raina slink across the stage and own it. Sex on legs. Glorious. Strong. The wings framed her body and somehow, despite the weight of them, she'd managed to leap and twist as though she might just take off.

Until the lights exploded and she ducked. And he saw himself leaping onto the stage and grabbing her, panic clear on his face. The video stopped when the lights died.

He hit PLAY again. Stopped when he saw his face again. Remembered the panic. The need to get to her. The certainty that he had to get to her. Remembered, with a sudden blinding flash, the first time he'd ever felt that way.

All those years ago. In Texas.

The explosion. Remembered the sound—a growling rushing roar—and then watching as, behind Alex, standing at home plate, half the stadium started to collapse.

The force of the blast had sent him rocking back but he kept his feet, half his brain registering the sight of Lucas falling to the ground while the other half tried to figure out what the hell had just happened.

It didn't take long. His ears ringing from the blast, he'd watched Alex running across the field, toward Lucas, uniform half streaked with black. Vaguely aware that around him, everyone else was running for the north exit. He stayed put until he saw Coach Paulson bend down to help Lucas to his feet. Lucas had shaken his head but the coach pointed at the exit and Lucas had grimaced and started to jog in that direction, limping slightly. Mal watched him go. The exit. That was the smart option. That way was safety. Which explained why most of the crowd was currently streaming in that direction, trying to get out of the stadium.

No way he going anywhere without his friends. He started toward them and the three of them met about halfway across the field. Lucas came to a stop, wincing, and Alex did, too. Mal stared past them at the flames and smoke billowing from what was left of the stand behind home plate. Lucas and Alex saw his face and turned, too.

"Coach said we gotta go," Alex had said. His face had been smeared with soot, his hair standing on end and black-smudged. One sleeve dangled from his jersey, nearly ripped off.

"There are people in there," Lucas said. Or that was what Mal thought he'd said. His ears still rang.

The three of them stared at one another a moment. None of them moved an inch.

"Okay." Alex nodded. "But we do this together. No one gets out of sight. No one does anything stupid."

It was stupid by definition. It was also the only goddamned thing to do. You couldn't run away when there were people in there. People who might be hurt or trapped. People who were smaller and weaker than he was. People who needed help. Stupid didn't matter. Only that he could do something.

He learned things that day. Learned the way that smoke stung your eyes and lungs as it closed around you. Learned that adrenaline could make you do things that you didn't think were possible and that you wouldn't remember clearly. Learned that he could feel completely terrified and keep running back into the flames.

Learned that he was one of the lucky ones. When they were done he had a burn across his forearm and a cut in his side where he'd stumbled against a twisted piece of metal but that was nothing. He was alive. The three of them were alive. Alex had busted his hand in half a dozen places and Lucas had done a number on his shoulder but all three of them were alive.

There were people who weren't.

People who'd died. Because on a perfectly sunny warm day they'd wanted to watch some damned baseball. Because they, too, loved the game. Died because some group of assholes had a gripe with the government or the university or something and thought they had the right to take it out on other people who were doing nothing more than trying to live their lives.

And he promised himself he wasn't going to let that happen again.

He shook himself out of the memory, breathing too hard. He hadn't remembered it like that for a long time. Not so clearly.

But he might have guessed that he'd be ripe for some sort of rebound, with the way he'd been pushing himself. He'd been half expecting one of his now rare nightmares. Combat and blood and death.

Instead there had been a girl wearing black-and-pink wings and leather in a darkened burlesque club.

There hadn't been an explosion.

Just a bang and a flash and a shower of sparks. And then pure reaction.

Dumb.

He leaned forward. Touched the mouse. Watched again. Watched Raina again. Stared at her, aching with the need to touch her.

Every move she made was clearly her. Strong and wild and free. Not someone who needed protection. Someone who couldn't be caged up. But someone who could keep up with him.

So much like Ally it scared him.

But different, too. Somehow he knew that. Raina didn't have that dark streak Ally'd had. There was nothing at the core of her, nibbling away at her, rotting her from the inside out.

He'd tried to fix Ally, to tame her. To keep her safe and in the end, he'd been defeated by Ally herself. Who didn't need him as much as she needed to try to run from whatever had been eating at her. Whether that was something the army had done to her or something from before he'd even known her.

He'd never know now.

There was no way to know.

But it wasn't too late to know Raina.

To let her in and let her be strong.

Which meant living with the fear of losing her.

He hit PLAY again. Watched her trying to fly across a tiny stage in a darkened club and completely enthrall a room full of people.

To try to stop her from being who she was would just make her smaller. Hurt her.

And then he'd lose her anyway.

So if he could get her to give him a second chance, he had to decide which Raina he wanted. The one on the screen, brilliant and bold and untamed, or a lesser version.

He could lose her, yes. That was the risk that anyone took if they let themselves be in love. But before then he could have her. Have all of her. If he let her be.

Leaning back in the chair, he played the video one last

time, pausing it on the first moment she was revealed. On the smile on her face and the wicked light in her eyes.

She wouldn't take him back if she couldn't believe that he wouldn't freak out again. So he needed to do what Lucas had said and remove the cause of his symptom. Find the creep who was trying to mess with her and make sure he got thrown into some cell for as long as possible. Give her back her peace so that she could be who she was in this video. And even if she didn't take him back, then Lucas was right, he could still give her that.

He just had to figure out how to catch the bastard.

The phone call woke Raina at about three a.m. She reached for it while she tried to make her brain function. "Hello?"

"Raina, it's Mal."

"Mal?" She peered at the clock on the phone. "It's the middle of night."

"You need to come to the hospital."

Her heart started to thump so hard she thought she might be having a heart attack. "Why? Is someone hurt?"

"Our feathered friend decided to make a move," Mal said. "Luckily, he underestimated Marly's abilities."

"Marly? What?" She bolted upright in bed. "Damn it, Mal, is Marly hurt?"

"Just come." He reeled off the name of the hospital. "Ned's on his way to come and get you. He'll be at Brady's place in fifteen minutes. He'll call you when he gets there."

He hung up before she could ask him anything else. Like how the hell he knew where she was staying and where the hell he'd been for the last two weeks and what the hell sort of first-contact-after-a-fight phone call did he think that had just been?

Her teeth clenched as she crawled out of bed, flicked on the lights, and tried to locate some clothes. Once she was sure that Marly was okay, she was going to kick Malachi Coulter's butt. Or something.

Chapter Twenty

Ned delivered her to the hospital—which was in Manhattan—about twenty minutes after he picked her up. The one bonus of three a.m. emergency trips was no traffic, it seemed.

She made her way to the emergency department at a jog. She'd sent Mal several texts on the journey in but he hadn't replied to any of them. She really was going to smack him when she saw him.

When she asked for Marly Eddison, the nurse gave her an odd look. "She's in Treatment Room One. Just down the hall. Are there going to be any more of you?"

"How many of us are there already?" Raina asked distractedly.

"At least four. Maybe five. I lost track," the nurse said. "Is she some sort of celebrity?"

"She's a Saint," Raina said with a grin. "We stick together."

She left the desk and found her way to the treatment

room. When she knocked, she heard Marly say, "Oh Lord, who else did you call, Mal?"

The worry in her stomach eased a little. If she was talking, then Marly couldn't be too badly hurt. Then it clenched again when she realized she was about to walk into a room that had Mal in it.

"It's me," she said as she pushed the door open.

Marly was sitting on the end of a bed wearing a hospital gown. She was holding an icepack to her head, and there were several small white strips on her face. The kind that went over stitches.

Stitches? "What the hell happened?" Raina asked.

Alex, Chen, Lucas, Maggie, and Mal all looked at her. And all started to talk at once. Which made the police office standing next to Marly hold up a hand and then bellow for everyone to shut up because he was taking a statement.

A statement?

Raina stepped into the room and closed the door. "Sorry, Officer. But I'd like to know what happened to my friend."

The officer rolled his eyes, looking exasperated, but then Marly smiled her killer smile at him and said, "Let me just fill Raina in, honey, and then I'll be all yours."

The officer went red and nodded. Marly was charming people while sitting on the end of a hospital bed with a beaten-up-looking face. Raina didn't know whether to be horrified or impressed. She went with impressed. Temporarily.

"What happened?" she asked again.

"What happened is Mal's plan worked. A little too well," Marly said.

Raina looked at her blankly. "Plan?"

"Malachi, please tell me you told Raina what you were doing?" Maggie said.

Mal stayed silent.

Maggie looked appalled. "What the—"

Alex put his arm around her. "Yell at Mal later, sweetie. Raina needs to know what happened."

"Yes," Raina agreed. "She does." She turned to Mal. Damn. He looked good. Tired, with more stubble than usual lining his jaw and clothes wrinkled to hell, but still good. Which ought to be against the laws of nature. Damned beautiful dark lord.

No. Don't think about the pretty. Find out what the hell he did.

"Mal?" she asked. "What the hell happened here?"

He pushed a hand through his hair, looking kind of pissed off. "We asked Marly if we could take over her Twitter account for a while. She had a couple more messages that ticked some boxes with us. So we started flirting back with the guys. Well, Chen and Marly did that part."

Marly smiled, then winced. "It was kind of funny at first. We just kept replying and seeing who kept coming back for more." She looked over at Chen. "Chen's pretty good at flirting with strangers on the Internet." She sent him one of her killer smiles .

Strangers on the Internet weren't the only thing Chen could charm, apparently.

"You used her as bait?" Raina asked, horrified. "And you didn't tell me?" She shot Mal a glare that should have, if there was any justice in the world, turned him into a pile of ash.

"It was fine. And it was needed to be a secret. Limit the number of people who knew," Marly said. "One of the security team always took me to and from Deacon and wherever else I was going. Chen here, actually." This time the smile she sent in Chen's direction was several degrees hotter than killer. Chen flushed and Raina heard Maggie bite back a laugh.

Marly and Chen. Well, well, well.

She realized she'd gotten distracted again. "In theory, that sounds like a good plan. But how did you end up here with stitches in your face?"

"They'll heal perfectly," Lucas said. "I did them myself."

"I'm sure they will, but I'm more interested in how they got there."

"Well, Chen walked me home tonight, and I let myself in and there was someone in my apartment. He jumped me but he didn't do his research too well if he was Internet-stalking me. Missed the fact that I studied tae kwan do in high school as well as dance. I got loose and that's when he hit me." She touched her faced gingerly, wincing a little.

"And that's when she brained him with the baseball bat she apparently keeps in her umbrella stand," Chen said, sounding proud. "I got the door open and found her standing over him. He was out cold. So I cuffed him and we called the cops, and then Mal, and eventually we wound up here."

"Are you okay?" Raina asked Marly.

"Yeah. My cheek hurts but Dr. Angelo here gave me something good for that and tells me it won't scar. I'll be back as soon as the stitches are out. Apparently I'm not allowed to put makeup over stitches." She frowned at Lucas.

"You need to let it heal. It will only be a week or so," Lucas said. "If you put makeup on and it gets infected then it will scar. Is that what you want?"

"No," Marly said, looking appalled. "Definitely not." Chen, who'd moved closer to her, looked like he agreed.

"And where's the guy now? Do we know his name?" Raina asked.

"Charles Buckley," Mal said. "He was a bit confused when he first woke up, and he gave the cops his real name. Then they found his van not too far from Marly's place. There was a bag of feathers in the back. Our feathers."

"He's the one then?" Raina said. "It's over."

"Let's hope so," Maggie said. "I want to focus on baseball, not break-ins."

"And now that Raina knows the story, perhaps we should leave Marly to finish giving her statement," Alex said. "Chen, will you take her home or wherever she wants to go? Marly, we'll pay for a hotel for you for as long as you want if you don't want to go home yet or if the police aren't done there. I'm sorry this happened to you. It's not exactly what I had in mind when I thought up the Angels."

"That's because you're sane," Marly said. "Thank you, I'm sure Chen will take good care of me."

From the look in Chen's eyes, Raina was pretty sure that he would, too. She followed the other four out into the hall. Maggie looked at her and then Mal and then yawned ostentatiously. "Well, I'm beat," she said. "Take

me home Alex. And Lucas, I'm sure you have somewhere to be."

"I do," Lucas agreed. "I have patients here I can look
in on in a few hours. Might as well go do some paperwork until then."

"You work here?" Raina asked.

"Sometimes," Lucas said. He bent down and kissed
her cheek. "Go easy on him," he whispered and then
hurried down the hall after Maggie and Alex.

Raina watched Lucas and then turned back to Mal.

"Not here," Mal said. "I'll take you home. We can talk
in the car."

Not being all that keen to have this particular conversation in a hospital hallway, she didn't argue, just followed him back out to where Ned and the big car were
waiting.

She climbed into the back and as Ned started the car,
she felt herself start to shake.

"Oh my God," she said, sinking back against the
leather seat. "You were right."

"What?" Mal said. Then his gaze sharpened. "You're
shaking. Come here." He slid across the seat and pulled
her close against him.

"I'm fine," she said but she wrapped her arms around
him anyway and tried to soak up his warmth as her teeth
started to chatter.

"You've had a shock," he said. "It's just adrenaline."

"I know what adrenaline feels like," she managed. "I
like adrenaline."

"Well, this is the less exciting kind," he said. His arms
tightened around her. "I'm sorry, I never thought he'd get
that far."

"You were right," Raina said. "There was someone after us." Then, to her horror, she burst into tears.

Mal just held her, kissing her hair and making soothing noises until she got the sobs back under control and lifted her head. "Sorry, I never do that."

"Adrenaline," he repeated. "It's weird stuff."

"But you were right and I got so mad at you."

"You didn't know I was right. I didn't know I was right. I'd rather I hadn't been."

"But you were *right*," she repeated and dropped her head back down on his shoulder, feeling horribly guilty.

"I wasn't right in the club," he said. "You were. I overreacted. I'm not sorry I grabbed you. You can't ask me not to try like hell to get to you if I think you're in trouble, but I'm sorry I got carried away. I'm sorry I didn't stop when you told me to. I'm sorry I scared you."

She lifted her face. "I'm sorry I got so mad."

"You were scared. I get mad when I'm scared, too. As I proved that night."

"Well, we make an excellent pair of idiots," she said. She looked up at him. "I missed you. Every minute. You didn't call me."

"You told me you wanted some space. After giving me quite the lecture about listening to you and stopping when you said stop. I thought that was a fairly clear message that not calling you would be the safest thing."

"Only until I calmed down."

"Ah. Sorry, turned my psychic powers off to save my batteries. I missed that part."

She laughed. "Okay, I deserved that. I'm sorry."

"I'm sorry, too," he said. "About a lot of things. I'm sorry Marly got hurt."

"I'm pretty sure Chen is going to make sure that doesn't happen again," Raina said.

"Chen?" Mal sounded puzzled.

"You didn't see how he was looking at her? He's got it bad. And she was flirting with him."

"Marly and Chen?" Mal repeated.

"You really didn't see how he was looking at her?"

"I was too busy looking at you," he said, absolute sincerity ringing in his voice.

She felt her heart suddenly melt into a puddle of goo. "You were?"

"I've spent the last two weeks wanting to see you. I caught a couple of glimpses at the home games but that's it."

"You weren't stalking me on the security feeds?" She'd looked up at the cameras sometimes. Just for a few seconds. Just in case he'd been watching. The thought of it made her feel like an idiot.

"I figured that would be the kind of thing you'd object to. But I wanted to. I missed you. I even missed the giant cat. My couches are way too pristine."

"I'm pretty sure he misses his cat tower," Raina said. "He keeps trying to climb to the top of Luis and Brady's bookcases and knocking things down. I think Luis wants to turn him into a rug."

"Poor Luis," Mal said.

"Poor Wash. Deprived of the luxury he's sure he deserves."

"And what about you," Mal asked. "Are you feeling deprived?"

Was she imagining things or had his voice just dropped down a few notches. She twisted her head up to look at him. And fell right into those hot dark lord eyes. Her heart started to pound all over again.

She was going to be out of adrenaline altogether if this kept up. "Deprived? Hmm, let me think about that. What would I have been deprived of?"

"Would you like me to tell you?"

Her stomach curled. She looked between the barrier that separated the back of the car from Ned. "That kind of depends on how soundproof that is."

"It's soundproof," Mal said. "I swear on every cent I have."

"So I get the Saints if you're lying?"

"One-third of them, sure. But what would you do with a baseball team?" Mal said.

"Turn 'em into winners with my awesome cheer squads," Raina said cheerfully. "Look how well I've done this year."

Mal shook his head at her but then he laughed. "I wouldn't put it past you. Though I for one would be sad if you had to give up burlesque to run a baseball team."

"You would?"

"I would," he said. "That outfit you wore with those wings has been haunting my dreams."

She felt her smile go smug. "It has? What exactly do your dreams entail, O dark lord?"

"You. Feathers. Maybe some rope. Me peeling that leather off you and making you come your brains out."

Her brain went blank at the mental image. "Oh. My," she managed. "And then what happens?"

He proceeded to tell her. In quite a bit of detail. Until she shut him up to prevent herself from bursting into flames by the simple method of climbing into his lap and kissing him.

Oh *God*. The taste of Mal. After all this time away from him. She let herself drink him in, tongue tangling with his as she squirmed on his lap, trying to get closer.

Mal held on to her and kissed her back with equal passion.

"Ever had sex in this car?" she asked when they broke apart for a second. She wondered if her own eyes looked as lust fogged as his.

He shook his head. "Not that I can recall."

"Well, that's just sad. What's the point of having a limo—"

"It's not a limo—"

"You have a driver, this backseat is huge, that's a limo in my book. Stop arguing, I'm propositioning you in your fancy car."

"So you are," he said. "I'm all ears."

She pulled her sweatshirt over her head. "Ears are not a body part that interests me right now."

His eyes were practically black now, the pupils huge. "Any body part you want. All yours."

She lifted her hips to swing her leg free and sit back so she could start to push her yoga pants down. "No one can see in here, right?"

"Right," he agreed. "No panties? Why, Ms. Easton, I'm—"

"Shocked? You woke me up at three a.m. You're lucky I found matching shoes. Underwear would've been wasting time."

"I was going to say pleased," he said. He slipped a hand between her legs, found her clit with his thumb as one finger slid into her. "But you can keep on talking if you want."

"No talking," she said. "Just you. Come here." She tugged him down so they were sprawled across the leather seat with him on top of her, pulling him against her, arching impatiently as he dealt with his zipper and then was inside her with one hard push that made her gasp.

"God," she managed. "Remind me to fight with you more often if this is how you do makeup sex."

"Not going to happen," Mal said. "You're not getting away from me again." He started to move and she decided she agreed with him. He wasn't getting away from her again. Not if she had any say in it. And then she stopped thinking at all.

Raina's haze of happiness lasted well into the next afternoon. Until Mal came looking for her as she was doing her postgame check of the wings.

"Hey," she said, putting down the feather she was holding.

"Hey yourself," he said. He leaned down and kissed her. "How are they holding up?" He nodded at the row of lockers.

"A couple of feathers adrift. Nothing me and Brady's magic glue technique can't fix. You don't have another home game for a week anyway. Plenty of time."

"If the team keeps playing the way they have, Alex is going to want to take the Angels on the road."

Raina froze. "On the road? I can't travel with the—"

Mal laughed. "I know. I was teasing. The other owners would have to agree to have the Angels perform at their games. I can't see that happening anytime soon."

"What about next year?" Raina said.

"Unless something drastic happens, I'd say we'll be the Saints and the Fallen Angels for a while yet," Mal said. "Even our Triple A team is asking for them to come and cheer at their games."

"What did Alex say to that?"

"Alex told them if they started winning like the Saints then he'd think about at least letting the Angels come meet the team."

"Sounds like a solid motivational technique for young guys," Raina said.

Mal nodded, but his expression turned serious. "I actually came down to see you about something."

Unease curled through her. "Why don't I like that expression?" she said. "Should I be sitting down?"

"Not sure," Mal said. "It's not exactly good news."

"Okay, I'm sitting," she said. She patted the bench next to her. If she was going to be upset, she might as well have Mal next to her. He was so nice to hang on to. "Come and tell me."

"Well, it's like this," Mal said. "I just got off the phone with the police. They've just finished interviewing Charles Buckley."

"Feather guy?"

"Feather guy. Who apparently has decided that he might as well confess all now that he was dumb enough to give them his name."

"That sounds good. What's the sentence for breaking and entering and assault these days?"

"Long enough that he won't be bothering anyone for a while. The police said they suspect he'd done this before. Stalked women. Maybe worse. They're going to keep working on him to see if they can get him to tell them anything more. But here's the thing. He admitted to doing the wings and to the Twitter stuff. Admitted to breaking into Marly's place, which was, admittedly, kind of hard to deny but he is denying doing anything to your truck or knowing anything about the stuff that happened at Madame R's."

Crap. Her heart sank. "That means I have my very own stalker out there?"

Mal shook his head. "I don't know. But I'm getting the feeling we're missing something. Graffiti and your tires—that feels more like trying to scare you off or something. It's not the same as the wings and online harassment. No one has been harassing you online, right?"

"No more than usual," Raina said. "I do burlesque, I get a certain amount of idiots, the same as anyone."

"I apologize for my sex," Mal said.

"Oh don't," she said. "I'm quite fond of your sex."

"Don't change the subject," he said with a grin. "So somebody is trying to scare you off." He stopped suddenly. "You haven't heard from Jeremy again, have you?"

She shook her head. "Radio silence since that first email."

"Good. Didn't think so. Then probably not him."

He looked somewhat smug. Which made her suspicious. "Did you do something to Jeremy?"

Mal shrugged. "I may have tracked him down and discussed the error of his ways with him."

It was wrong to feel happy about that, right? She decided she didn't care. And that she didn't want to know what Mal's discussion had involved.

"It was only a discussion," Mal said, seemingly reading her mind. "I didn't beat him up. It was tempting. But unnecessary. Usually is with bullies."

"That's very restrained of you. Are you giving up your dark lord ways?"

"Not entirely," he said, eyes glinting at her in a way that made her shiver with remembrance about exactly what they'd done the night before.

She fanned her face a moment, trying to clear the fog of the heat. "Weren't we talking about something?"

Mal laughed. "Yes. Right. Back on topic. The incidents at the club. New theory. Maybe it's not you they have a problem with, maybe it's the club?"

"You thought it was me originally," Raina said. "Why the change of heart?"

"Originally that was the most obvious solution. But if feather guy isn't guilty, then obviously that might not be the way to go. Maybe it's not personal. Maybe it's business. So who has an issue with your club? Got any burlesque enemies?"

"Corsets and pistols at dawn? No." She snorted. "I really don't know. It's not like we're a strip club. We get a lot of women and couples coming. We're not near any schools or day care centers or churches or anything. I made sure of that when I picked the location. It's mostly bars and restaurants and small businesses and young-and-upcoming couple types."

"Young and upcoming," Mal mused. "Yeah, I saw the for sale signs on some of the buildings in your street. Lots of condos going up."

"People buying up cheap after the global financial crisis," Raina said. "The way the market has been, people are happy to sell. I got a great lease because my landlord couldn't find a tenant at the time. Locked him up for five years with an option for five more."

Mal lifted his eyebrows. "Landlord? Now, there's someone who might be unhappy if the market is picking up and he has a tenant in a building he might want to sell. Does your lease have cancellation penalties?"

Raina nodded. "Yeah, he can kick me out with six months' notice but it would cost him."

"Unless you decided to break the lease yourself?" Mal suggested.

Raina stared at him. "It couldn't be that, could it? I mean, I've always known that Phil was a weasel but that's pretty low."

Mal smiled grimly. "I don't know. But I vote we find out."

"Me too," Raina said. "Got time for a little field trip?"

"Hello, Phil," Raina said silkily as she stalked into her unfortunate landlord's grimy office a few blocks away from Madame R. She'd slicked her mouth with red and found her spike-heeled boots again. Her black leather jacket kind of matched Mal's. The thought pleased her.

Phil was middling height with a rapidly expanding waistline, bushy black eyebrows, and graying hair slicked back with gel. He hadn't grown any more pleasant smelling since the last time she'd had to deal with him in person. She fought not to wrinkle her nose against the smell of stale cigarettes, old fast food, and slightly too-long-unwashed male.

Phil got to his feet. "Raina? Late with the rent, are you?"

"You know I've never been late with my rent even once," Raina said pleasantly. She looked at the pile of papers on the chairs in front of Phil's desk. It wasn't often he had visitors. The few times she'd been here the place had been deserted other than two or three of the younger guys he always introduced as his nephews hanging around doing nothing much. She picked up the papers and dropped the pile on his desk then settled herself on the chair. Mal did the same with the other chair, saying nothing.

"Who's your friend?" Phil asked.

"This is my . . . security adviser," Raina said with a sunny smile. "We had a couple of incidents at the club. So we decided to get some advice on our security setup."

"You do anything like that and you have to pay for it," Phil said. "Check your lease."

"Oh I know," Raina said. "I pull it out every so often to read it. That non cancellation clause makes me happy every time. It's so nice for a girl to have some security in these uncertain times, don't you think?"

Phil frowned at her, brows drawing so close together that she wondered if the extravagant hairs ever tangled together. The expression made him look like a bushy-faced bulldog. Not attractive. "I'm a busy man," he said. "You gonna tell me why you're here?"

"Sure," Raina said. "It's like this, Phil. I'd like for you to stop trying to drive me out of my club. And in return, I won't sue your ass for harassment and vandalism."

Beneath the red patches on his cheeks, she saw Phil turn pale. *Bingo.* Phil had a guilty conscience.

"I don't know anything about any harassment," he sputtered.

"Are you sure about that, Phil?" Raina asked. "Because Mr. Coulter here has been telling me all about some fascinating innovations in security technology. Did you know they can even get fingerprints off things like scraps of paper ? Like, say, a half-burned firecracker."

Phil bristled. "What's a firecracker got to do with me?" Then he frowned. "Did you say Coulter?" He jerked his head at Mal.

"Oh, didn't I introduce my adviser?" Raina said. "Phil Longoria, this is Malachi Coulter. He owns MC Shield, among other things. Maybe you've heard of him."

Phil's eyes widened. "You're one of those guys who bought the Saints."

Mal nodded. "That's correct." His tone wasn't friendly.

"What's a guy like you doing working security for a two-bit burlesque club?" He pronounced the word *burlesque* like he really wanted to say *hooker*. Or something worse.

"Perhaps you hadn't heard, Phil. I've been doing some work for the Saints. I've always been a baseball fan," Raina said.

Phil had gone another few shades paler. "You work for the Saints?"

"Yes, she does," Mal said in the deadly deadpan voice. "And at the Saints, we take the welfare of our employees and contractors very seriously. Particularly when one of the incidents Ms. Easton is referring to took place on Saints property. That's the sort of thing we dislike. A lot." He smiled then. The expression was more disconcerting than his serious face had been. It involved a lot of bared teeth. Phil shrank back in his chair a little.

"You can't prove anything," he said desperately.

"You really want to make that play?" Mal asked. "Perhaps this is the part where I mention that MC Shield is one of the biggest security outfits in the country? And the fact that I'm ex-special-forces. You really think I can't take down a two-bit little property shark like you, Phil?" He leaned forward, smile now distinctly unfriendly. "So tell me, Phil. Which way do you want to do this? The easy way or the hard way."

"I'd be happy with the hard way," Raina chimed in. Yanking Phil's chain was proving quite entertaining. She'd obviously watched far too many gangster movies.

Phil, however, didn't seem very happy about it. "What's the easy way?"

"Raina?" Mal said.

She straightened in her chair. "Well, that would be the one where Phil signs another contract with me. One your lawyers draw up to say that if he sells my building I have first right of refusal at a reasonable market value set by three independent parties and get at least twelve months' notice if I decide not to exercise that option."

Phil turned a truly impressive shade of purple, "You can't do that," he sputtered.

"Yes, she can," Mal said. "And said contract will have an additional clause that says I have second right of refusal with the same terms."

Raina turned her head toward him, mouth falling open. "It will?"

"It will," Mal confirmed.

"Okay," she said. Happiness bloomed through her. Mal would buy the building if she couldn't. She wasn't so sure how she felt about that, other than pleased that it had obviously pissed Phil off even more than he'd already

been. But the fact that Mal was willing to do something
like that for her was definitely a good thing. A very good
thing.

She smiled at Mal, trying for a Marly-style killer
smile. "Phil, what do you say? Do you want make a
deal today or let Mal go to work and find out all the loose
ends that are going to lead back to you? Because now that
I think about it, some of those nephews of yours look
about the right height for the guy we have on tape interfering with my truck. And throwing firecrackers. Do you
think they love their uncle Phil enough to go to jail for
you? Or do you think they might start talking as fast as
humanly possible to save their scrawny asses?"

Phil looked like he was going to explode. For a minute she thought he was going to keep fighting but then
he deflated like a popped balloon—or one of her poor
truck's tires—and leaned back. "Fine. I'll sign your stupid contract," he said.

"Good," Mal said. "I'll have something couriered to
you tonight. If I don't have it back on my desk first thing
in the morning, then I'm going to start digging, Phil. And
it will be a very deep hole you'll be standing in." He stood
then. "Come on, Raina, Phil needs time to find a pen."

Raina followed him out of the building and back down
onto the street before she starting laughing. "That,"
she managed between sputters, "was kind of fun." She
gained control with an effort and then tilted her head up
at him.

"I don't need you to buy a building for me, you know.
I can do it myself."

"I know you can," he said. "But it never hurts to have
a backup plan. If I end up having to buy it because Phil

tries to pull a fast one, then you can just buy it off me, when you're ready."

"You'd do that for me?"

"Well, Lucas suggested I try to give you the moon but this seems more you."

"It is," she said. "So you'd be my landlord?"

Mal grinned. "I guess so. Why, are you going to try and wrangle a rental discount out of me?"

"Are you susceptible to bribes?" Raina asked.

"Do they involve you and nakedness?"

"Of course."

"Then absolutely," he said. "In fact, I might insist on them."

"I'll start practicing," Raina said. And then she started laughing again because he was just so damned gorgeous. "Hey, Malachi Coulter, I love you, you know that?"

He went still and then the smile she received was the best one yet.

"Me too, Raina Easton," he said, and he kissed her to seal the deal.

Epilogue

Damn. It smelled like a ballpark. Mal breathed deeper as he stood at the edge of the field, trying to ignore the headache that was fighting back against the ibuprofen he'd downed earlier. He closed his eyes and let the grin spread across his face. It smelled like *his* ballpark. Like Deacon Field.

Still the same heady mix of grass and sweat and old beer and stale popcorn and wood and metal and leather that spelled baseball.

Home.

"How are you feeling?" Alex said.

Mal opened his eyes, glanced at his friend sitting in the first row of seats a few feet back from where Mal stood by the railing. "Slightly worse for wear. You?"

Alex toasted him with the bottle of bright yellow Gatorade in his hand. "I have a certain leaning in that direction. I think we're getting too old for that kind of party."

"It was certainly a party," Mal agreed. He wasn't going to admit to feeling old. Not today.

"If every end-of-season party is like that," Lucas said from where he lay across several seats, next to Alex, "remind me to get into training a few months ahead."

"Not sure surgeons are encouraged to do that much drinking," Mal said.

"I could write myself a prescription," Lucas said. Then closed his eyes again.

"Next year will be worse," Alex said cheerfully. "Next year we're going to make the play-offs."

Mal shook his head. "Don't remind me about that." The Saints had lost their final game last night. The final game that stood between them and a play-off spot. Lost by two lousy runs to the goddamned Yankees, just to add an extra sting to it all. Things had been pretty quiet back in the locker room.

"Like I said last night—"

"As I remember," Mal said, cutting Alex off before he could start making another speech. "It went something like, this is our best result in decades, so fuck it, let's celebrate."

"I'd like to think I was a little more eloquent than that," Alex said.

"Yeah, yeah, you were inspiring," Lucas said. "Stop talking so loud."

Alex's speech had been inspiring. Mal had to credit him with that. He'd marched into the locker room, Maggie in tow, climbed up onto one of the benches, and then made one of the best damned speeches Mal had ever heard. At least, what he could remember of it had been good.

After that, the mood had flipped and everyone had charged onto the buses for the trip back to Deacon Field. Everyone except Maggie and Alex, who'd vanished.

Back at Deacon, the field had been transformed with a giant marquee and the booze had been plentiful. The party started with a bang and just grew crazier from there. When Alex and Maggie reappeared, Maggie had been smiling so widely, Mal thought she might blind people.

Then Raina, who'd been leaning against him, having done him the honor of taking a night off from Madame R for the last game of the season, had said, "Oh *my God* look at that rock, it's bigger than Sara's." And Mal had suddenly cottoned on to why Maggie looked so happy despite the loss.

Raina had squealed and rushed over to Maggie, along with every other female in the room. As the news had spread through the marquee, the party went to a whole other level. Culminating in Maggie's announcement that she wanted them all to celebrate her engagement the next day with a staff and players game, "before the weather turns completely crappy."

It had seemed like a pretty good idea at the time. But now, the thought of having to run around a baseball diamond was kind of appalling.

"Everyone's going to be arriving soon," Alex said.

"Shut up," Lucas groaned and Mal laughed. At least he wasn't alone in his suffering.

An hour later, Raina watched Mal standing at home plate grinning like a lunatic while he shouted something rude at Lucas. Who promptly replied with a fastball that

made Mal duck. Which earned him a slow clap from all
the players and a triumphant grin from Lucas. That
might have been why Mal slammed the next pitch out
over the practice field boundaries.

"Go Mal," Raina yelled. "Show that surgeon boy." She
put her fingers in her mouth and whistled as Mal began
a slow saunter around the loaded bases.

Besides her, Sara groaned. "You're as bad as they are.
Look at them all. Don't they know how to lie down and
recover quietly from a night of debauchery like normal
people?"

"Is that why Lucas is off his game?" Raina asked in-
nocently. "Did you wear the poor boy out last night?"

Sara went pink. Raina thought it was pretty funny
that someone engaged to someone as hot as Lucas still
blushed so easily.

"No comment," Sara said.

"I know what that means," Raina said, laughing. "Mal
was very . . . enthusiastic when we got home last night.
That man can hold his liquor. Among other things. My
grandma would so have approved of him."

Maggie, having just gotten a free ride from third base
to home courtesy of Mal's hit, jogged over to them after
doing a little victory dance in front of Alex, who was
catching for Lucas's team.

"You sure you don't want to play, Raina?" Maggie
said, panting a little.

Raina passed her a bottle of water. "I'm sure," she
said. "I have a show tonight. Besides which, Sara got
lessons before she had to play. I want lessons first. I
haven't played anything resembling baseball since ju-
nior high."

"Lessons can be arranged," Maggie said, waving her left hand magnanimously. Sunlight sparked off the massive diamond that graced her ring finger.

"Hey, watch where you're pointing that thing," Raina said, pushing her sunglasses up her nose to stop the glare. "It's dangerous."

Maggie just grinned at her. "It's gorgeous and you can't make me stop admiring it. Not for a few months at least. Alex has good taste."

"I'm surprised either of you can walk around upright with those rocks weighing you down," Raina said.

Sara laughed. "Well, you just wait. Mal's very competitive. You'll end up with the biggest one of us all."

"Early days," she said.

Maggie and Sara both looked like they didn't believe her.

"So what do you girls do around here for fun when it's not baseball season?" Raina asked, desperate to change the subject. Mal was hers and she had no intention of letting him go but she wasn't quite ready for the M word.

"Well, Shelly's getting married in Hawaii in ten days," Maggie said. "And then Sara and Lucas on New Year's Eve."

"Ooh, do you think you and Alex could organize your wedding before spring training starts?" Sara said.

Raina made her escape before the wedding bug rubbed off on her. She walked over to where Mal was standing by the edge of the field looking very pleased with himself.

"Good hit," she said, standing on tiptoe to kiss him. She'd intended for it to be quick but apparently Mal had other ideas. The kiss went on and on until she started to see stars and everyone around them started applauding.

It took her a minute to catch her breath when he let her go. A minute during which she tried to figure out if there was anywhere they could sneak off and take that kiss a bit farther. But she didn't think she had much chance of enticing Mal away from his game. Not just yet, anyway.

"I take it you're feeling better?" she said, putting her arms around his waist.

"I am," he said.

"You're not upset about losing?"

He bent down and kissed her again, this time soft and slow. "We lost the season but I'm thinking I still came out a winner," he said. "After all, I got you. Have I told you today that I love you, Raina Easton?"

"No, but flattery will get you everywhere," she said with a grin, feeling her heart expand. She hooked her fingers through his. "Just how much better are you feeling?"

He wriggled his eyebrows at her. "You'll just have to wait, woman, there's a ball game to win."

She laughed. "You're really not mad about losing, are you?"

He shrugged. "We did good. Better than anyone expected. And like I said, many good things have happened in the last twelve months. Besides . . ." He grinned and kissed her. "Next year we get to do it all over again."

Read on for an excerpt from
Melanie Scott's next book

Playing Hard

Coming soon from St. Martin's Paperbacks

Wall-to-wall hot men and all she really wanted was more comfortable shoes. It was official. Her life was sad. If there was a list of people who had lost their mojo, it would clearly say "Amelia Graham" at the top. Amelia winced at the mental image and tried to find the party spirit. But her feet hurt—stupid new shoes—and the wall-to-wall hot men seemed far more interested in the hordes of superhumanly glamorous women in the room than in her. She looked good but these women were New-York-model-level gorgeous. And if the sky-high stilettos most of them wore were hurting their feet, they were far better at ignoring the fact than Amelia was.

Which only proved that her name belonged on the sad list. If Em could see her now, she'd be rolling her eyes in disgust. Of course, it was Em's fault that Amelia was stuck at this party in the first place. Her best friend had steadfastly refused to move to New York, remaining at home in Chicago. Which meant that when Em's brother

Finn—Amelia's de facto brother by way of lifelong best friend-hood with Em—had been transferred from the Cubs to the New York Saints, Amelia had inherited Finn-watch. Something she'd been used to when Finn was in high school where being three years older gave her and Em a little leverage over Finn. But now, at twenty-nine, it was kind of weird to be asked to keep an eye on a guy who was a professional baseball player blessed with the same dark good looks as his sister and, sadly for Amelia, a distinct fondness for a party.

Still, it had been hard to say no when Finn had invited her out tonight. The Saints were celebrating the fact that they'd made it to the play-offs for the first time in a long time. Amelia liked baseball, having kind of absorbed her knowledge of it through Finn, so a baseball party should have been fun. Besides which, having to explain to Em why she hadn't gone when there was nothing else pressing in her social calendar would not have been fun. So she'd come. And now, somewhat predictably, she was watching Finn dance with random women, and she was bored.

She sighed and rattled the two rapidly melting ice cubes that were all that was left of her drink. There really had to be something wrong with her. All these gorgeous men and no one had caught her eye. Which was troubling. She had something of a thing, to her chagrin, for guys who oozed confidence, and professional athletes did that. But all too often it seemed that that confidence had a downside. Too many of them were a little too fond of themselves and a little too sure of their place in the universe. Aka, standing firmly in the center of it. It had been that way with the jocks in high school and it was the same way with the men she met on Wall Street. They also leaned toward master-of-the-universe. They just did it in expensive suits rather than baseball uniforms.

She'd resolved in the future to find herself a nice guy. Maybe the fact that she was bored meant she had a chance of succeeding. But probably not tonight. So maybe she should just give it another hour and make her excuses to Finn and leave. Go home to comfy slippers and whatever was on her TiVo. Be sensible. Like the guy she wanted. She sighed and put the empty glass down on the small high table near her elbow. If she was going to stay, she at least needed another drink. Though maybe a soda first. Whoever had made the cocktail she'd just finished definitely hadn't skimped on the alcohol.

Maggie Jamison and Raina Easton definitely knew how to throw a party. Oliver Shields took his tequila from the bartender and turned to survey the room, taking in the heaving mass of partying Saints players, wives, girlfriends, and whoever else had been invited. The play-offs. The Saints had made the fucking American League Division Series for the first time in God only knew how many years. Of course, he should know, having spent the last ten years playing for the Saints, but after his first tequila had gone down far too fast, the statistic, one that most of the time he was only too pleased to forget, refused to come to the top of his head easily.

He was finally going to play in the play-offs. Halle-fucking-lujah. He had to hand it to Alex Winters. He hadn't liked the man when Alex had first bought the club with his two best friends, Lucas Angelo and Malachi Coulter—not least because Alex had succeeded in getting Maggie

Jamison to now be technically Maggie Winters—but the terrible trio knew what they were doing. This was the third season since they'd purchased the Saints from Maggie's dad and the team had made the goddamn play-offs.

Which was why they were currently blowing off steam for one night of crazy partying before it was back to the grindstone and seeing if they could achieve the next seemingly impossible goal—making it to the World Series.

Ollie sipped his tequila—one of the other things Raina Easton knew how to do was stock damn good tequila in her burlesque club—and watched the crowd. Across the room he saw Maggie's dark head next to Alex's blond one and found himself smiling. They were good together. They worked. In the way that he and Maggie, as much as he'd never wanted to admit it, never quite did.

Damn, that was way too serious a thought for tonight. Tonight, he'd decided, was for celebrating. He'd been pretty damned dedicated this season. Practically a monk. But even monks needed to give in to temptation occasionally and this room was just chock full of temptation.

Though no one had actually caught his eye yet. Which was why he was still drinking tequila alone at the bar instead of busting a move down on the tiny dance floor with some gorgeous woman. Like Raina was with her fiancé, soon-to-be-husband, Mal Coulter. Raina was an ex–Broadway dancer among other things, so she was making Malachi work hard to keep up, but the two of them were both grinning at each other like fools. Next to them, Finn Castro was dancing with a short blond who Oliver didn't recognize.

The sight soured his mood slightly. Alex had bought

Castro cheap from his previous team. And while the guy could play, he was pretty much a grade-A jerk. One who had his eye on Ollie's first baseman slot. Well, Castro could look all he wanted, but Oliver wasn't going anywhere.

He drained his tequila, savored the smooth burn for a minute, then decided that maybe it was time to slow down. He'd driven tonight, not wanting to break training too much. And because, if he did find some temptation to yield to, he preferred to drive them back to his place under his own steam rather than use a driver.

Turning back to the bar, he waved at the skinny bald guy tending bar and said, "Club soda," at the exact same moment as a woman slid through the crowd at the bar and ordered the same thing.

She turned to look at him and said, "Snap," with a smile in her big blue eyes that were almost the exact deep shade of the Saints' logo. He found himself smiling back automatically. She had a pretty face, curving lips and dimples to go with the eyes. Her hair was pulled up into some sort of messy bun arrangement at the back of her head, wisps of it coming loose around her face. In the low lighting of the bar, he couldn't really tell what color it was . . . maybe blond, maybe red, maybe something in between.

The bartender slid two glasses across the bar toward them. Ollie nodded at her. "Ladies' choice."

"Thanks," she said and leaned forward to take the nearer glass. Her dress was sleek and black and finished north of her knees, showing off a very nice pair of legs and equally sleek black high heels, but it wasn't the usual plunging, painted-on type thing that girls who came to trawl Saints parties for talent wore. Who was she exactly?

He reached for the other glass, using the movement as an excuse to move slightly closer. "So, what has you hitting the hard stuff tonight?"

She stirred the soda with the straw. There were no rings on the slim fingers. "I could ask you the same question."

He started to say, "I'm in training," then stopped. For once he didn't feel like being Oliver Shields, first baseman. "What if I said I'm on duty?"

Her eyebrows arched slightly. "On duty? Are you security? One of the guys' bodyguards?"

She didn't know who he was. This could be fun. "I could tell you, but then I'd have to kill you. And that would just cause problems." He hit her with a smile. "Now I've told you, your turn."

"Me? I'm an economist at Pullman Walters," she said. "Wanna hear about the outlook for South East Asian currencies in the next few months?"

He nearly choked on his soda, and she burst into laughter. Deep throaty laughter that sank into his gut and spread outward and downward. Damn. His vague curiosity about her kicked itself up to "very interested." "Sounds fascinating." He didn't really know what an economist did, but he was willing to find out.

"Really?" Amusement lurked in her eyes.

"'Round here, the conversation revolves around baseball, so it's something new."

She laughed again, and his body reacted in the same way to the sound. He curled his fingers a little tighter around the glass.

"You get points for not falling asleep immediately."

"I find it hard to believe that anyone could fall asleep on you," he said.

She tilted her head, but her smile didn't fade. And there was a glow in those big eyes he liked. "If you're going to flirt with me, you should tell me your name," she said.

Damn. He didn't feel like giving up his anonymity just yet. "Ladies first."

"Oh no, you started this, you go first."

There was a sudden loud cheer from the direction of the dance floor. He turned to see one of Raina's performers balancing on Sam Basara's shoulders. The kid—who was shaping up into a very nice pitcher—was grinning like all his Christmases had come at once as the girl on his shoulders did a pretty good bump and grind given she was standing where she was.

"Interesting," said his mystery woman from beside him.

He turned back to her. "These guys get a little crazy when there's something to celebrate."

"Oh?" She closed her lips around the straw and sipped, and he suddenly found his attention riveted by the deep pink of her mouth. Its curves were edible. He leaned slightly forward and a hint of her perfume—something heady and rich—reached him. His gut tightened.

Who was this girl?

"Not too crazy," he said. Though right now he felt like getting a lot crazy. If crazy involved her.

"Everyone has to blow off steam sometime," she said. "So what are you celebrating?" Her eyes were laughing again.

She had to be teasing him. "You don't know? Did you crash the party or something?"

"I'm here with a friend."

A friend. That could mean a lot of things. A flash of

disappointment hit. Of course, she was here with some-one. But she definitely wasn't dating any of the guys on the team. He knew all the wives and girlfriends. There were a few guys who were single. Like him. But none of them had mentioned bringing a date. Maybe she was here with a girlfriend?

"A friend—" he started to say, then stopped as Finn Castro muscled his way up next to them and grinned. Oliver felt his jaw tighten.

"Milly. There you are. I was looking for you." Finn turned his focus to Oliver and his smile died. "This guy bugging you?"

She shook her head. "No, we were just talking while I got my drink." She looked from Finn to Oliver and back again.

Oliver smiled at her and then narrowed his eyes at Finn, trying not to let his annoyance show on his face. Castro. Of course, she had to be here with Castro. Because the gods apparently had it in for him. "Finn," he said, trying to sound polite.

"Shields," Finn replied. He jerked his head toward the dance floor. "Come on, Milly, let's dance."

Milly—what was that short for?—held up her glass. "I haven't finished my drink."

"You can finish it with me."

"Finn, you're being rude." Her expression had turned exasperated. Her tone wasn't annoyed girlfriend, more sisterly irritation. Interesting. Oliver felt a flash of hope that she might actually stay and talk to him.

"I'm just looking out for you," Finn retorted. "Shields here likes to sleep around. He's not the kind of guy for you."

Oliver stiffened. "Excuse me?"

Beside him, Milly said, "I'm a big girl, Finn. I've been choosing my own dates for a long time now."

Finn scowled. "Yeah, well, don't pick Shields. He has a different girl every week."

Oliver bit back the urge to tell Finn exactly where to go. That wasn't going to help the situation or impress Milly if she really was a friend of Castro's. Besides which, Finn was clearly on his way to drunk. A bit glassy-eyed. And he was full of just enough youthful arrogance and stupidity to pick a fight. Which was the last thing anybody needed.

"I believe that's a case of the pot calling the kettle black," Milly said. She glanced up at Ollie, a mixture of resignation and wariness in her eyes before she focused on Finn again. "What happened to the blond?"

"I came to find you. You said you'd dance with me."

She studied him for a long moment. Sighed. "Okay, I'll dance with you. But how about we get you a cup of coffee first?"

Damn it, she was going to go with Castro. Time to step back from the plate. "Good idea," he said. He smiled at Milly. "It was nice to meet you, Milly the economist."

And then he turned and walked away.

Amelia watched Finn dancing with the same short blond he'd been flirting with earlier and tried not to think about Oliver Shields. Or give into the desire to smack Finn for ruining things. She managed to pour one cup of coffee in him and they'd danced for a song or two, but then the blond had returned bearing beer and Finn had abandoned her.

Leaving her with nothing better to do except think about Oliver. Oliver of the night-dark eyes and dimples and pirate grin. Oliver who, as Finn had been all too happy to tell her, was a player as well as a baseball player—why hadn't he told her that?—and therefore really the master-of-the-universe type. Exactly what she was trying to avoid. Though she was fairly sure she might have thrown common sense to the wind and thrown herself at him if Finn hadn't come along and been Finn at exactly the wrong moment.

Really, she was resigning from Finn-watch after tonight. Finn was an adult. He was going to have to figure out how to be one. If he was hell-bent on screwing up, there wasn't much she could do about it. And she drew the line at letting him screw things up for her as well.

Oliver Shields was mighty pretty. And mighty appealing. And even if not Mr. Right, it had been too long since the last Mr. Wrong. A man as gorgeous as Oliver really couldn't be terrible in bed, could he? One-night-stand material, definitely. But hopefully a memorable one night stand.

And now she'd never know. Because it was pretty clear that Finn and Oliver did not get along. The last thing Amelia wanted to do was cause a problem between Finn and one of his teammates. If Finn couldn't make it work at the Saints, then he could be in trouble. Amelia was fairly sure there was more to Finn being traded to the Saints than just baseball team shuffling. Em had been tight-lipped but that alone spoke volumes. So Finn needed to keep his nose clean at the Saints and not cause any problems. So even though she was resigning from Finn-watch, she didn't want to do something that could make life harder for him. So she, Amelia Graham, would take one for the team and not try to seduce Oliver Shields. Though, of course, there was always the possibility that he might have turned her down. She thought of that smile again. And the dark warmth in his eyes. Nope. She didn't think she'd been calling that play wrong.

Bloody Finn. He was a flaming hypocrite.

Sucking warming club soda through a straw, she watched him dancing with the blond. Close dancing. In a way that made it clear that he was planning on introducing her to some extracurricular activities later that night. She suppressed an eye roll. Finn had always been surrounded by willing women. One day he was going to meet the woman who would tell him no and Amelia very much looked forward to standing on the sidelines when that happened and cheering her on. But it didn't seem like tonight was going to be that night.

Which meant that she might as well call it a night. She didn't really know anyone else at the party, and if Finn had abandoned her for the blond, then he wasn't there to introduce her to anyone new. It was getting late and her feet were hurting more than ever. It was time to just go home. Back to Manhattan. Where she would curl up in bed alone and try not to think of Oliver Shields's pirate smile.

Somewhere around one a.m., Maggie Jameson ambushed Oliver as he made his way across the club looking for distraction. It was well over an hour since Finn had pulled his bullshit and Oliver had struggled to shake the nasty mood that had settled over him in the aftermath. Castro. Grade-A prick. Still, Maggie didn't deserve to get caught in the crossfire of his lingering irritation, so he forced a smile when she stepped in front of him.

"What's up, Mrs. Winters?" he asked. "Come to your senses and decided to leave Alex for me?"

She grinned at him, looking beautiful as always, her long frame wrapped in a bright red, very short dress that matched the red gems gleaming in her ears. "In your dreams, Ollie."

He grinned back. Once upon a time, Maggie had been his dream. But that was a long time ago. "Are you out of official party-wrangling mode yet?"

Maggie and Raina and Sara—the third of the trio of women who ruled the owners of the Saints—usually worked like a well-oiled machine to ensure Saints functions ran like clockwork. Which Ollie thought was rather unfair. It meant they didn't always get to relax and enjoy the parties as much as they deserved to.

"Just about," Maggie said. "Things will wind down soon." She studied him for a moment. "Meet anyone nice tonight?" she asked.

That was Maggie-speak for "Are you hooking up?", he thought. Or maybe "When are you going to settle down, Oliver?" Which was a subject that he considered to be none of her business since she'd long ago declined to be a candidate for said settling.

"Still looking," he said, trying not to think of Milly the economist and her perfume and her pretty eyes.

Maggie smiled. "Oh good, then you won't mind doing me a favor."

Crap. He'd walked into that one. "Define favor," he said suspiciously.

"Helping out one of your teammates," she said. "With a ride. You drove, right?"

"Maybe."

"I saw your car parked outside the club."

Busted. "All right, yes, I drove. Who needs a lift?"

She hesitated. Just for a second. Then, "Finn."

"Castro?" Ollie said disbelievingly. He did his best to get along with Castro at the club, but he had made his opinion of the guy clear to Maggie on several occasions. And his act earlier hadn't improved that opinion one bit.

"Yes. He's had one or two too many. Alex and Mal and Lucas think it's time for him to go home."

Translation, the guy was wasted and Maggie was in damage control mode. "So put him in a cab."

"He's not that drunk. He'd probably just get the driver to take him to another club as soon as they got out of sight."

True. Castro was a little too fond of partying, Ollie thought. The last thing they needed was him doing some dumbass thing while under the influence and getting the Saints' name plastered in the papers or on some gossip show.

"He was here with someone earlier. Milly or something." His jaw tightened at the thought of her. And of Finn chasing her off. Though she'd let herself be chased off. Sort of. So maybe she hadn't been interested in the first place. Or maybe she was just a good friend. Dammit. He needed to stop thinking about her.

"If I'm understanding Finn correctly, then she went home," Maggie said.

"So send him home with someone else." He understood Maggie's reasoning for not wanting to trust Castro with a cab or one of Alex's or Mal's or Lucas's drivers, but he really wasn't in any mood to help Castro out.

"He lives about one block from you," Maggie said. "You're the best candidate."

He'd been vaguely aware that Castro lived somewhere near him. He should have paid more attention. Then Maggie would be trying this with some other sucker. "How do you know I won't succumb to the temptation to kick him out of the car halfway across the Brooklyn Bridge?"

"You won't do that," Maggie said.

"Why not?"

"Because you think I'm awesome," she said with another brilliant smile, and he resigned himself to having a very unwelcome passenger for his trip home.

They drove in near silence. Castro hadn't said a word since Mal and Dan Ellis, the team coach, had practically escorted him from the building and into Oliver's car. He'd pulled out his phone and started texting someone as soon as Oliver had started the engine. Which suited him just fine. He really wasn't interested in talking either. He focused on the road, suddenly tired. The adrenaline of the win and the party was fading, and now he just felt every one of the twenty or so hours he'd been awake.

As they hit the end of the Brooklyn Bridge and eased into Manhattan traffic, he yawned.

Finn looked up. "Tired, old man?"

Jesus. The guy didn't let up. No wonder the Cubs had sold him cheap. He was a decent batter and a good fielder, but he was trouble. He shook his head. "No, just bored by the company."

"Yeah, well, you can just let me out at SubZero and I'll be out of your hair and you can go home to bed."

Un-fucking-believable. "Not gonna happen. I'm stopping nowhere but your apartment building."

"Shit. You sucking up to the bigwigs or something? Just take me to the damned club."

"Look, Castro, I don't know who gave you the bug up your butt, but let me give you some advice." Oliver let the car glide to a halt as the light ahead turned red. "When the owner of your club and your coach evict you from a party for being wasted, the smart thing to do for your career is to go home, sleep it off, and apologize in the morning."

"If I wanted advice, I'd ask for it," Finn snapped. "As if you've never partied."

Apparently the kid was determined to dig his own grave. The light flashed green, and he stepped on the gas. "Fine. But I'm still taking you to your apartment. You can do what the hell you want after that. It's your damned funeral."

The SUV that hit them halfway across the intersection came out of nowhere.